MY SECRET ROCKSTAR BOYFRIEND

Eleanor Wood lives in Brighton, where she can mostly be found hanging around in cafes and record shops, running on the beach, pretending to be French and/or that it's the 1960s and writing deep into the night. She used to make a photocopied fanzine, moved on to embarrassingly personal blogging and has written for magazines like *Elle*, *Time Out* and *The Face*. She has a fringe, is fond of eyeliner and wishes she had a dog.

You can read her blog at
http://eleanor-wood.blogspot.co.uk
or chat to her on Twitter at @eleanor_wood

Lanc
Bow
Pres
www

D0419938

MY SECRET ROCKSTAR BOYFRIEND

ELEANOR WOOD

MACMILLAN

For my parents

First published 2015 by Macmillan Children's Books
an imprint of Pan Macmillan
a division of Macmillan Publishers Limited
20 New Wharf Road, London N1 9RR
Associated companies throughout the world
www.panmacmillan.com

ISBN 978-1-4472-7787-3

1 3 5 7 9 8 6 4 2

A CIP catalogue record for this book is available from
the British Library.

Typeset by Ellipsis Digital Limited, Glasgow
Printed and bound by CPI Group (UK) Ltd, Croydon CR0 4YY

All characters appearing in this work are fictitious.

Nevermind the . . . ?

OK, I may not have been born yet when Kurt Cobain died (hey, does that mean I could be his reincarnation? I've got the right hair for it,[1] if nothing else) but have you LISTENED to Nevermind lately? That's Nirvana's breakthrough second album, in case you are unlucky enough not to be familiar with it already. It was released in 1991, but I swear if it came out tomorrow it would still sound new.

Let's not forget that Nirvana were the most groundbreaking band for a whole generation[2]. I can only imagine what it must have been like when Nevermind really was brand new, released into an unsuspecting world of 80s pop, a time when the edgiest rock scene still consisted of Guns N' Roses and similarly big-haired buffoons.

I'm not saying there's nothing good around these days – that would be stupid (and, hello? Have you heard of Grimes, or the Internet, or Nando's, or any of the other excellent stuff that wasn't even around in 1991?) I'm just saying I'm really, really happy to live in a time when I have the luxuries of modern life AND Kurt Cobain's back catalogue at my fingertips, to ransack to my retro little heart's content.

---

1 i.e. Unintentionally yellow/bleached-blonde mess that I cut myself with the kitchen scissors.
2 This may not be MY generation, but I still get a say. I am a spiritual child of the nineties, so humour me. Please?

Comments

As usual, Chew — you are the voice of someone else's generation. And that's why you're pretty unique.
seymour_brown

Chew, tell Seymour to stop being such an enabler — you both need to get out more. If he tells you otherwise, don't listen. Maybe you should try an open relationship. Seymour, FYI, there's no such thing as 'pretty unique'. A thing, or person, is either unique or it isn't. End of.
Nishi_S

Aw, you guys. Et cetera. By which I mean STFU, both of you. Open relationship? Nish, I'm so telling Anna you said that. Anyway, I'm off — MIC is starting and you know how I hate to miss it. I'm not even joking. I've got a date with E4 and a pack of Hobnobs. Living the dream.
Tuesday-yes-that-is-my-real-name-Cooper

'No, but seriously – don't you think that I might be pre-empting a big comeback? When all the hipsters are wearing them in six months' time, who'll be laughing then?'

'I will,' Nishi says. 'In six months' time, Chew – I will still be laughing. At you. Because you're wearing those dungarees.'

'But –' I open my mouth to protest, even though I kind of suspect she's right.

These dungarees aren't really doing anything for me. Probably because they're shiny leopard print, frayed at the edges and have a crotch that's veering perilously close to looking like I've done a poo in it. Possibly, at some point in this garment's weird life, somebody has.

I give it one last go. 'You don't think it has just a teensy Debbie Harry at CBGB's sort of a vibe to—'

'No, Chew,' Anna interrupts, accepting no arguments. 'Nishi's right. Just . . . no.'

'Now take them off,' Nishi adds. 'We'll meet you next to household tat, OK?'

I close the curtain of the makeshift changing room and take one last look in the mirror. I'm not too bothered about the fact that my arse looks approximately the size of a small country. Well, I kind of am, if I'm honest, but I try my very best not to think about it. I bring other skills to the table, so there's not much point wasting my life wishing I looked like some dreamy Alexa Chung type. It's never going to happen – sad but true – so I'm pretty sure that coming to terms with the truth this early on in life makes me about 37% more productive. Whenever I catch myself obsessing – about my wayward weight, my lack of cheekbones or my weird knuckles – I remind myself that it's wasted time I could be spending on my blog, or learning Arabic, or eating a delicious pizza. It doesn't always work, but I'm nothing if not a trier.

Anyway, chub aside, I am most definitely bothered about the fact that I don't look cool. In any way, shape or form. I look like a demented toddler. I am forced to admit that my friends are right.

So I begin the laborious task of peeling myself out of the second-hand dungarees – worryingly their synthetic fabric is already making me a bit sweaty – and back into the pale blue second-hand nightie I'm currently wearing as a dress, along with white tights, ballet slippers and a ratty old-man cardigan. I'm going for Courtney Love circa 1990 – back when she had her old-old nose.

This is to go with my current hair – the bleached-blonde disaster. I make a point of dyeing my hair a new colour once a fortnight at the very least. I try to go for a strong enough statement each time that I have to formulate a completely new look around it. Sometimes I even try out a slightly different personality. I don't have the pain threshold for piercings, and my attention span is way too short for a tattoo. The idea of something that lasts forever scares me. Hair dye – bright, brash, but not a long-term commitment – is the ideal mini-rebellion for the essentially cowardly girl. Everyone notices it and comments, but if you really don't like it, all you have to do is stay in and wash your hair ten times in a row. Better yet, dye it another colour over the top.

'Hang on a minute – did you say household tat?' I shout from behind the curtain. 'You two aren't *nesting* already, are you? You've only been going out for about five minutes.'

Fully dressed again, I push the curtain aside, to find that there's nobody around to hear me. Anna and Nishi have already disappeared out of sight. The charity shop is almost silent, and the only person I can see is the old lady behind the till, who is giving me evils like I'm about to stab her for her pension cheque. I smile at her as sweetly as I possibly can as I hang the hideous dungarees up where I found them. I make sure that they are in exactly the right place and very, very neat – showing that the younger generation can in fact be courteous and helpful.

I find Anna and Nishi tucked away in a corner, examining a vintage tea set.

'It's been four months actually,' Anna says – unlike me, waiting until I'm standing next to them, and using her indoor voice.

'And you're already buying shared crockery.' I sigh. 'That must be true love.'

'Hey, what does a lesbian take on the second date? A removal van.' Nishi cackles at her own joke.

'Am I allowed to laugh at that?' I ask seriously.

'No,' Anna tells me, giving Nish a cautionary look. 'Because it's not funny. Anyway, how long have *you* been going out with Seymour?'

I suppose I ought to know this. I have to think hard, and I'm still not sure.

'Well, I must have known him properly for nearly a year, I suppose. Because when we met him at that party it was definitely summer – I remember because I had on that yellow playsuit I got in Beyond Retro. You know, the one with the palm-tree pattern that looks a bit like something Lucille Ball might have worn in an *I Love Lucy* Hawaiian holiday special. I have no idea when we actually started going out. Ask him – he's way more likely to remember the specifics.'

'Oh, he'll definitely remember the exact date. He'll probably remember what he was wearing and every single witty remark he made.' Once again Nishi cracks herself up. 'Come on, don't look at me like that – you know what Seymour's like. He's quite . . . self-involved, isn't he?'

'I'm obviously drawn to self-involved characters,' I say sanctimoniously. 'I seem to be surrounded by them.'

Nishi, clever as she is, doesn't turn a hair at this. 'Hey, I'm just looking out for you. That's what best friends are for. Keeping things real.'

Anna and I look at each other and roll our eyes fondly.

'Chew's right, Nish – let's go and get some food,' Anna cuts in, diplomatic as usual. 'I'm starving.'

Unbelievably we leave the charity shop empty-handed. This is almost unheard of, but it's been a slow day for chazzing. At least my mum will be pleased – she doesn't understand our 'morbid fixation on dead people's crap'. She's always trying to throw my stuff out when she thinks I won't notice, or she decides she's going to 'draw the line' at taxidermy, or that scary Victorian doll I once brought home.

We troop across the road to our favourite cafe, Macari's. It's like a cross between a school canteen and a 1950s diner. We grab our favourite booth and take it in turns to go up to the counter and order. The others get baked potatoes, but I feel like I want to have at least some indulgence in my life on a Saturday afternoon, given the failure of our shopping trip and the fact that I still have a hard-earned tenner burning a hole in my pocket. So I order cheesy chips, an ice-cream sundae, a chocolate milkshake and also a Coke because I am thirsty.

'Impressive,' Nishi notes with a sarcastically raised eyebrow.

She's right, even if she does have a slightly smug attitude and a worrying obsession with kale. By the time I'm done, I feel sick. I make sure to leave one overcooked brown chip and exactly half of one ice-cream wafer, so that it's like none of it actually happened; I didn't finish all that food, so it doesn't count.

'What are we doing next?' I ask, slurping air from the bottom of my milkshake.

'Falling into a diabetic coma?' Nishi suggests.

I've known Nishi since we were five. We've been best friends since junior school. We're more like sisters by this point – I'm an only child and Nish has all brothers. By this, I mean that we argue like siblings and don't feel any need for good manners or common courtesy around each other. I feel totally myself with Nish, in a way I don't always in the outside world. Nobody else quite gets the two of us.

However, I am properly delighted that she and Anna have got together. They met online, on a Riot Grrrl message board; then it turned out that Anna lives really near us, even though she's a year younger and goes to the fancy all-girls school on the other side of town. Sometimes if we have a free afternoon Nishi and I try and convince her to bunk off and hang out with us, but she's far too strait-laced and we're not exactly major rebels, so we usually make do with going to Macari's or the noodle bar together at lunchtimes or after school. Anyway, Anna's always embarrassed about us seeing her in her navy-blue school uniform when we can go to college in our jeans. Or revolting second-hand nylon nightdresses in my case.

Even though – as I have just been reminded – we have only known Anna for the past four months, she fits right in. It's great having her in our tiny little gang. They don't make me feel like a third wheel, and it's like we're kind of a family, as I've been there with them since the beginning. I feel a bit like their child or something. A slightly overgrown child who will probably be living with them when she's thirty, eating all their food and not giving them a moment's peace. Actually that sounds like a pretty good plan for my future adult life – I must suggest it to them; maybe they can get a house with a spare room for me one day.

When they had their first 'in the flesh' date, after

months of messaging and then awkward phone calls, Nishi arranged to meet Anna in a Starbucks and made me secretly sit at the table behind her, in case Anna turned out to be a freaky old man or something. I sat there wearing a beret and reading a newspaper, mostly trying not to laugh and make a spectacle of myself. Nish ended up calling me over to introduce me, and the three of us spent the whole afternoon hanging out in town together. It's pretty much set the pattern for their whole relationship.

Most of all, it's nice to see Nish so happy for once – I love my badass friend, but it's actually kind of cool to see that she *does* have a soppy side. In all the years that I have known her, I never would have guessed it could happen, but they are properly in love.

It's a good thing I've got Seymour, otherwise I might feel left out. The fact that this has happened is basically a small miracle – as I would never previously have dreamed I'd be able to get a boyfriend like Seymour. I'm still not entirely sure how I managed it. I'd casually admired him from afar at college for ages, but never thought much of it – just like half the girls in my year, which is unsurprising, as he is so good-looking *and* plays in a band.

Then, somehow, we got chatting in the common room one day when he saw me reading a vintage copy of the *NME* that I'd bought off eBay. He seemed genuinely sweet and interested, so I even forgot to be nervous as I explained to him the cultural significance of *Meat Is Murder* by the Smiths. We kept hanging out together and actually became friends – he started coming round to borrow my charity-shop records or even to ask advice on his band's demo tapes. It took a while, but things kind of went from there.

It's probably a good thing that we were friends before we got together, as I know I'm not really pretty enough to be going out with someone like him – luckily for me I somehow eventually won him over with my incessant chatter and encyclopaedic knowledge of Jared Leto films. Handsome boys love that sort of thing, right? Seriously, he looks like when they put glasses on a ridiculously handsome actor in an American teen movie, to make it obvious that he's the 'clever' one. He plays guitar and sings in a band called Terminal Ghosts. Despite Nishi's sniping, my friends think he's cool; my mum loves him. Actually my mum mostly loves him because he has a slightly posh voice and unusually good table manners, plus he once sided with her against me in an argument about which of the Bee Gees are dead – but that's not the point. Even when he's being annoying, they all generally take his side. It's always like, 'Chew, what did you do?' Fair enough, really. I guess we all know I'm punching above my weight.

Sometimes I have to remind myself that I bring different qualities to the table – like the fact that I do better than him at college, and that before he met me he thought Iggy Pop was just some old guy in insurance adverts.

Anyway, I really shouldn't have to remind myself that life is pretty sweet at the moment. It's nice to have this brilliant little group around me, after years of just Nishi and me doing our own thing against the tide. It's like the world has caught up, and being the slightly odd, clever kids has suddenly paid off for us.

We've got our A levels coming up in a couple of weeks' time, and I'm weirdly excited about the whole thing. I really like all the subjects I'm studying, particularly English, which has been my favourite subject for as long as I can remember. I love writing, and it's been awesome to leave maths and science behind. I'm not a fan of any subject where there is only one correct answer – if something is set in stone like that, it's so boring; that just isn't how my brain works. It's probably why I also love really rubbish reality TV – I'm all about the journey.

This is partly why I'm trying to spend a lot of time working on my blog at the moment. It's a really fun hobby; obviously it's grossly self-indulgent because it's all about me and the music and other stuff I'm into, and nobody reads it except for my friends and my mum. Still, I think it's good practice for my writing. I would love to be a journalist one day; it's my dream to become a writer and move to New York. Or at least London.

'We could go and try on ludicrous clothes we can't afford in Urban Outfitters?' Anna suggests for our next Saturday-afternoon activity.

This is pretty much our favourite thing to do. Which is why she's Nishi's kind of girl – and mine. She doesn't need to ask us twice.

Monkey Gone to Devon

What is it, dear reader, about people called Kim that makes them so awesome? Just this morning, my Musician Boyfriend was making fun of me for my weird love of Kim Kardashian and her whole family (although I would like it to be known that Khloe is my favourite Kardashian sister, hands down. I'm not too proud to admit it; I'm all about the no-brow, me. I never want to be someone who pretends they're cool all the time).

Anyway, I reckon Kim K is basically the new Liz Taylor. And we could do with a bit more of that in the world. I had to point out to my mocking Musician Boyfriend that I am also a big fan of other such amazing Kims as Kim Deal (bass player from the Pixies, and also the Breeders, who are a great old band and you should really listen to their song 'Cannonball' if you don't already know it) and Kim Gordon (basically the sexy bass-playing godmother of grunge, out of Sonic Youth – Kurt Cobain's favourite band, fact fans!). Actually it got me wondering whether Kim Kardashian might secretly be a really good bass player . . .

I had to remind Musician Boyfriend that he owns a Sonic Youth T-shirt but precisely zero of their albums – whereas I own TWO WHOLE Sonic Youth albums so I WIN. Then we had a Skype dance party to Bikini Kill and all was once again right with the world. Good feminist Musician Boyfriend.

But he does have a point. Sort of. Please let's not

forget that Kim Deal and Kim Gordon should be equally as important to the Youth of Today – women who can play instruments; bands that made songs so great I can legitimately say lame stuff like, 'They don't make them like they used to.'

To recap for any new readers – hi, Mister Nobody and Ms Nobody-hyphen-Jones! – my name is Tuesday (yes, that's my real name – don't ask) and I am an expert in romanticizing an era that I am too young even to remember. I just want to make that clear, so that I can stop getting comments that all say I'm a sad old lady at the age of eighteen.

Yes, I mean you, Musician Boyfriend! And you, Token Lesbian Best Friends (TLBFs for short – catchy, right?). And, OK – hi, Mum. *waves*

Literally nobody else ever reads this blog. Can't think why. Oh, what's that you say? It's because I'm a sad old lady at the age of eighteen? Meet you at Grey Gardens.

Comments
Token Lesbian Best Friends? Really?
anna-banana

Really, Chew – have we taught you nothing? You're fired.
Nishi_S

Musician Boyfriend? I'm with the Token Lesbian Best Friends on this one. Nought out of ten for imagination.

Oh, and hi, Tuesday's mum!
seymour_brown

THIS IS MY *ART*, MAN! No more criticizing or I'll block you all. I've got loads of other readers. Loads. *tumbleweed*
Tuesday-yes-that-is-my-real-name-Cooper

Tuesday, I thought you were supposed to be revising for your exams up there?
Carrie_Cougar

I'm not kidding. Don't think I won't block you just because you're my mother.
Tuesday-yes-that-is-my-real-name-Cooper

Dinner's ready . . .
Carrie_Cougar

We *are* having chicken curry, right? If it's stir-fry again, consider yourself blocked.
Tuesday-yes-that-is-my-real-name-Cooper

Gruel for you at this rate, young lady.
Carrie_Cougar

This is getting weird. I can actually hear you typing. I'm coming downstairs now so that we can make our hilarious jokes face to face for a bit.
Tuesday-yes-that-is-my-real-name-Cooper

'What do you think about leather trousers?'

Unfortunately I think she's serious.

'*Mum*! Isn't it a bit, like, try-hard sexy housewife?'

'And your point is . . . ?'

I think for a moment, doing my best to be genuinely helpful. 'Carol Vorderman. Probably, like, Susanna Reid.'

'Oh . . . I see.' Her face falls, as well it might. 'Thanks for ruining my fun. You don't let me do anything.'

'That's what teenage daughters are for, isn't it? To totally cramp your style.'

'Apparently so. Remind me, when are you leaving home?'

My mum grins and grabs another slice of pizza, turning away from her laptop. Although, I do notice that she first shuts down the window she had open on Topshop.com showing skinny leather jeans. I've done her a favour, seriously.

She concentrates instead on the crap film we're watching while we eat our Saturday-night takeaway. I've kind of lost track of the plot, because we've been chatting too much – but I think Leighton Meester is dying and Ryan Gosling's going to give her a kidney or something. Tonight's Netflix was Mum's choice, not mine. I wanted the new Lars von Trier, but she wasn't having it.

I don't mind; in fact, there are few things I enjoy more than dissecting – and secretly enjoying – my mum's rubbish taste in films. It is quite nice just to chill out with my mum on a Saturday night for once. I've been out with

Nish and Anna all day, and she's been on an afternoon coffee date – we both arrived home at about the same time, impromptu, so we decided to put on our pyjamas and order a pizza.

My phone beeps. I quickly check the message before going back to squirting ketchup on to a pizza crust.

'Was that Seymour?' my mum asks.

'Mm-hmm.'

'What did he say? Have you replied? I hope you were nice to him. How come you're not seeing him tonight, anyway?'

'Calm down, Mother. His band are playing a gig in Reading tonight. There wasn't room for me in the car, but it's OK – it was a bit far for me to go anyway, since I have revision and blogging and stuff to do this weekend. God, the way you go on, I'm sure you like Seymour more than you like me.'

'You're lucky, that's all,' she says. 'You've got this gorgeous boy wanting to go out with you, and I couldn't get a boy to call me back after the second date when I was your age. Still can't actually.'

'Hey – not lucky, just sensible! I've learned from your mistakes. Don't go for the douchebags.'

'I wish I could learn the same lesson . . . Well, send Seymour a kiss from me.'

'Coo-coo-ca-choo, Mrs Robinson.'

'Daughter, has anyone ever told you you're too witty for your own good sometimes?'

My mum is definitely feeling restless at the moment – I

know all the signs. It's been about six months since she and my last ex-stepdad broke up. She gets cross with me when I say things like 'my last ex-stepdad' because she thinks it makes her sound bad. To her credit, I suppose I should add that at least she's never made me wear a hideous bridesmaid dress or tried to make me call any of them 'Uncle Andrew' or 'Dad', or anything repugnant like that.

'After all, you've only had two stepfathers, barely even plural – you make it sound so much worse than it really is,' she protests. 'People would think I was Henry VIII, the way you go on!'

But it *is* technically true. It's now getting to the point when this is about the longest she's ever been without a serious boyfriend. Since she was fifteen, as she's always telling me. She hates not having a boyfriend, or preferably a husband. I sometimes think she's a bit like the Sandra Bullock of relationships – a great actress who has the tendency to pick really bad films.

I honestly don't understand it. I'd never had a boyfriend before Seymour, and I'm still not really sure what having a boyfriend is supposed to be like. We just ended up hanging out together so much as friends that I suppose it seemed like the logical thing to do – unromantic as that sounds. We didn't ever really have a conversation about it, and it was like one day he had decided that I was his girlfriend. I wasn't about to complain, and everyone is *still* telling me how lucky I am to have a boyfriend like Seymour. They don't know that he secretly spends forty minutes every morning making his hair look like he hasn't tried, or that he only pretends to have read Jack Kerouac.

It's not really what I always imagined – but, to be fair, it's probably for the best that it hasn't been like all my crazy Kurt/Courtney or Sid/Nancy fantasies. We're both still taking things very cautiously, even after a year or however long it is – which, most of the time, suits me just fine. I think we're still both finding our feet with figuring out what being more than 'just friends' entails – we can both be pretty awkward.

Luckily I've always been determined not to be one of those girls who gets carried away by having a boyfriend, forgetting all her friends and letting her principles fly straight out of the window. So far, that definitely hasn't happened and I don't think either of us is in any danger of getting totally carried away.

I suppose it's unsurprising that I might choose to be more sensible than my male-fixated mother, but I don't like to sit about getting too Freudian about it. I can't stand people who feel sorry for themselves and blame everything on their parents. I've got better things to do, like just getting on with it.

Whenever I am in danger of feeling down about having no dad – not to mention a mum who sometimes forgets that I exist – I remind myself that other people have it a lot worse. From what I've heard, having a nuclear family can be very overrated. Sometimes I just feel a little bit left out that I've never had one, that's all. It's yet another one of those things that I Just Don't Think About. Sometimes it gets a bit exhausting trying to remember all the millions of things I choose not to obsess over, but it's better than the alternative. If I'm not careful I'll get neurotic about *not* being neurotic.

Besides, I really like my mum – or Carrie, as she's more commonly known. Leaving to one side all her own neuroses, general madness, failed relationships and the fact that she chose to call me Tuesday, we really get on. I was named after my mum's favourite actress, Tuesday Weld – who, as far as I can tell, was famous for being beautiful, a child star and a girlfriend of rich and famous men. I am not, and nor do I ever intend to be, any of these things.

'Anyway, do you think you'll see today's date again?' I ask her.

'Put it this way – he said that he'd bet I was stunning when I was thirty. This from a man with a paunch and quite alarming hair growth from his left ear, who picked his nose behind the menu.'

'Yikes.'

This is not only rude but grossly unfair. My mum is better-looking in her forties than I am at eighteen. Seriously. This is not only due to our respective ratios of skinny leather jeans to second-hand granddad cardigans. Our looks are about as similar as our life priorities – my mum is tanned and toned with meticulously highlighted hair; she's into yoga and spinning, and she tries every celebrity diet fad going. I've rarely ever seen her without lipstick on, and I don't think she has ever left the house with unshaven legs or bedhead. She really makes me laugh sometimes – in fact, we baffle each other in equal measure – but most of the time we manage to go for a 'live and let live' kind of tolerance policy in our little household. With frequent but well-meaning jokes at each other's expense.

I must admit – although I want her to be happy – I'm enjoying this interval of it just being my mum and me at home, before I go off to university. It's relaxing, and it's nice to spend time with her when she's not obsessing about a man and putting him first.

Obviously I hope she finds herself a lovely new husband immediately once I'm out the door – after all, that's what she'd like most of all. A really nice one this time, who'll stick with her and realize that she's even more amazing than she looks.

Although men have drifted in and out of the scene, it's really always been just me and my mum, when it comes down to it. My dad moved out when I was three and never came back, so I don't even remember him. I've never had a father figure who has lasted for any notable period of time. I think my mum spends more time worrying about this than I do. I've trained myself not to lose too much sleep over the fact that I don't have a proper dad, or even a decent stepdad.

I'm too busy pondering the important things: like the perfect winged eyeliner, or whether I would still fancy Kurt Cobain and River Phoenix if they were middle-aged rather than dead; how I can make myself more like Lena Dunham or Tavi Gevinson, but with Jemima Kirke's looks and wardrobe. I don't have time for the trivial stuff. Honestly . . .

Sweet for Sour Apple

My first-ever crush was on Leonard Cohen. Not even kidding. I mean, so what if I was eleven and he was seventy-five – in ten or twenty years, who would care about the age difference anyway, right?

Then, when I was nine, I dressed up as David Bowie for Halloween (Ziggy Stardust era, natch). Strong look. And, yes, there is photographic evidence.[1]

Therefore I would say it's pretty unsurprising that, as a precocious thirteen-year-old, my favourite band was Sour Apple. Yes, dear reader, my bedroom wall was plastered with pictures of Jackson Griffith.[2] Jackson said himself that Sour Apple was a band for sixteen-year-old girls (I was precocious, remember?) and their mums – he was right. Sour Apple are about the only band my mum and I agree on. We had a picture of Jackson stuck on the fridge for a while, and we always listened to Come On Over (Please Leave Quietly) on repeat on the way to school, singing along and for once in total harmony (on a metaphorical level, you see; neither one of us can actually sing in tune). My mum liked them because they were modern – and she had even more of a crush on Jackson Griffith than I did. I liked them because they sounded a bit like a cross between Nirvana and Cat

---

1 No, you're not seeing said photographic evidence.
2 Alongside Kurt Cobain, Bruce Springsteen, Bob Dylan and My Aforementioned Geriatric Fantasy Husband. HOT.

Stevens. We both still love Jackson Griffith.

So, my mum and I have both been saddened to read about Jackson's current, ahem, difficulties. I hope the news that he is taking a break due to 'exhaustion' is true – that he just needs a really long nap in front of the telly and he'll be back on top form again, rather than something more sinister. Hugs not drugs, Jackson!

Comments

That model he was married to left him, right? Hey, I can overlook the rehab rumours for a voice/face like that. Your next stepdad?
Carrie_Cougar

MOTHER!!! HE'S STILL ONLY 23 YEARS OLD!
Tuesday-yes-that-is-my-real-name-Cooper

Lighten up, kiddo. I'm hoping that my fifth husband hasn't even been born yet. And aren't you meant to be revising? Boom.
Carrie_Cougar

hey I don't think i've ever had a mom and daughter fight over me before – this is pretty cool . . . nice website and i'm not just saying that cuz you said sweet things about me – ps dont believe everything you read!!
jackson_e_griffith

Ummmm . . . . . .
Tuesday-yes-that-is-my-real-name-Cooper

hey.
jackson_e_griffith

*This is a joke, right? Someone is winding me up, and
given the scale of my readership, that narrows it down
to one of about four people. Nishi, is that you?*
Tuesday-yes-that-is-my-real-name-Cooper

I hope so, or I should probably be worried right now! :-/
seymour_brown

*I think I can say with quite a lot of certainty that you
don't have anything to worry about, seymour_brown
!! x*
Tuesday-yes-that-is-my-real-name-Cooper

Seymour and I are sitting at our favourite table in our favourite Japanese restaurant. I can't believe that I am a person who would actually have a favourite Japanese restaurant with 'my boyfriend'. Still, it's just the weird way it's worked out – I'm not changing for anyone.

As if to prove this, I am wearing old three-stripe tracksuit bottoms and a ripped checked shirt with the same granddad cardigan I've been wearing all week. You know what it's like when you have one item of clothing that's all you want to wear, at least for a while? Everything else just feels wrong, until the next favourite item of clothing comes along and replaces it. I think I've got quite a badass look going on, but my mum actually laughed out loud before I went out the door. Then she rolled her eyes and muttered something about it being a wonder that I had such a handsome boyfriend, or any boyfriend at all. Which I guess proves that I fulfilled my chosen objectives with tonight's outfit. It's a good thing I'm not easily offended.

Anyway, I'm not totally out of place. When I say 'favourite Japanese restaurant', don't go picturing some Michelin-starred celebrity haunt. It's a really cool, authentic cafe called Moshi Munchers, with plastic chairs and strip lights, where you order food by number at the counter and the only drinks you can get come straight from cans in lurid colours with Japanese writing on them, so I have no idea what they actually are.

I've got a row of tiny bowls in front of me filled with miso soup, pickles, steamed dumplings and octopus balls (yes, really – they sound gross but they're the best), so I am happy as I fill my face clumsily with my chopsticks.

'How did the gig go?' I ask Seymour, through a mouthful of food.

'Chew – *chew*,' he says in mock exasperation.

'So-*rry*,' I reply sarcastically.

I open my mouth to show him both its contents and my annoyance at him trying to tell me what to do – Seymour can be very squeamish, not to mention prim and proper, sometimes. He looks away and waits until I've swallowed before replying.

'It was quite worthwhile, I think, thank you. I talked to some other bands and some promoters. It was good. I'm sorry you couldn't come; I think you'd have enjoyed it. What did you get up to?'

'What do you *think* I got up to?'

'OK, let's see . . . Hanging out with Nishi and Anna? Buying crap from charity shops? Writing your blog? Exchanging fashion and beauty tips with Carrie?'

'Ha ha. You're almost exactly right. You know me so well. Carrie sends you a big kiss, by the way. With tongues, probably.'

'Thanks for that, Chew. Nice image, not weird and gross at all. I'm just glad she likes me. She's cool, your mum.'

'Yeah, I know. I'm pretty lucky actually,' I agree. 'How are all your lot?'

I have to force myself not to make an involuntary face as I say it. Seymour, unlike me, has the most nuclear of families. His parents are still together. He is the oldest of four children. His grandpa even lives in an annexe next door. All of Seymour's family are ridiculously 'lovely', in a way that means they do not understand anything or anyone who is not completely and appropriately 'lovely' at all times.

The first time I went round there for Sunday lunch I tried to help by carrying some plates through from the dining room into the kitchen – where I overheard Seymour's mum, Elaine, talking about me and using the incomprehensible abbreviation 'NQOT'. It was only when I asked my mum about it later – careful not to let on where I'd heard it – that I found out it's a horrible, snobby phrase that means 'Not Quite Our Type'.

I've never said anything about it to Seymour or anyone else – and I just made a massive effort with Elaine from then onward. I'm pretty sure I've won her over by now – I hope so, anyway – and she's quite nice to me these days, even if she isn't the funnest person in the whole world. I would never upset Seymour by saying anything critical about his family, so there's no point even thinking about it. Bygones and all that.

It's only occasionally I still worry about that sort of stuff around Seymour's family now. Like, I'll inadvertently use the wrong fork or admit to liking *TOWIE* and they'll ban me from their house forever.

'How are my family? What do *you* think?' Seymour laughs, pushing his glasses up his face as he does so. 'My mum's on my back twenty-four hours a day about

A levels, even though they haven't even started yet. She and my dad actually sat me down after Sunday lunch and asked me when I was going to consider giving up the band for the sake of my "academic career". It's a bit worrying actually. I tried to tell them that it's not likely to happen any time soon, but I don't think they really get it. So then of course –' he looks over at me guiltily – 'they said I should probably lay off seeing you so much, at least until the exams are over.'

I've seen this one coming for a while; I'm surprised he hasn't. I try my very best to compose my face into a neutral position, as I know there is absolutely no point getting cross about this, and Seymour gets very upset at the slightest sign of conflict.

Inside, I feel really unfairly got at. Because of how we both are, just due to our natural personality types, people seem to make a lot of assumptions about Seymour and me. I mean, he's the one who's in a band, even though to look at him he may not seem like the most rock 'n' roll type. In fact, he lives and breathes it – and as a result he doesn't care about college nearly as much as I do.

Elaine might like to think that I'm 'NQOT' – I suppose because I'm loud-ish, not particularly posh and definitely not smartly dressed – but if she bothered to ask me, she'd actually find that I'm a pretty good influence on her outwardly quiet, sweet son. I'm more focused on my writing than anyone else I know of my age. I know my blog is just a small, silly thing, but I work hard on it. I'm desperate to go to a good university and do something interesting with my life.

Sometimes I really wish I could be more the quiet, enigmatic type. Quieter, smaller – *less*. Life would be a lot easier. But whenever I try, no matter how hard, it's impossible to keep it up for long. It feels like trying to hold my breath underwater. I've always been crap at swimming.

'Well, what can you do?' I shrug and give Seymour a reassuring smile. 'I mean, you can understand why they'd want to make sure you give it your best go.'

In reality, although it annoys me that Seymour's parents would jump to conclusions about me as usual, this time I do think they have a point. In a small way it's a bit of a relief. I want to make sure I do the best I possibly can. This actually might prove to be the perfect excuse – Seymour can be a bit touchy, and I don't want to risk an argument.

'You're so cool,' Seymour says blithely. 'Look, shall we go? It's a weeknight and it's nearly ten. You know what my mum can be like. I'd rather not be butchered in my prime.'

'Sure,' I find myself saying, even though it's closer to half past nine and I really fancied a pudding. Hopefully my mum will be around when I get home – I need to stay up and finish a blog post I started earlier anyway, so it'd be nice if she and I could hang out together for a midnight chocolate feast.

Seymour, like the well-brought-up gentleman he is, offers to walk me home. I only live ten minutes' walk away and it's kind of on his way – but it's still nice of him.

'Do you want to pop in and say hi to Carrie?' I ask when we're turning the corner into my road and I can see that the lights are still on in my house.

'No, thanks – I'd better not.'

'Are you sure?' I persist.

Even as I'm saying it, I already know what his answer will be and I kind of wonder why I bother putting myself out there at all.

'No, I really do have to get home. Sorry,' he mumbles awkwardly, surprising neither of us.

I try not to take it personally, or get all hung up on things, but sometimes I have the sneaking suspicion that Seymour should be a bit less sensible. He knows that if he comes round to my house, my mum is much more lax about stuff than his parents are – if he wanted to, we could still have a clear hour alone in my bedroom, while my mum watches telly downstairs and pays us no attention. Way too often, Seymour is more interested in getting home to play guitar or spend hours chatting to other people on Facebook. I'm not sure if it's me or him, but I'm pretty sure this is not normal.

Before we get too close to the house, we stop and kiss goodnight. We both know the drill by now; we've done this enough times. No tongues – Seymour takes quite a bit of warming up before that's permitted, and he is remarkably prudish when a parent is within approximately a two-mile radius, so it's not even worth me giving it a go. I'm not risking getting shot down again so soon.

After five seconds or so he pulls away and starts walking towards my house again, not pausing to wait for me. He always walks me all the way to the front door.

'Hey, I just remembered,' he says, 'did you see that weird comment on your blog? Some guy pretending to be Jackson Griffith. I hope he's not some nutter that's going to start bothering you.'

I laugh it off. 'I don't think we need to start worrying quite yet – I'm just pleased that someone other than you and my mum has looked at my blog, though I still think it's probably Nish winding me up. Hey, maybe it really *is* Jackson Griffith.'

'Then I really should be worried. My mum wouldn't have to stress any more then – I'm sure you'd dump me in a nanosecond and run off to LA, or wherever it is that he's rock-'n'-rolling himself to death these days.'

'Yeah, right. I don't think you need to lose any sleep over it tonight. Thanks for walking me home – text me when you get in, yeah?'

'Of course, and I'll see you at college tomorrow. Night, Chew.'

I stand on the doorstep and wave until he disappears. I'm glad my mum is still awake, because I'm not tired at all.

PJ Hardly

When I was a kid, my mum used to listen to Kate Bush a lot in the car. My earliest memories are of wailing along from my booster seat in the back, along with the whole of The Hounds of Love and Never for Ever. I still know all the words now. 'Running Up That Hill' would be one of my Desert Island Discs. I spent a lot of time perfecting my crazy Kate Bush dance moves.

Crazy was the key, you see.

I'm sure it was the early influence of Kate that got me into the idea of beautiful, talented and mad women for evermore – from PJ Harvey to Björk to Florence. It's a deep lifelong love in me.

Basically I wish I could be beautiful and talented enough to be that barking mad and get away with it. I want staring eyes and cloudy hair like Kate Bush. I want to stand on a hillside in a thunderstorm quoting the Brontë sisters in shrieking verse. There's something deeply sexy about being that mental, right? Well, so long as you're good-looking enough. Then you're fascinating and different, and just too divine for this world. Otherwise, you're just mental and/or a bit silly.

If I tried this, my mum would tell me to brush my hair and my friends would all laugh at me. (They frequently do anyway, obviously – have you met me?) So I'll stick to dancing in my room in my old jazz leotard with my charity-shop shawl, thanks.

Comments

Aw, Chew – you are a special little snowflake. Now brush your hair. Love ya!
Nishi_S

nice piece. I only found yr site cuz I was googling myself . . . but I've stuck around for the writing! Stay beautiful!
jackson_e_griffith

The canteen at college is so much better than school ever was. It's massive and there are different stations where you can get pizza or baked potatoes, instead of just one rubbish shepherd's pie with grey meat.

Nishi and I are sitting at our usual table. It's not like it's a particularly amazing table but we're creatures of habit.

'How was your date with Seymour last night?' Nishi asks me.

'Date?' I screw up my face. 'And how *was* it? You know us so well you might as well have been there. We went to Moshi Munchers; we had miso soup and those really amazing dumplings, and I ate about a million of those octopus balls that everyone else thinks are really gross. He walked me home, then I watched telly with my mum and stuffed my face with chocolate biscuits because I am a fat, disgusting piglet with no self-control gene. Standard. It was fine.'

'Then why do you think I'm asking you a polite and uncharacteristic question like that, Chew? Think.'

She pushes her plate away and looks at me, eagle-eyed, as I absent-mindedly pick up one of her wholemeal sandwich crusts and gnaw on the end of it while I ponder her question.

'I don't know. Really. Dunno. You're going to have to tell me.'

'Because I want you to ask me about Anna, of course!' Nishi exclaims, with a look of exasperation. 'You're so desperate for everything to be great all the time that you don't even ask any more.'

This strikes me as grossly unfair, but I suppose she's right, in a way. Nishi usually is. I *do* want everything to be great. I don't see what's so wrong with that. It's why I didn't tell Nish about Seymour's mum not wanting him to see me any more; I just said my evening with him was 'fine' so as not to bore her stupid with all the less than perfect details. There's no point.

I suppose that's why I like writing so much; it gives me some power over my sad little life – you can at least try to be funny, or make a crap party sound so much better than it was just by concentrating on the little details or making a joke about its very crapness. Those details are always there if you look for them – the tiny sparks of glitter and neon in a doomy, dark Wednesday. Even if it's just doing a good job on painting your nails for once, or eating a particularly crispy-skinned baked potato.

So I take a deep breath before I reply. If things aren't great between Nishi and Anna, then I'm not sure I want to know.

'OK. How are things with you and Anna?' I ask, trying to keep the tone of dread out of my voice.

I recognize this feeling. It's not quite so bad on this occasion, obviously, but it reminds me just a tiny bit of all those times – from my dad onward – when my mum would sit me down and say she had to talk to me about something. She'd tell me she was breaking up with whoever the guy was, always say it wasn't my fault, then she'd cry a bit and pretend not to; then we'd usually get a takeaway and watch a crap film together to cheer ourselves up. That was the drill.

I'm hardly the traumatized child of a broken home, but it would be nice not to go through that again. Ever.

'How are things with me and Anna? See, that wasn't so hard, was it?' Nishi starts to roll her eyes at me, in her usual sarcastic style – but halfway through she fails miserably and her face crumples. 'Oh, Chew, I just don't know . . . I don't know if she likes me any more. I don't think she does, at least not as much as she used to.'

She leans her elbows on the table and clutches her face with both hands. Her sharp bobbed undercut flips over on itself so all I can see is the contour of her shaved head underneath. I instantly forget about my own self-absorbed worries. Even abandoning Nishi's leftovers, I drop the crust and rush around to her side of the table, accidentally kicking my plastic canteen chair over in the process. I bundle in and hug Nishi from behind, as tight as I can.

Nishi's not really the hugging type, but I want her to know that I'm here for her. She stiffens and brushes me off – although I know she doesn't mean it nastily – so I walk back around the table, pick up my chair and sit back down in my own seat. Usually Nishi's as reluctant to talk about her feelings as I am, if not more so – which means this must be pretty bad.

'Oh, Nish . . . That's not true. It can't be. You and Anna are perfect together.'

'What, like you and Seymour are?' She says it in this slightly snarky voice, and for a second she looks over at me with a cocked eyebrow and a very odd expression. 'Oh, forget it.'

'Come on, Nishi. We've got this far. Talk to me. What's the matter? Has Anna said something?'

'No, she hasn't *said* anything – but she's being off with me, I know it. She's been weird for a while.'

'But I saw you guys on Saturday; we spent the whole day together – she was fine. We all had a good time, didn't we?'

I can't help feeling personally wounded by this possible state of affairs. The three of us get on so well – or so I always thought – that I might as well be part of this relationship. I couldn't stand it if Anna dumped both of us. I've had stepfathers I've cared about less.

Embarrassed at my own train of thought, I have to give myself a strict reminder that this is not all about me.

'Yeah, of course we did,' Nishi agrees, and I inwardly breathe a sigh of self-serving relief. 'The three of us always have a wicked time, don't we? It's when it's just the two of us that the problems start.'

'What do you mean?'

Maybe I really *am* more important to this situation than I thought. Maybe this *is* kind of about me. God, I hope Anna isn't secretly in love with me or something. Again I have to remind myself that this is not an appropriate thought process and shut my own stupid brain down before it can really get started. Bad Chew.

'Well . . .' Nishi looks uncharacteristically bashful. 'I mean, I don't really know how these things are supposed to work. You know I don't have a lot of experience in that department. But it's all a bit . . . awkward. Can I just ask you, what are things like with you and Seymour?'

'What *do* you mean?' I blurt out in the voice of a shocked Victorian spinster, forgetting in my surprise that this is probably quite a big deal for Nish and I ought to be making it easier on her – not make her feel bad the one time she decides to share.

'You *know*.' She rolls her eyes and snaps at me rather than admit her own embarrassment. '*Sexually*. I'm presuming that you and Seymour, like, *do it*. We're eighteen – well over the age of consent, after all – and we're all in proper relationships. So it shouldn't be a big deal, right? Otherwise I just have to assume that she doesn't really fancy me.'

Once she's finished speaking – a long and personal speech by Nishi's usual standards – she props her head in her hands again. I suspect this is due only partly to despair, and as much to avoid looking me directly in the face. With her undercut, pierced nose and her uniform of buttoned-down shirts and skinny black jeans, it can be easy to forget that Nishi is not always as tough as she looks.

Occasionally I'm forced to admit that she and I are not like normal girlie best friends. Neither one of us is particularly interested in discussing things like crushes or make-up at any great length – and although this shouldn't matter, sometimes it feels as though that's all the other girls at college ever talk about. Plus, much as we love each other, we'd rather have a laugh than sit about having emotional discussions or crying, or some miserable crap like that.

Over and above all of that, we do not – repeat *do not* – talk about sex. I don't know why Nishi is so reticent; that's her business and I don't really want to know. Well, maybe I kind of do, secretly, but I would never ask.

For myself, I know the reason why I would rather eat glass than discuss my sex life. The simple fact is that I don't have one. Everyone assumes I must be doing stuff with Seymour – we've been going out for a while and he is gorgeous, so they assume that of course I would want to. And I do want to, I think. We never really talk about it, but he just seems kind of . . . uninterested. I mean, isn't it supposed to be boys who are desperate to have sex and girls who are trying to stop them, not the other way around?

I've never had a boyfriend before Seymour, so I don't know what the norm is; maybe I've just watched too many American teen films. It's great that I don't ever feel pressured by him, or like I have to compromise my feminist principles in any way – but it also means I don't ever feel very, well, sexy. I'm actually glad Seymour isn't like that, but occasionally it seems to go a bit too far the other way – sometimes it can feel a bit like going out with Morrissey.

'Oh yeah, of course,' I bluster, going back to fiddling with the sandwich remains and not quite looking Nishi in the eye. 'I mean, yeah. Obviously. We've been going out for ages, so . . . I don't really like to talk about it. It just seems disrespectful to Seymour. You know what he's like – he'd be really upset if he thought I was gossiping about all that . . . you know, stuff.'

This is a stroke of genius on my part, I reckon. Because, if there was actually anything to tell, I'm pretty sure this actually would be Seymour's attitude. So it's not really a lie. Which is fine. Right?

Unfortunately Nishi gets the same weird look on her face that she had when we were talking about Seymour a minute ago.

'Chew,' Nishi says, 'is everything all right with you? That was kind of why I wanted to bring this up, as well. I don't just want to be totally self-obsessed for once! How are things with you and Seymour?'

'Fine, thanks,' I find myself saying automatically.

It's funny. There are things I *would* like to talk to Nishi about, now that I've got the chance for once – she is looking at me across the table with genuine concern – but for some reason I find I *can't*. Admitting that anything is less than perfect just seems too scary. Even though I know I'm being stupid and I should take this rare window while I can, I can't seem to stop myself from forming my face into a silly grin and waving her words away like I don't care. I can't even make myself look her in the eye.

'Tuesday,' she says, in her usual no-nonsense tone, 'it's up to you whether you want to talk to me or not, but I'm your best friend and I'm here. No matter what. I'm not going to go all soppy, but I want you to know that. OK?'

There's a pause, in which I worry that I might actually burst into tears. Nishi, being my best friend in the entire world and all of history, lets me have a moment to pull myself together if I want to.

'Yeah,' I say eventually. 'I know.'

We do look at each other this time, across the table. Dead on. Eyes level. We don't have to say any more – thankfully for both of us. I take her hand and squeeze it, just for a second; I drop it quickly before she tells me to get off.

'Hey.' I smile once more. 'Shall we get pudding? Go crazy for once. I'll buy you a treacle sponge and custard or whatever canteen delight they have today.'

'Yeah, go and see – tell me what they've got.'

I jump up to have a quick look at the blackboard and report back. I am laughing so much when I get back to the table that I can barely speak.

'It's spotted dick!'

'My favourite,' Nishi replies, totally straight-faced.

You Remind Me of the Babe

Because we have nothing better to do with our time, recently my friends and I decided to rewatch a childhood favourite film, Labyrinth.

When I was a kid, I was unfazed by this film. There was singing. There were funny goblins and animatronics, and weird flamingo-esque creatures whose heads came off. It was hilarious and fun, and only a tiny bit scary in just the right kind of way (i.e. not very).

So I was pretty shocked when I saw it now that I am an oh-so-worldly and cosmopolitan eighteen-year-old. It's pure filth! Reader, I was appalled. And pretty excited.

David Bowie wears a catsuit and a codpiece! He sings weird pervy songs to a teenager that say things like 'How you turn my world, you precious thing' and 'Everything I've done, I've DONE FOR YOU.'

When I was seven, I kind of wanted to be Sarah from Labyrinth *because she got to wear a pretty white dress and hang out with weird creatures and talking animals. Now I kind of want to be her because she is really hot and – spoiler alert – has the chance to hang out for eternity in the labyrinth with the Goblin King. Who is, like, David Bowie. And, fact fans, she grew up to be Jennifer Connelly.*

I hope I don't feel like this if I start rewatching all my beloved childhood classics; it's way too disturbing.

There's nothing in The Lion King *that's going to give me weird sex dreams, is there?*

Comments
Ahh, Labyrinth *— yep, that was definitely one for the mums.*
Carrie_Cougar

Ew.
Tuesday-yes-that-is-my-real-name-Cooper

I love the Labyrinth *— how come nobody invited me?*
seymour_brown

Because it was girls only. Although Bowie's codpiece was clearly wasted on the TLBFs. I'd be *well* up for watching it again, BTW. If that wasn't obvious. In fact, I might buy you a catsuit and a Bowie wig for your next birthday.
Tuesday-yes-that-is-my-real-name-Cooper

Hey, if only I knew that chicks dug catsuits so much, my whole life would have been a lot easier. I might not have bothered with that whole boring 'learning to play guitar to get girls' thing. Thanks for the tip!! Anyway, I'm rambling now but I really love Bowie. I know it's not cool but I'm really into his plastic soul 80s period — great pop tunes, man! You seem like a girl who knows her music, so I bet you'll shoot me down and say you only

like Ziggy Stardust or whatever – but I'm just gonna put myself out there! Feel free to think I'm totally lame and never speak to me again! Also, just wanna say I really like your writing – you're funny!
jackson_e_griffith

Um, thanks? I'm not sure what to think about this . . . ?
Tuesday-yes-that-is-my-real-name-Cooper

I walk through the front door and the atmosphere in my house feels different. It's familiar, but I haven't sensed this for a long time.

First of all, my mum's home before I am for once. Her car is already parked in the road outside. This hardly ever happens; I usually have a minimum of an hour by myself, for watching TV and eating snacks before dinner without consternation. Usually I have at least three rounds of toast and get started on cooking dinner before Mum gets in from work.

As I walk into the house, kick off my shoes and dump my bag in the hallway, I register that music is playing somewhere, the windows are open and my mum's work clothes and belongings seem to be scattered liberally about the house.

'Hello, darling!'

I hear her voice and follow it outside, where I find my mum sunbathing in the last rays of afternoon sun hitting our minuscule garden. As she sits up, I realize she's topless and wearing only an ancient pair of yellow shorts that won't quite do up. Prince is playing on her laptop.

'Um, what's going on?' I ask, feeling a bit of a frumpy spoilsport.

'Well, it was such a beautiful afternoon I decided to work at home for once. Do you know what nobody ever says on their deathbed? "I wish I'd spent more time at work."'

'Oh god, what's *actually* going on?' I ask again, more suspicious by the millisecond.

I know what she's going to say before she opens her mouth. It's been a while, but the signs are so clear it's embarrassing.

'I've met someone!'

I kind of have to admire her optimism. Sometimes I can really see where I get my annoying cheerfulness from. The way she says this, if you didn't know better, you'd honestly think she was my age and had never been kissed before. Not a woman who's been divorced three times (so far) and has had more unsuitable boyfriends than I own ridiculous American Apparel leggings. And – trust me – that's a lot. She basically epitomizes that old quote about the triumph of hope over experience. Bless her – I wouldn't change her for all the world. Maybe one day she'll even be right.

'Actually, before we discuss this in detail, do you maybe fancy putting your boobs away?' I ask.

'You teenagers these days are such prudes,' she tuts. 'Pass me my top then. It's getting a bit chilly anyway – shall we go inside?'

'You don't have to ask *me* twice, Mater.'

As soon as we're back in the kitchen – and my mum, thankfully, has pulled on a T-shirt with a picture of a parrot on it – she turns to me with shiny eyes and a naughty smile, desperate to spill.

'Go on then – who is he?' I ask as required.

It feels like our roles have been reversed as I pour myself a glass of orange juice and eyeball her beadily.

'Well . . . we met on that dating website I'm on,

but we've been chatting for a while now.'

'Sneaky.' I wag my finger at her.

'Shut up. We've been emailing a lot and this afternoon we just spoke on the phone for the first time. He's Welsh; he's got a lovely voice. We're meeting up this weekend.'

'How come he's got nothing better to do on a weekday afternoon than chat on the phone to you – doesn't he have a job?' I'm grinning as I say it. I want nothing more than for my mum to be happy, but we have to be able to have a little fun about it. 'You have to laugh or you'd cry' has so often had to be our philosophy about my mum's love life.

'Actually he's a teacher. A history teacher, in fact. He had a free period.'

I mock-groan. 'Of *course* he is. A Welsh teacher who's going to lock me in the coal shed to teach me some good old-fashioned respect, right? What's his name?'

'Richard Jenkins.' She says it in the same way that I might say 'Jackson Griffith' or some other world-class hottie – Kurt Cobain, if he wasn't dead.

'What a boring name. Probably suits him. I bet he wears a lot of brown corduroy and reads the *Guardian* and clears his throat all the time, right?'

'Ha!' my mum shoots back. 'That's where you're wrong. Did you know that Richard Jenkins was actually Richard Burton's real name? If it's good enough for the most handsome classic movie star who ever lived . . .'

'Oh, that's good,' I say, all faux innocence. 'A couple more marriages and you'll be up there with Elizabeth Taylor – you must be made for each other!'

For a second, I think she's going to tell me off; it doesn't happen very often but, according to my mum, there's a line and I don't know when not to cross it. Then we both start laughing and crease up in absolute hysterics. It's the only way forward.

Fortunately my mum then appreciates that it really is a bit chilly and goes upstairs to put on a pair of jeans. I follow her up there and we end up getting into pyjamas instead and lolling about on her bed, putting the TV in her room on.

After a couple of episodes of *Bake Off* that we've had saved up, we can't really be bothered to cook a proper dinner. We shuffle downstairs in our pyjamas to make scrambled eggs and cups of tea to take back to bed. In a stroke of brilliance I grab a packet of Jaffa Cakes from the cupboard and stick them in my pyjama pocket to bring up the stairs along with my dinner on a tray.

We stick yet another rubbish film on – something to do with Anne Hathaway and a stray dog – and, unsurprisingly given our viewing choice, I end up falling asleep. I wake up at four in the morning in my mum's bed with the TV still on; I switch it off and creep back into my own room, making sure my alarm is set.

As I climb back into my own bed, still only semi-conscious and drifting straight back into sleep, the thought of Richard Jenkins the history teacher randomly comes into my head. I really hope he's nice and it all works out for her – but I need to make the most out of this kind of quality time while I can. We don't get to do these kinds of things when my mum has a husband.

Like a Lead Balloon

I think maybe it's because I don't really have a dad — it's fine, don't worry, this isn't some 'boohoo, my sad childhood' post; there are plenty of other places to go to for that. But it does mean that my taste in music — although I would hasten to say that I myself am most emphatically NOT — is maybe a little bit . . . girlie. Please note that I do include a lot of classic Riot grrrl under said banner of 'girlie'. I don't sit about listening to Adele's saddest songs and weeping all the time. Don't stereotype me, man.

For some reason, I had always decided in my head, for no good reason, that Led Zeppelin was 'boy music'. I've never listened to them much, despite my well-documented obsession with the 70s. Until now, dear reader.

I found a copy of Led Zeppelin I *in my favourite charity shop the other day and a strange thing happened. I felt weirdly drawn to its cover and had a sense that it would be the perfect addition to my collection. Suddenly this seemed like a gaping hole in my musical education — and, you know, I can't be having that. Hey, apparently Led Zep are Tori Amos's favourite band — so if that doesn't blow my previously misguided theory out of the water, I don't know what does.*

So it now sits in front of me as I type, and I am going to explore the world of boy music. I shall report back from the trenches of testosterone rock in due course. Wish me luck.

Comments

Good start . . . led zep one is a worthy addition to the collection. i have a hunch you'll like dazed & confused, great track, let me know what you think.
jackson_e_griffith

Look, thanks for the recommendation and I don't mean to be rude but WHO ACTUALLY ARE YOU? Not being funny, but pretty much nobody reads this silly little blog of mine except for my friends and my mum, so I find it pretty hard to believe that this is the real Jackson Griffith. I'm really pleased that you seem to like my crazy ramblings, whoever you are – so obviously I don't mind you *not* being THE Jackson Griffith. But as you seem to be hanging around in my virtual living room quite a bit, it might be nice if we could do proper introductions. Excuse me if this is incorrect blogger etiquette – it's totally up to you where you spend your online surfing time, so don't feel under any obligation or anything – but I wouldn't know because I've never really had a real-life anonymous reader before! I'd just like to keep things cosy and polite. Thanks.
Tuesday-yes-that-is-my-real-name-Cooper

hey, weird I know but it is me. I mean, I am me. guilty as charged. I goggled myself, ok?? Goggled, Googled, whatever – I'm an egomaniac! i hope you don't think me too forward but i saw there's an email address listed here on your site – emailing you now with proof of the

pudding! This mystery will soon be solved. The MYTH!
The MYSTERY – woooo!
jackson_e_griffith

Chew, seriously – stop feeding the trolls. Just ignore this
guy and he'll go away.
seymour_brown

relax, dude . . . I know my reputation precedes me but
it ain't all true! I'm just hangin out. I don't mean any
harm. Peace – JEG.
jackson_e_griffith

I can't believe it. I literally cannot believe it. I am sitting on the sofa with my laptop, drinking Nesquik and eating a peanut-butter sandwich with the TV on – the usual afternoon routine before my mum gets in from work – and suddenly the world has gone completely mental. This has got to be a joke.

I have just received an email from 'Jackson Evan Griffith', sent from his personal email address, no less. The guy who has been leaving comments on my blog and, according to the stats, looking at it most days. It's Jackson Griffith. It's really him.

It even begins 'Dear Tuesday'. It dawns on me that I now have Jackson Griffith's personal email address.

I know how unlikely this sounds – and that I sound like a totally gullible fangirl – but, against all odds, I'm pretty sure it must be him. Not only because his style of writing does actually sound like a Sour Apple song – and I should know because I've listened to them all enough times. Not only because he explains to me that he has just moved from New York to LA, via hospitalization for 'exhaustion' – I know this is true, but then so does pretty much everyone who reads the tabloids and/or music websites. Not only because he has sent me a list of random, personal facts about himself, like that his favourite fruits are bananas and avocados ('they're a fruit, you know!' he tells me helpfully), he prefers dogs to cats, drives an ancient blue Jeep, hates anchovies on pizzas and is currently reading *Infinite Jest* by Dave Foster Wallace.

No, I can be fairly certain that it's him because of the

slightly out-of-focus selfie attached. It is a bit grainy and obviously taken in a hurry, but it is most definitely Jackson Griffith of Sour Apple. It's a slightly different Jackson Griffith to the one I'm used to seeing in the papers, but this somehow makes it more authentic – he's got a bit of a beard and is wearing a burgundy beanie hat and a ratty old sweatshirt. He looks tired and a little bit baggy around the eyes – but he is half-smiling and still looks young for his age, even though I know he is now twenty-three, no longer the teenage golden boy of pop music. In the background I can see an empty-looking room; an open laptop is resting on the wooden floorboards and it's displaying my blog.

In case I still didn't believe him, he is holding an American driver's licence, which even in the blurry photo I can make out is in the name 'Jackson Evan Griffith' and bears a picture of him. A picture within a picture, as if he stretches into infinity.

Despite this exciting piece of evidence, my gaze is drawn first not to this important official document, but to the famous blue eyes, the sandy surfer-boy hair only half hidden by the hat, the lanky build that's easy to make out even in a head-and-shoulders shot, the mischievous look on his face . . . It's a few minutes before I am able tear my eyes away and minimize the window, going back to the email itself.

He goes on to say: *'if you still don't think that I am me, you can call my agent Sadie Steinbeck – I'm sure in this modern world you can look up all the details. I don't know why I care* so much whether you believe me or not. I don't usually go to this much effort where girls are concerned. Not being arrogant, but you don't have to if you've been in a famous band since you were eighteen years old. Anyway, for some reason, I do care. I guess it's because I like your writing, and I think you're funny and cute. That's pretty rare in my world these days.'

I have to deep breathe for a few minutes. My eyes start swimming as in a daze I see he's signed it: 'I hope I haven't gone too far and freaked you out by getting in touch, I was only playing, but I remain yours etc., JEG x'.

Slowly and carefully, I bite down on the side of my index finger as hard as I can, really sinking my teeth in until it hurts. Pulling away, I observe the deep purple-red tooth-marks and wipe off the gross sheen of saliva. I suppose this is real then. I laugh out loud in the empty room.

I switch off the TV so that I can concentrate, and start typing a reply. My brain is spinning so fast that I can't think my words through too carefully. I probably sound like a complete moron, but I'm not going to start changing my style now that I know he's a real pop star. Not only that, but a real pop star who I had a poster of on my bedroom wall when I was thirteen years old.

I hurriedly finish up – not even thinking about how my spelling and grammar are doing with my wobbly hands – with: 'I've got to be honest, I never expected Jackson Griffith as a pen pal – but I'm seriously thrilled that you like my writing. Maybe I can send you some interview questions and we could do a special feature on my blog; bet it's always *been your dream to appear on a random girl's website with a readership of approximately four (five now, including you) – welcome to the big time. Anyway, got to go – this peanut-butter sandwich isn't going to eat itself, and I *do* have some glamorous English lit revision to do – but I'm very pleased to make your acquaintance or whatever. All very best, Tuesday (yes, that is my real name!) Cooper. PS I don't want to say 'I love your work' but, um, I really do – and my mum would kill me if I didn't mention that she does too. Seriously, thanks for getting in touch – means a lot. Txx.'*

I hit send before I can think about the ramifications. As soon as I've done it, the voices of doubt start to creep in: mostly Seymour telling me that this is just some random nutter who somehow Photoshopped a picture of the real Jackson Griffith – probably some obese middle-aged weirdo who lives with his mum in Bournemouth or something. It's not only Seymour though – I know that Nishi would be telling me to stop being an idiot. Probably in a much louder voice than Seymour's.

So I distract myself with the obvious thing to do at this juncture. I start Googling Jackson Griffith. I look at pages and pages of photos of him – looking just like he does in the photo that he sent especially to me; a bit glossier in his official promotional pictures; quite a lot messier in paparazzi snaps from the worst of the gossip magazines. Always, I have to admit, looking unfairly, preternaturally gorgeous, in the way that only the famous and genetically blessed would be able to dream of.

Seeing multiple versions of his face actually makes this

whole weird situation feel less rather than more real. He looks like another species. So I shut it down and go to his Wikipedia page to remind me of the hard facts. Most of it is pretty familiar by now, to me as well as to so many other people.

Jackson Griffith was born in the prosperous town of New Canaan, Connecticut, the youngest son of an ex-model and a banker

– seems a most unfair advantage, that combination as a start, I reckon.

His parents divorced acrimoniously when he was eight years old; he grew up with his mother, Gill, and three sisters. Griffith was a prodigiously talented guitarist from a young age. Despite a well-documented misspent youth, he excelled at the progressive private school he attended. He had in fact started at a prestigious Ivy League college to study anthropology, before he dropped out after one semester as his band, Sour Apple – which he formed as a teenager with two school friends – had been offered a lucrative record contract.

Sour Apple's first album, *Come On Over (Please Leave Quietly)*, was a worldwide hit, due to a combination of their radio-friendly 'bubble grunge' sound and Griffith's pin-up good looks. Sour Apple became an overnight success, gracing every magazine cover and touring the world. Griffith in particular became known as an erratic live performer and an eccentric, if charming, interviewee. The band were noted for their relentless touring schedule, with some industry insiders questioning their management team's judgement in light of the band's youth and naivety.

Amid an international tour that would last for more than three years in total, the band released their more experimental – and, many would say, patchy – follow-up album, *Your Friends All Hate You And So Do I*. The album failed to fulfil expectations, despite reaching number one in Spain, France and Australia. However, Sour Apple were still considered one of the biggest bands in the world. Griffith became well known for his party lifestyle and was a familiar fixture on the celebrity social circuit, often appearing dishevelled and the subject of many rumours regarding his unhealthy lifestyle and turbulent love life. After being linked with many renowned beauties, he unexpectedly married the French model Célia Le Masurier in a secret ceremony after a whirlwind romance. Griffith was quoted at the time of his marriage as saying his new wife had changed his life and rescued him 'from a path of self-destruction and shallowness'.

Following his marriage, Griffith retreated from the public eye. He moved to the French countryside with Le Masurier and announced that Sour Apple would be taking an indefinite hiatus. For two years he remained quiet, apparently retired from public life and enjoying his new domestic idyll. At the age of twenty-two, he was – by choice – no longer the new face on the music scene, though many new bands continued to name Sour Apple among their influences.

Jackson Griffith returned, unexpectedly, at the Glastonbury festival in the UK the following summer. Not listed on the official billing, he invaded the stage when old friends, the seminal Liverpool band Creation, were playing the headlining set on the Pyramid Stage. He was spotted playing a tambourine, forgot the words to his own songs when Creation's Noel Moore tried to instigate a duet and fell off the stage after being booed and jeered by the crowd.

By all accounts a very public meltdown ensued. Griffith hit the party scene once again with a vengeance. This time around, many started to feel that his charming persona and boyish good looks were wearing thin. Célia Le Masurier filed for divorce, citing irreconcilable differences, following only seventeen months of marriage. Griffith broke his wrist in a late-night brawl and announced that he could no longer play music, so he would be going on tour with Creation, as their roadie. He became a regular fixture onstage, playing various toy instruments and singing backing vocals. His physical deterioration was evident, with fans being shocked by his appearance. After a gig in Liverpool in February, he was rushed to hospital, although the reasons for this remain unclear and rumours that he had died were confirmed to be an Internet hoax.

Upon discharge from hospital, he sold his flat in New York and checked into a controversial therapy programme in the Philippines. His agent, Sadie Steinbeck, released a short statement stating that her client was seeking treatment for 'exhaustion', and asked for privacy at this very difficult time. When Griffith returned, he moved to Los Angeles, where – at the time of writing – he is reported as living quietly and writing an acoustic solo album. He has not made an official public appearance since his disastrous visit to the Glastonbury festival, and sightings of him these days remain rare and largely unconfirmed.

I'm scanning the references at the bottom – lots of them, slightly worryingly, are headlined things like 'Jackson Griffith's public meltdown: all the details!' and 'Jackson Griffith denies going on a 48-hour drinking binge with Kate Moss and Cara Delevingne'.

'Chew, what on earth are you doing sitting in there in the dark?'

My mum's voice brings me back to the real world with such a bump that I literally jump out of my seat. My laptop goes crashing to the floor along with my still half-eaten sandwich. I hadn't even noticed that it had got dark. I forgot that I switched the TV off ages ago, and the room feels weirdly quiet.

'Chew, sweetheart – are you all right?' Mum asks in more concerned tones when no response is forthcoming.

'Yeah, yeah,' I reply quickly, still all discombobulated and blinking as I emerge into the bright hallway. 'I'm fine. Totally. Just . . . I had a really tiring day at college today, and I think I actually dropped off for a minute there while I was in the middle of my revision. Crazy, I know.'

I follow her into the kitchen, where she takes off her jacket and dumps her briefcase on the table. I grab a glass and fill it from the tap, downing one and then another.

'Oh, Chew,' my mum says in genuine sympathy, laying a hand on my forehead. 'You've always been such a hard worker. I hope you're not overdoing it. I know how stressful A levels are; I remember it well, even though it was back in the Dark Ages when I did mine. You just relax and I'll cook dinner tonight.'

I'm not sure I've ever felt so guilty. I've never had any reason to before. I hope it's not a sign of things to come.

La Belle Epoch

Yeah, I got a B in French GCSE. What of it?

OK, French was compulsory up to Year Eleven in my school. But even if it wasn't, I would have taken it anyway, because I like the idea of speaking French. I still get a thrill from such sexy gems as 'Où est la gare?' or 'J'ai dix-huit ans'. Impressive, non?

So I was basically hysterical with joy when – yes, in my trusty local chazza, of course – I found a double CD called La Belle Epoque: EMI's French Girls 1965–1968. It's full of jaunty beats, 60s joie de vivre and girls called things like Michèle and Véronique.

It is thus my favourite new thing to play as I dance around my bedroom, wearing a beret and a stripy T-shirt, and wishing I could be a hot French chick. Meet you at Café Rouge, yeah? It's the closest I'll ever get at this rate. Quel dommage.

Comments
Don't worry, Chew! I don't mind your boring old non-exotic Anglo-Saxon self.
seymour_brown

hey I was married to a hot french chick and i can tell ya they aint all they're cracked up to be . . . i nearly went out of my mind with boredom if you wanna know the real truth. gimme a smart, sweet writer chick any day o' the week! i don't wanna alarm you or be too

forward but I am really starting to think you're a special girl, Tuesday.
jackson_e_griffith

Um, thanks? *blushes* I'm not going to say 'ditto', because obviously you're a famous pop star and you don't need me to stroke your ego for you (or anything else, for that matter – ha ha).
Tuesday-yes-that-is-my-real-name-Cooper

and i thought I was the one being too forward, you English writer girls are crazier than I thought! I didn't say nothing about stroking. Officer, it wasn't my idea!!! She started it!!! OK . . . you're it – go . . .
jackson_e_griffith

Pfft, you're clearly way too used to girls throwing themselves at you so you're misinterpreting my perfectly innocent comment. *prim face*
Tuesday-yes-that-is-my-real-name-Cooper

That's hot.
jackson_e_griffith

I'm extremely busy and important and I am not listening. La la la la la . . .
Tuesday-yes-that-is-my-real-name-Cooper

Hahahahahahha – you kill me, I knew i liked ya . . .

been in the studio these last couple days working on some new ditties, aint nothing special but maybe you can get a journalistic scoop and be the first to hear 'em. I'd appreciate your advice anyway. So, it's five in the morning here in LA and I haven't been to bed yet so i'm gonna check out and leave you alone (temporarily, I hope). N'night, Ruby Tuesday (anyone ever call you that, ha ha). X
jackson_e_griffith

WTAF??!!??????
seymour_brown

Chew??
Carrie_Cougar

Seriously, Chew – what the hell is going on here?
Nishi_S

As we know, dinner at Moshi Munchers is usually my favourite thing to do. *Usually*. I am sitting in my customary corner seat with the full array of miso soup, dumplings and octopus balls laid out in front of me. I am sucking an edamame pod of its delicious oil and salt coating. I should be at my absolute happiest. 'Should be', you will note, being the operative part of that sentence.

Instead I feel like I'm up in front of a firing squad. A firing squad made up of the people who are supposed to be on my team.

'You're being deluded, Chew,' Seymour says, labouring his point, as he has been for the past ten minutes. 'There's no way that this is the real Jackson Griffith. Don't you think he would have better things to do than to read silly little blogs by small-town English schoolgirls? No offence.'

I hate it when people say 'no offence' after they've already said something really hurtful. I can't even be bothered to pull Seymour up on being so disrespectful, as he's already decided that I'm the one in the wrong, and Nishi and Anna both seem to be backing him up. He's being as bad as those girls who say, 'I'm not being a bitch, but . . .' before they say something really, horribly bitchy. Whatever else, he knows that my 'silly little' blog means a lot to me and I'm sure he's just being nasty on purpose because he's annoyed with me. It's really unlike him, but he's acting very weirdly in general about this.

'Well, he's got quite a lot of time on his hands since he came out of therapy,' I try to joke feebly.

I know now is the time to pull out my trump card, get out my phone and show them the photo evidence of the driving licence, and thus prove my triumph once and for all. But I don't. I tell myself it's because I can't be bothered, that they won't believe me anyway. But, if I'm honest, I think it's kind of because I want to keep something for myself. Especially when they're all sniping at me like this. I just want to drop it, before they make me feel like crap and ruin the whole thing for me. It's probably really wrong of me, but I want to enjoy my little secret for at least a bit longer without them taking all the fun out of it.

'Can't you be serious for once?' Seymour insists. 'I'm really worried about this. You've got some crazy guy stalking you via your blog – and not only are you joking about it, you're encouraging him! What do you think, Nishi?'

Typical Nishi – totally ignoring my pleading glances, she *actually thinks* about her considered, balanced opinion on the matter. Doesn't she realize that, as my best friend – and especially after everything she said in the canteen the other day – she should just take my side? I can already tell by the pained expression on her face that I'm not going to like what she has to say. Damn her and her strict moral code.

'Well . . . whoever he is, Chew,' she says, 'you've got to admit that those comments on your last post were really inappropriate. I can see that the attention must be flattering, but you need to shut it down. Not cool.'

I stop listening as they go into a flurry of pious agreeing with each other, all still saying that they don't believe it's him anyway. Like I'm not even here.

Worst of all, they clearly can't decide whether A) I've turned into some loyalty-free harlot who's going to run off with Jackson Griffith and become a professional groupie at a moment's notice; or B) I'm a poor easily led child who's being groomed by some weirdo perv posing as Jackson Griffith, and my mum probably needs to put parental control on my Internet access. I genuinely can't decide which one is more offensive. They're both pretty derogatory.

'Fine,' I say, holding my hands up. 'I've said I'm sorry. I already deleted the comments. I'll leave it alone. Can we please talk about something else now?'

Unfortunately for me, I am sure I must be the world's most rubbish liar. Yes, I'm lying – I *know* it's the real Jackson Griffith, but there is no point in pursuing that conversation with my friends.

'You're right,' I add for good measure. 'You're all absolutely right.'

However I feel so freaked out by lying to my friends, and how obvious it must be, that I suddenly feel all physically awkward – I don't know what to do with my hands or where to look. So I shove an octopus ball into my mouth, whole, without even bothering with chopsticks. I regret this immediately and promptly start choking.

For about half a second I'm quite glad to have created such a cunning diversion, however inadvertently. Then

I realize that I am actually, properly choking. I start to feel like I might die. I suppose it would be no more than I deserve.

'Stop mucking about, Chew,' Seymour says, barely even looking at me. 'We get it, we'll forget the whole thing – you don't have to try and be funny to distract us.'

I attempt to breathe and only succeed in inhaling more deep-fried octopus into my lungs. Clutching blindly at the table in search of my drink, I misjudge and come away with a handful of nothing.

'Guys,' Anna says quietly, after a few more seconds of me being asphyxiated in the corner. 'I think she's really choking. Her face is turning purple.'

Seymour and Nish don't get themselves together to do anything useful, so Anna starts pounding me on the back as hard as she can. It hurts a surprising amount considering she looks like the daintiest little thing you can imagine – I swear she has more genetically in common with a small woodland creature than she does with me.

Thankfully it finally works – she jabs an elbow into my side and I puke octopus balls right into Seymour's lap.

'Oh no, my new red jeans!' he exclaims, and I think it is pretty telling that this is his reflex reaction.

However he soon rights himself and makes all the appropriate soothing noises while he grabs about two dozen paper napkins and starts the mammoth task of mopping up his trouser area.

'Sorry,' I manage to whisper.

My throat really does hurt, and out of nowhere I feel

surprisingly teary, like not only has this evening been a disaster but it's just all too much. My near-death experience has pushed me over the edge and I feel weirdly emotional about all sorts of things. I'm probably just being silly. Plus I think I still have a chunk of batter lodged behind my nose somewhere. It feels disgusting.

'Look, I'm really sorry but I think I'm going to go home,' I say, standing up on slightly wobbly legs. 'I actually don't feel that well. You can all have the rest of my dinner – if you want it.'

Seymour and Nishi look like they might actually take me seriously for the first time ever when they see that I really am prepared to leave the remainder of my food. This has literally never happened before. They are both speechless.

'See you both tomorrow then,' I add, forcing a smile in the hope that they'll leave me alone. 'And see you soon, Anna. Night, everyone.'

I'm honestly relieved that neither Seymour nor Nishi offers to walk me home, even though they both live really near me. However, I can't help but wonder if they are all going to start talking about me behind my back the second I exit the building.

I'm past caring; the fresh air actually helps as I spill on to the pavement outside and start walking. It only takes me a few steps before righteous indignation kicks in and powers me along.

'Hey, Chew – wait!'

I'm barely listening. Expecting Seymour or, less likely,

Nishi to be the owner of the voice shouting out behind me, I don't bother to turn around and just keep walking.

'Tuesday,' Anna gasps as she catches up. 'I'm glad I caught up with you.'

She's panting and grinning, but she isn't even red in the face like I would be – Anna always looks very together. She's basically an indie Audrey Hepburn.

'Actually,' I say, which starts off as a croak but soon begins to go back to normal, 'since you just saved my life, I'm probably the one who should be chasing you around, offering to do good deeds or something.'

'That's OK.' She shrugs. 'Somebody had to do something. I learned everything I know from *Mrs Doubtfire*. Anyway, I wanted to talk to you.'

'Really?'

I don't mean to sound sceptical. As I've said a billion times before, I really like Anna. It's just that we have never really hung out, or spent any length of time one on one. Now I come to think about it, the longest times have probably been when Nishi has been to the loo in Macari's. Nishi can be a bit possessive of both of us, I suppose.

Oh god – my conversation with Nish in the canteen springs to mind. I hope Anna *isn't* secretly in love with me. I mentally roll my eyes at myself – I'm such an idiot; no wonder my best friend and my boyfriend both appear to hate me.

'Yeah,' Anna goes on to explain. 'I just wanted to say that I think the other two are both being really harsh. And I don't think it's right for Nishi to gang up on you with Seymour like that – she's supposed to be your best friend.'

'Well, thanks a lot – but you were a bit quiet too when this was actually happening . . .'

I know I'm being uncharitable and I should just be grateful for the support now. None of this is Anna's fault.

'I'm not proud of myself, OK?' she says quietly. 'I'm working on it. It's just that sometimes, with Nishi, it's really hard to speak up. I'm sure you don't understand because you're really good at holding your own, but she can be so forceful and she just automatically assumes that I have to agree with her about everything. Like, if I'm not with her I'm against her. God, you must think I'm so pathetic.'

'Oh, Anna! I really, really don't – I promise. I understand exactly what you mean. Nishi's always been like that. When we were eight and anyone asked her what she wanted to be when she grew up, she would always say she was going to be the Queen of the World. It was only when we were fifteen and she started studying politics that she downgraded to Prime Minister. I wouldn't be surprised if she is, one day.'

'It's why we love her, right?' Anna agrees. 'It's just that sometimes . . . I don't know, I feel like she just likes the idea of me, and she would rather I didn't ever say or do anything to spoil it.'

'I do know what you mean, totally,' I tell her, gabbling to hide the panic that's invading my stomach again. 'Sometimes I think Seymour's the same. I never feel quite good enough, if I'm honest. But Nishi loves you – she really loves you. She thinks you're amazing. You're the best thing that's ever happened to her. Honestly, since she met you, she's been a way nicer person. I mean, she's always been nice, but . . . You know what I mean!'

'Sure.' She sounds hesitant.

'You do love her as well. Don't you?'

'Oh, Chew – I really do. So much. *So* much. She's the coolest person I've ever met, and she's really beautiful and clever – how could I not? I think it's my fault; I'm crap at speaking up for myself. I'm going to work on it. I wanted to start with telling you what I thought. Next, maybe I can even tell Nishi!'

We both laugh, both relieved.

'Well, maybe I can help you,' I suggest. 'I'm used to standing up to Nishi and her craziness. I'll give you lessons.'

'Do you know what? That sounds great. It's really helped talking to you, Chew – thanks. We should hang out more, just the two of us sometimes. I ought to start spreading my wings a bit.'

'Yeah, that'd be cool,' I agree.

For the first time today, I feel like I'm doing something right and not everyone is against me. The least I can do is help Nishi and Anna out. Maybe Nish will start being a bit nicer and seeing things from my point of view if I can heroically save the day and help to solve her relationship problems.

'Anyway . . .' Anna changes the subject with a sly grin.

'Enough about me. I don't know if you know this, but I'm a big Sour Apple fan as well.'

'Right . . . ?' I hope I'm not going to get it in the neck again; I'm kind of over discussing this subject for one evening.

'So I've been doing a bit of research and I really think your mystery commenter *is* the real Jackson Griffith.' Her eyes are shining and she sounds almost as excited as I have been. 'The style of writing, everything he says – it fits. And he's known for randomly chatting to fans and stuff like that; this is just the sort of thing he would do. It's not that crazy an idea.'

At last. Someone. I haven't told anyone about the photo with the driving licence, or the emails that Jackson and I have been exchanging since. All anybody knows about are the public comments on my blog, and just that has caused enough of a backlash – Seymour and Nishi have made their position clear and I haven't even wanted to tell my mum for fear of her reaction. This is so huge and I have been forced to keep it totally to myself – which is *so* not me.

It might be stupid and childish of me, but suddenly the urge to spill is too much. Even if this is a very risky thing to admit to my disapproving best friend's girlfriend.

'Anna, can you keep a secret?'

To: Tuesday Cooper
From: jackson evan griffith

Hey there Ruby Tuesday!

I'm stoked that you replied to my email. I don't wanna repeat myself and start boring you, but I really think that you're a cool girl. And they're rare around these parts, believe me.

Don't take this the wrong way, but you remind me of my sisters. The kind of girls I grew up with, before things got so crazy . . .

I loved those interview questions that you sent me. But I have a better idea. Maybe.

So, this is top secret and I'm probably nuts but I have the weirdest feeling that I can trust you. I maybe mentioned that I have been working on some new solo tunes. Man, this is top secret!! And I mean TOP secret.

Anyway, I like it over in Europe and I'm kind of bored of LA. Don't know if you've ever been here but it's a pretty boring place. Scratch that – I shouldn't say it in case that means you don't ever want to come here and visit me! LA's GREAT! Honest! Shangri-LA, baby!

So, I feel like it's time for a change of scene. Overdue, in fact. My management's lining up some secret appearances for me in the UK. Good old Blighty as you would say, right?! They always liked me better over there. I'm gonna do some shows on the down low, do some press . . . And if that goes well, face my old nemesis at Worthy Farm when festival season comes around. But let's not go there yet.

I'm rambling cuz I'm nervous to ask you. I never have to ask girls things like this, I don't wanna seem too eager! But I arrive in London in around a week's time. I'm gonna be staying at a hotel over there, I can check which one and let you know. I'll be there a couple weeks, then staying with my buddy who lives in England, travelling to do some shows. Then, who the hell knows, maybe Glastonbury. That's still not a definite. But I will definitely be on your side of the pond for a few weeks at least.

Will you come and meet me? I don't mean to alarm you but I really wanna meet you so bad! It doesn't have to be 'a date', just a friendly meeting. It will be innocent, sweet, unimagined . . .

Whatever you wanna do. We can have coffee, climb a tree, eat kippers (that's what you people do, right?). Whatever. Go to Nando's!! I've heard of that place, never been!

Let me know. Meet me next to Nando's!

Yours, JEG XXX

To: jackson evan griffith
From: Tuesday Cooper

Dear Jackson,

I believe that honesty is the best policy and I am a terrible liar. Like, really bad. The worst.

So I ought to tell you now that I would love to meet

you in London, but I will be unable to do so. I am truly sorry.

I am probably being very presumptuous and childish here, but I should also tell you that I have a boyfriend. His name is Seymour Brown and he is in a band as well (it would be disloyal and you don't need me to tell you that they are not exactly on the same level as Sour Apple). He is eighteen and we go to college together.

In fact, I don't know how much you know about me from my blog. I am eighteen. I go to college, where I am studying for my upcoming A levels (I think that is like American SATs?) and I am hoping to go to university in the autumn. I live with my mum in a small, boring suburban town about thirty miles outside of London. I am quite a small, boring person.

I just do my blog because it's a fun project and I want to be a writer. I don't know if you have seen some of the pictures on my blog or on Facebook but I'm just a loud, somewhat 'kooky' (I hate that word, but let's face it) girl who's trying to make the best of what she's got and stand out in the crowd. I am very ordinary, really. I am not a model or an actress or a pop star.

I do well at school and I love my friends, but I am not the coolest, or the prettiest, or the most special by any means. I am of average height with unusually short legs (the uncharitable might call me dumpy). I have naturally brown hair that I dye myself very badly whenever I am bored, which is often. My clothes are all from charity shops and smell of dead people. I have a scar on my left cheekbone from the time a horse kicked me in the face when I was seven. Oh, and I can't ride a bike. And I am rubbish at climbing trees.

I don't know if you really do want to meet me. None of my friends (well, except Anna, but that's a whole other story) even believes that you are really 'you'.

My boyfriend is, to say the least, not too delighted about our correspondence. In fact, I am now worried that I may have been inadvertently fraudulent in our communications and given you the wrong idea. I'm so thrilled that you like my writing, and thank you for your support, but it's probably better if you don't post comments on my blog any more.

For all of the reasons above, I'm sure you will understand that I cannot meet you in London. Much as I would like to. If you even really wanted me to anyway.

With very best wishes and my sincerest apologies,

Tuesday Cooper (Ms) x

I haven't blogged. I am behind on my revision timetable, even in English. I can't think about anything else.

I send my email to Jackson Griffith, which I must say is very mature, sensible and reasonable of me – although it kills me, *kills* me to send it – and I have to resign myself to the fact that this is the end of the short-lived, weird, possibly fake affair. I am, just as Seymour and Nishi told me to do, shutting it down, once and for all. It is simply the right thing to do, or so I tell myself. I love my best friend, and I am very lucky to have a boyfriend like Seymour, and I am doing the right thing. Well done me.

Then I go up to my room with a jar of peanut butter, a loaf of white bread and a copy of *The Notebook* on DVD (my mum's, not mine – I hasten to add even at such a time of trauma), and I proceed to cry hysterically for the next two hours. Fortunately my mum is out at a work dinner until late tonight, so I am free to wallow.

I know I'm being ridiculous. I know that it's technically impossible to miss something you've never had. But it's letting go of the idea that's the hard part. It was a flash of excitement in my boring little life, and I'm extinguishing it before it's even got started. For a tiny window in my ordinary existence I've been able to entertain the fantasy that a gorgeous (not just in my opinion but Official Fact – he's been listed in the 50 and 100 'most beautiful people' by several trashy magazines) and talented pop star could be interested in me, Tuesday Cooper – an average girl with a weird name, too-big ambitions, chubby thighs and delusions of grandeur. It was so fun while it lasted.

Whether it was true or not. It added a sprinkle of magic to my dull little life.

Because I'm tired and miserable, and allowing myself to break my usual code of Putting A Brave Face On It At All Times, I take the opportunity to feel thoroughly sorry for myself and think about every single bad thing that has ever happened to me in my entire life. I'm too fat. I don't have a dad. My mum is always chasing after something that doesn't exist and there is nothing I can do to help. My best friend and my boyfriend are making me feel like utter crap. I'm terrified about the future. I hate my thighs. The most exciting thing ever to happen to me is about to disappear and I don't want to be a grown-up about this at all.

Then – because I'm Tuesday Cooper, always putting my foot in it, always making a joke, never serious and never a drag – I pull myself together. I wipe the thick rope of snot that has somehow made its way past my chin and into a clump of my hair, rub the black eyeliner off my cheeks and tell myself that's enough.

After my sob-fest, I immerse myself in a boiling hot bath with one of my mum's old Jilly Cooper novels. A fat brick of a book from the 80s, that's really saucy and has a lot of horses in it. That's always guaranteed to cheer me up. I really go for it, with candles and music on and everything. I manage to stop myself from listening to Sour Apple, and put on a bit of old Neneh Cherry (hard-copy charity-shop find) to cheer myself up.

It mostly works and that's a good thing because, by the

time I get out and change straight into my pyjamas, my mum might be home at any time. I don't want to have to get into a whole stupid discussion with her as well. It wouldn't do for her to catch me weeping and dripping about the house – I don't want to worry her for no good reason.

It's not that late, but I'm just going to go to bed. I'm not in the mood to get anything useful done, like college work or blogging, and I'm not even much in the mood for watching TV. I'll just check my emails first.

I sit down on the edge of my bed with my laptop – an old work one of my mum's, passed on to me, which I have duly decorated with a wide variety of ridiculous and/or sparkly stickers – and that's when I see that I have twelve unread messages. Other than one that is trying to sell me a cheap holiday to Latvia, they are all from Jackson Evan Griffith.

The first is just one word. 'Please.' The second says only, 'I really wanna meet you!!'. The next few follow on from this along much the same theme. There is another iPhone photo of Jackson Griffith, doing a sad face. He looks like an adorable puppy. A very sexy, adorable puppy.

After that, the photos and random messages continue and it should be creepy, but somehow it's not. It's weird but it's sweet. Next is a wonky photograph of a chain-link fence with a pink flowering plant growing up it, the California sunshine bright and a big blue car in the background: 'the view from my new place here in Los Feliz . . . wish you were here. I live opposite the old high school where they filmed the movie Grease. I have a weird feeling you *might like that movie. I think it's OK, as is the country Greece. Write, call, email, text any time. Come round for dinner.'*

After sifting through them all, I come to the final email. It just says, 'I will cease being a pest now. Yours etc., JEG X.'

I am still staring at it when I hear my mum's key in the door. I quickly snap my laptop shut. With lightning speed, I switch off the light, leap into bed, pull the covers up to my chin and screw my eyes so tightly shut that it hurts.

I think I would feel better about my decision to blow off Jackson Griffith if Seymour and Nishi could just be a bit more bloody gracious about the whole thing.

'Hey, Chew,' Nishi greets me in the canteen, where she is already sitting with Seymour – most annoyingly, he is in my usual seat. 'How's it going? Meet any pop stars in double English this morning? I've noticed that new caretaker out on the sports field looks a bit like Harry Styles; maybe he reads your blog!'

She's looking at me like I should know why her tone is so nasty, but I have no idea.

'Wow! Why are you being so bitchy this morning?' I ask, genuinely taken aback.

'Oh, don't be so touchy,' Seymour chuckles. 'Nish is only kidding. You've got to admit, the whole thing has been a bit of a joke.'

I smile along as best I can, just to show that I'm not being 'touchy'. And I'm not, I don't think. They're not being fair – I'm really trying here. This is fast turning into one of those 'jokes' that becomes a running theme and is used to make a person feel bad at every possible opportunity.

It's weird that they're teaming up like this – and I'm not sure I like it. I've always wanted them to get on, but this is a step too far. Nishi has never really taken Seymour seriously, and he's always been a little bit intimidated by her, so they've kept each other at a comfortable arm's length before now. Both Nishi and Seymour can be quite judgemental sometimes – I should have predicted that this would happen if they ever had cause to join forces.

'I've noticed there hasn't been any more action on your blog. Has the nutter given up and left you alone?' Seymour asks.

'I guess so,' I agree, taking a massive mouthful of my macaroni cheese and burning the skin off the roof of my mouth in the process. 'That's the end of it. I've learned my lesson; you guys were right. I won't reply to anything like that ever again.'

It feels as if they're both looking at me a bit too hard. Maybe it's unlike me to give in like this, and not put up a fight or at least try to make some sort of 'hilarious' joke out of the whole thing. I just can't be bothered. I feel like I've cut off contact with Jackson Griffith for their sake, and now they're being so mean to me it doesn't seem even a tiny bit worth it. I can't help but feel a bit begrudging. I shovel down a bit more cheesy pasta to avoid having to make conversation.

'Watch it, Chew,' Nishi warns. 'You don't want to chuck up your dinner all over Seymour's jeans again!'

She gives off another drain-like laugh and looks mildly disappointed when Seymour doesn't join in. If she knew him as well as I do, she'd be aware that Seymour isn't as great at laughing at himself as he is at laughing at me. In fact, he's pretty good at being the touchy one himself.

'Anyway.' I decide to try changing the subject. 'How's things with Anna, Nish? You guys do anything yesterday?'

She shoots me a look that freezes my blood. I instantly understand where all this animosity is coming from; it is not anything to do with comments or my blog or with me and Seymour.

'I really wouldn't know,' she snaps. 'You're the one who walked home with her after she left me the night before last. I've barely even heard from her since. I've got to go.'

She pushes her half-eaten quinoa salad aside and leaves the table without even saying goodbye to me, stomping out of the cafeteria.

'Bad move, Chew,' Seymour says, shaking his head and taking the last bite of his sandwich. 'I'd better go after her. I know you didn't mean anything by it, but I really think you'd better apologize to her. See you soon, OK?'

He pats me vaguely on the shoulder and trots off after Nishi. This is unbelievable. What I want to know is, how come it's all right for the two of them to gang up on me, yet the one time that I speak to Anna on my own I'm suddenly the one in the wrong? Nishi and Seymour just love blaming things on me – that's Chew, too loud, always putting her foot in it, always getting things wrong, let's say it's all her fault.

At the moment I feel like I can't do a single thing right. I am gripped by that pointlessly reckless, self-destructive feeling I get sometimes, which I know by now always ends in disaster. Or at least leaves me feeling completely rubbish about myself.

I shove the whole bowlful of macaroni cheese into my mouth within seconds, barely chewing. I wash it down with a can of Fanta, practically in one gulp, followed by a bag of salt-and-vinegar crisps that sting my mouth after the boiling hot cheese sauce.

I think of Nishi and her healthy lunches, and how Seymour can take about three hours to eat a two-finger KitKat, and it feels like I'm laughing in their faces, showing that I don't care. Too bad I'm the only one who will get fat.

I take a deep breath and plaster on some fresh orange lipstick – bright tangerine to match my vintage blouse – as I fear I have none left on by now.

I have a free afternoon and I had been planning to ask Seymour if he wanted to go to the cinema or something. But apparently he's too busy running after Nishi, so I have nothing to do. God, it's a good job she's a lesbian. There's enough to worry about here as it is.

I march out of the college building and start pounding down the road in an attempt to dispel the furious, pointless feeling. I have no idea where I'm going. I'm too jangly to concentrate on college work or anything else useful.

So I just keep walking. This is probably where I would smoke an angry cigarette, if I smoked. Fortunately I don't.

After a while the fist-clenching frustration passes. However, the deeper emotion that lurks beneath – the recurring one that I can't quite put a name to – does not.

I admit defeat and sit down on the nearest park bench. As if magnetized, my hand creeps into my pocket and closes around my phone. It's an old BlackBerry – another cast-off from my mum's office – so I can pick up my emails on it.

I barely even look at it as I automatically thumb out a message. I certainly don't stop to think about what I am doing.

I only type four words, but the gravity of each one hits me like a punch in the chest. I have a feeling that this is huge. I don't know what I'm getting myself into, yet I'm totally aware of all the potential ramifications – and I am doing it anyway. I don't care that this might ruin my cosy little life in so many ways.

I hit send. Four words: *OK, I'll do it.*

To: Tuesday Cooper
From: jackson evan griffith

Ruby Tuesday,

I gotta say I was pretty delighted to get your message. But surprised as well. I don't want to push you into anything or pressure you, or anything like that. I'm not so stupid that I don't realize this situation is very weird and it has been instigated by me. I know I can be crazy. I just really like you.

Please excuse my insane moment of sending you all those emails. It certainly wasn't my intention to hound you. I just get carried away sometimes – addictive personality, I guess. Some days I can't seem to help myself.

I'm doing so much better now though. I feel like I've come back to myself, you know? I like just being quiet, doing some work. Being a productive human being, you could say. Trying, anyway!

I'm glad I found your website. It's funny, you know – cuz I feel kind of like I know you through your writing (when I found it, I went back through and read the whole thing) so I kind of forget that I don't really know you. Not really. I know enough to know I like you. I like your writing, you've got smart opinions, you like great stuff . . . I've seen your picture as well, you know . . . You're really . . . OK, how to say this without being cringey or completely grossing myself (and you) out?! Sorry. Look, you're cute. As in, pretty. Really pretty.

I think I did fairly well with not pestering you, like I

said. But I confess I have been thinking about you, kind of a lot.

I know you might have really good reasons for saying you didn't want to come and meet me (OK, you listed a lot of them and there are some big ones). I'm not so egotistical as to not realize that you just might not want to! But I couldn't help noticing in your last [electronic!] letter that you sound so down on yourself. Let's be real: it sounded kinda like you didn't wanna meet me because you think you're not pretty enough. If I've got this wrong, then sorry to patronize you or whatever – but it sure sounded like it. I know you're not a model or an actress or any of those things – and that's part of why I'm attracted to you. I don't wanna sound jaded or braggy, but I've had enough of those types of people to last me a lifetime. Honest. Call me crazy, but I just have the weirdest feeling that you are the kind of person I need in my life right now.

So, in case you're nervous or whatever, I just want you to know, whether we ever meet or not . . . A) I'm not that shallow, and B) You are so much cooler than all those other girls.

As I have said a million times, I really wanna meet you – but only if you want to and it's the right thing. I just think you're a very cool girl. I am attaching the details of my trip and my cellphone number. I hope to see you, but if not I will understand.

Yours respectfully, admiringly and hopefully

JEG

To: jackson evan griffith
From: Tuesday Cooper

Dear Jackson,

I'm starting to suspect that I might be as mental as you are. (Ha ha, no offence!) I don't know if this is a good thing or not. Maybe it actually is.

I've known everyone in my life for so long, sometimes I feel like they make assumptions about me and they don't always really listen. You know, good old Tuesday . . . I'm the one sounding all cheesy now, but I feel like you're the first person to really see me. Does that even make sense? I'm not just saying this because you said I was pretty! Flattery will get you everywhere, apparently. God, I'm such a predictable girl sometimes.

If you feel like you know me through my writing . . . Well, I have been listening to your music for years and I think you are a pretty amazing human being.

Enough! Look . . . I know I've been sort of mucking you about, but I WILL come and meet you in London. (Note to self: how can I not?!) If you really do want me to, and this isn't some big sick elaborate joke at my expense.

I have some conditions:

1 We meet in a public place. Safety first, you know? Plus I read the odd tabloid – I know all about your terrible reputation. Ha ha.

2 Remember, I am a Serious Music Blogger. I'm
   going to interview you, like a proper journalist. I'm
   basically thinking of it as a business meeting.
3 There is cake. I just really, really like cake.

Hey, get me – making demands on pop stars. But I feel
I have to do something to preserve my own sanity amid
all this.

Oh, one more thing. So I know you're going to turn
up and you're not winding me up: the day of our meeting,
I want you to Instagram a picture of yourself holding a
sign saying the word 'falafel'. No explanations.

See you anon . . . ?

Tuesday Cooper, Serious Music Journalist and Girl
About Town

From: jackson evan griffith
To: Tuesday Cooper

Whatever you want. Seriously. I mean it. I can't wait.
J x

He's done it. He's really done it. He Instagrammed a blurrily snapped 'falafel', scrawled on hotel notepaper. I spent the entire train journey here staring at it on my phone and reading all the mystified comments and speculation – 'BUT WHAT DOES IT MEAN?!' – by a million fangirls.

In fact, looking at them all, it occurred to me that even they are mostly so much prettier and more glamorous than I will ever be. Not for the first time, I am absolutely stumped with wondering what the hell he wants with me. I can't shake the feeling that this must all be a mix-up, or at least some sort of elaborate cosmic joke. I mean, he used to be *married to a French model* for goodness sake.

It's probably a good thing that it's too late to back out now. Otherwise I might chicken out and not even get to see what could happen in my own life. I've made my excuses at college – an emergency dentist appointment – and Anna's the only person I've told where I am really going, only in the interests of safety. I remember those 'stranger danger' talks in junior school. In fact, I still have the occasional nightmare about strange men offering me sweets or asking me if I want to look at some puppies.

She's sworn to total secrecy, but under strict instructions to call me if I haven't texted her by four o'clock to let her know I'm safe, and to call my mum/Nishi/the police/the media and confess all if I haven't got in touch by six. I feel bad for putting her in this position; I downplayed the whole thing as much as possible, so that she wouldn't burst with excitement and not be able to tell anybody, but it was pretty hard for the two of us not to get carried away. I *may* have sort of given her the impression that I had been invited to a press event, rather than a one-on-one meeting in a cafe. I mean, it's an interview. Not a date – right? In which case, I probably feel way too excited at the idea of seeing this intriguing, talented boy in the flesh.

Jackson – and I think the odds are good that that's really who he is, rather than some crazy Internet stalker – even offered to travel out of London to meet me, if it would be more convenient for me. Much as I was tempted by the idea of bumping into half the people I know in Macari's while I was just casually having a coffee with Jackson Griffith, I told him I'd be happy to come into London. I don't know whether to feel relieved or disappointed that, as I walk around Soho trying to find the random cafe we agreed on, I am completely anonymous.

I thought I'd better dress like my character for the day, to keep me on the straight and narrow. I took the Serious Music Blogger theme and ran with it, so I'm in jeans and an old Nirvana T-shirt, rather than my usual vintage tomfoolery. OK, I'm still wearing a ratty leopard-print cardigan and slightly smeary red lipstick. But I think I look pretty cool; I can actually almost kid myself that I am a professional. I'm just here to do a serious interview, honest.

Of course, I am still struck by a complete crisis of confidence as I realize I am standing outside the cafe. It's just an ordinary cafe, nothing to be frightened of. I've walked past it more than a few times before, usually on trips to the massive Topshop with my mum or record-shopping expeditions with Nishi. I hover on the threshold until a tall, modelly woman with a cardboard coffee cup and a briefcase shoves past me and tuts loudly.

At least it propels me through the door, where I stand and look around the crowded, bustling room. In one corner, I see a tall, hunched figure in a hood, their face obscured. I have a strong feeling that it must be him, but I'm not sure enough to go over.

Then I see the cake. The table is completely covered in small plates bearing slices of it. The hooded figure looks up – even though he appears to be wearing a half-hearted disguise, made up of a baseball cap and a pair of thick-framed glasses, it's immediately obvious it is him. He looks different from all the mere mortals in the room. He has a force field around him. In the flesh, underneath it all, he's absolutely breathtaking. He's like a beautiful lion. Seriously. Don't laugh.

He finally looks up and grins over at me – a heartbreaking, perfect, crooked crocodile grin – and raises his coffee cup in salute.

Everyone else in the room seems to disappear as I make my way over to him, through the crowds and the tiny gaps between the tables. I can't feel my legs, and my stomach has fallen out somewhere around the door. Obviously I knew he was good-looking – he's Jackson bloody Griffith after all – but up until now that had seemed purely conceptual. I wasn't expecting him to be so breathtakingly *beautiful*. I can't take my eyes off him.

'You said to get cake.' He shrugs. 'I didn't know what kind you liked, so . . .'

He gestures helplessly around the table. There are at least five varieties of cake in front of him.

He stands up in a slightly awkward show of politeness. As he bends down, I suppose to hug me or kiss me on the cheek or something, I feel a rush of panic and find myself ducking to one side, so that he headbutts the side of my shoulder. What an idiot. I'm only glad I ducked so that he can't see my hideously blushing face.

Seriously, he is so good-looking in the flesh that I can't believe he's actually real. I'm starting to see where all those clichés come from, as I expect that any minute now I'm going to wake up in my normal boring life.

When I force myself to look up, like staring straight into the sun, he is still staring back at me. His sleepy, amused eyes make my heart stop, just for half a second. It's a physical reaction to his unsettling beauty. Yeah, I knew he was a gorgeous pop star – but this, *this*, is like being so close to some priceless artwork masterpiece that you're scared to breathe. He's still smiling, and he looks surprisingly young and somehow pure. Somehow I know instantly that he's a nice person and I don't have to be worried. My heart calms down a notch, in a good way.

'I'm so happy you came,' he says slowly, not taking his eyes off me. 'What's your favourite kind of cake? We've got carrot, chocolate, banana, something I don't know what it is, or something called lemon drizzle. Isn't "drizzle" what you guys call the weather over here? Sounds kinda fun, anyway. Let's get you a cup of tea. You English girls are crazy for tea, right?'

'Yes, that's right.' I grin back at him. 'And we all sing "God Save the Queen" every day at three o'clock. Actually,' I concede, 'I'd love a cup of tea, please.'

He calls over the waitress, who is clearly – understandably – charmed.

'So you're the cake girl,' she says to me, with a sideways look at Jackson. 'Lucky you.'

'It's just an interview,' I blurt out, coming over all prim and proper, not wanting to embarrass myself by getting carried away and thinking I could possibly be on a date with this person who is so clearly out of my league. 'I'm a music blogger, you see,' I add lamely.

Is it just my imagination, or does Jackson's smile drop, just slightly, just for a second? Yep, I'm definitely getting carried away and being stupid.

'Well, I think the music blogger would like a cup of tea, and I'll have another coffee, please.'

'I brought some questions with me,' I tell him when the waitress leaves.

'Um, OK. If that's what you wanna do. I'm glad I've got coffee. Although you should really know that I don't usually buy journalists this many types of cake. Hit me.'

I fish my battered notebook out of my bag and, as I turn to my page of questions, feel suddenly self-conscious. I take a giant forkful of the chocolate cake, and then wipe my mouth with a napkin before I remember that I had red lipstick on.

'What do you think is the worst song you have ever written?'

This sounded really cool and funny when I wrote it down in my bedroom – and when I practised it in my head on the train here. Not too fawning, a bit off the wall. Now I think I just sound silly and a bit rude. Not quite the vintage *Popworld* vibe I had hoped for.

Jackson bursts out laughing. 'All of them? Which one do *you* think is the worst? It's pretty much all that keeps me going – the hope that one day I'll write a decent song.'

'But you've written so many *great* ones!' I wail, totally overcompensating. 'I basically love them all. Well, nearly all of them. I even prefer your second album, even though people said it wasn't as good as *Come On Over (Please Leave Quietly)*!'

'Wow. You really tell it how it is, don't you?'

'Sorry.'

'No, I kinda like it. Makes a change, I can tell you. Hey, leave some of that carrot cake for me! OK, next question?'

'What's your favourite word in the dictionary?'

'"Superlative". I also enjoy "ululate". Next.'

'What's your favourite flavour of crisp?'

'My favourite flavour of *what*?'

'Um, crisps. Like . . . chips?'

'I still don't understand the question. Like, salt? Barbecue?'

'Never mind. Who would you invite to your dream dinner party?'

He looks me in the eyes seriously. 'Joan of Arc, Gloria

Steinem and Sylvia Plath. And you. We'll have a riot. Have we had enough questions now? Hey, how about I interview *you*?'

'Um . . .' It feels awkward to have the tables turned, although mainly I'm wondering why he would even want to – but I don't have much of a chance to argue.

'What's your favourite book? Whatever it is, I want to read it.'

I'm glad he started with an easy one; I don't even have to think. '*I Capture the Castle* by Dodie Smith. Have you read it?'

'Nope, but I'm definitely going to. I'm trying to become more well read.'

'Well, I really think you'll like it,' I find myself enthusing, forgetting where I am and who I'm with. 'It's really lovely. It's all about this girl called Cassandra, and she has this mad family, and she keeps a diary –'

'Kind of like you then.' He grins. 'Right. It's on my reading list. This is supposed to be an interview, remember? I know it's an obvious one, but what would your superpower be?'

'Actually I've thought about this quite a lot. It would definitely be the ability to read minds. It would be useful in so many ways, although obviously I might not want to know what people are thinking about me sometimes . . .'

'Wanna know what I'm thinking right now?'

I find myself blushing and concentrate on my teacup. 'That you'd choose the power of invisibility?'

'Hey, I probably would. No, I'm thinking that you're

much prettier than your photos even.'

'I . . . I, um, thought this was supposed to be an interview?' I stammer like an idiot.

'Tuesday, I don't want to speak out of turn here, but who are you trying to kid? You said yourself that your boyfriend doesn't know you're here – so you can't even put an interview with me up on your website. Can you?'

He's right. Somehow I really hadn't thought this through. He's looking straight at me, direct and clear-eyed; I start to realize that, despite his slightly shambolic persona, he's actually got a sharp brain. He's easy-going but nothing gets past him. My respect for him actually goes up a small level – if I'd suspected he wasn't just a pretty face, now I know it for sure.

'I'm sorry. I've been an idiot. It's just . . .' I can't even explain it.

'It's OK. This is a weird situation. I understand.'

He reaches over the cake plates and takes my hand, and I swear a bolt of lightning goes through me. His hand feels cool and dry and perfect. It's calloused from playing guitar and it belongs to Jackson Griffith. I can't even speak.

'Look, Tuesday . . . Let's be real, OK?'

I nod mutely, still staring at his hand.

'How about we just finish our cake and have another cup of tea?' he continues. 'And quit pretending this is an interview or whatever? Just hang out together, have a nice time. What do you say?'

*

I get home feeling like I have just had the strangest dream. I honestly can't believe that any of today really happened. It's a good thing that the house is in darkness and my mum is still out at work, or she would probably think I am on drugs, or that I have actually gone insane.

In the end we just talked. Me and Jackson. All afternoon and into the evening. About everything. And nothing. About music and books and favourite films and childhood pets; about Irish poetry and roller-skating and otters and 'desert-island condiments'. Once we started, neither of us seemed to be able to stop. One story led to another, until we were snorting tea out of our noses and had forgotten what we were supposed to be talking about in the first place.

We had so much fun that I forgot 'who' he was and could only see the person sitting in front of me – a goofy, clever, lovely boy with the prettiest eyes I've ever seen in my life. It was so comfortable and easy, it was almost like chatting to my mum or Nishi – until I looked at him and my insides turned the consistency of Nutella when you put it on hot toast. Delicious, hot . . . toast.

'This is amazing,' he said, in words that will surely be engraved into my cerebral cortex for the rest of time. 'I know it sounds really tacky and cliché, but I really feel like I can be myself with you — which, by the way, almost never happens. This kind of connection doesn't come along too often.'

We stayed until the cake was finished and we had drunk so much tea we were sloshing.

'I have to go,' I told him, knowing I had to but half hoping he might argue.

Outside the cafe, it looked like he might. We hung around like a couple of losers, Jackson scuffing his feet on the pavement and me making lame jokes, suddenly all awkward again. Then our eyes met and we both burst out laughing. Jackson took a step towards me.

Then, out of nowhere, there was some kind of kerfuffle across the road from us – a couple of cars pulled up and I could see people starting to crowd around. It took me a second to twig that all this might be because Jackson had stayed in one place for too long and we had both forgotten about his rudimentary 'disguise'. The hat and the glasses came off hours ago.

I watched as his whole being changed before my eyes. Gone was the easy bearing and amiable lollop; he was suddenly tense and twitchy. He shoved his hood up and hunched in on himself so I couldn't see his face.

'Man, I thought I'd lost these guys this morning,' he muttered under his breath. 'I really don't want you to get caught up in all this. Seriously. It wouldn't be good for either of us. I'll call you, OK? I've got to run.'

It wasn't a turn of phrase. He turned and ran. I just stood there and watched him until he disappeared around the corner, and then I found my slightly shellshocked way to the nearest tube station – entirely unnoticed by the crowd around me.

Now I'm home, feeling like a stranger in this familiar setting – as if the world has changed since I left the house this morning – and not sure whether I should be walking on air or kicking myself. It was the loveliest day I have ever had, but it ended so abruptly it felt like a full stop.

I'm lying fully clothed on my bed, staring at the ceiling in the darkened room – when my phone blasts out its signature ironic rendition of *Single Ladies*. I don't even dare to hope. I make myself wait until the end of the chorus before I move, holding my breath so as not to tempt fate. Even when I see 'unknown number' flash up on the screen, I don't let myself hope. He might have lost my number. He might not really want to see me again. He's definitely got better things to do.

'Hello?'

There is a pause. A cough. Enough time for me almost to combust.

'Ruby Tuesday?'

My entire body breathes a sigh of relief. I flop back on to my bed, falling through the darkness until I land on my back. My grin must be floating in the air of its own accord, like the Cheshire Cat's.

'Hi,' I say.

'I know I ought to say thanks for a wonderful afternoon and sorry I had to run out on you like that – and I will, promise. But first, I really wanted to ask you – where do you stand on peanut butter?'

My laugh echoes all around the empty house.

'Well,' I reply thoughtfully, 'I'm pro, generally. But the crunchy kind is the best, obviously. And not that weird organic, sugar-free stuff that my mum buys in the health shop. Actually, it's funny that I like crunchy peanut butter, because I only like orange juice with *no* bits. Orange juice with bits in is an abomination.'

'Are you crazy?' Jackson asks. 'Real fresh orange juice is the best. My mom lives in Florida now and the orange juice there is crazy good. You ever been?'

'Nope. I've basically been to Broadstairs and Spain. Oh, and France on a school trip once. What's your mum like?'

'Well . . .' I hear him exhale at length while he has a think. 'My "mum" is pretty cool. She's a nice lady, you know. Super pretty – she used to be a fashion model; now she renovates houses. We didn't get on when I was younger and kind of wild, but now I like to hang out with her and my sisters when I'm back home. Doesn't happen very often.'

'Are your sisters older or younger?'

'Two older, one younger. By the way, Tuesday – will you come and meet me again tomorrow? I really want to see you again.'

'Tomorrow?' I can't; I have to. I can hardly breathe. 'I'd love to.'

'I was hoping you'd say that. Come to my hotel if you like – it's nice. Get there as early as you can so that we can have the whole day together. Anyway, I've told you about my mom and my sisters. What about your family? It's just you and your mom, right?'

I tell him all about my mum, and college and my friends, and somehow I don't even worry that I'm boring him. I can tell that I'm not. I hear my mum come in and potter about in the kitchen, and I take my voice down by a notch but don't even think about hanging up.

Even with my mum downstairs, right below me – there in the darkness, lying on my bed with the bedroom door closed, Jackson's voice is low and soft in my ear, and, as it gets later and later and we keep talking and talking, I feel like we are the only people in the world.

I wake up in the morning, still in my clothes and with my phone squashed against the side of my face, stuck in my hair.

Random Chaotic Ramblings

Are you there, Internet? It's me, Tuesday.

Sorry, I've been crap. This is the longest I've ever been without blogging since I started up this little electronic journal about three years ago.

I'm feeling weird, and A levels are really looming. I think maybe I am more stressed about this than I have fully realized. Not to sound melodramatic – I know they're technically only exams.

But I really want to do well at them. This feels like my one big chance. To get out of this small town and go to university. To try to become a writer one day. To do something with my life and be something other than ordinary and boring.

But then there's a flipside to that – of course, there always is. Leaving my friends. Leaving college, which I have loved so much. Maybe not living with my mum any more. Growing up.

I'm welling up here. I'm just overtired, honest.

From time to time it all feels like too much. Please forgive me if I don't blog a lot these days.

Comments
[No comments.]

This time it's different. I can't pretend it's an 'interview', or that I am doing this for any reason other than the fact that I am desperate to see Jackson again – and this time I believe that he wants to see me. I can't kid myself that I am not completely, stupidly, verging-on-insanity crazy about him. Not any more. I am so excited I can hardly breathe. But at the same time, I am now a liar. There's no going back from that. No excuses.

I am supposed to be at college. Right now, English literature – my favourite class, no less – is going on without me. Just when I need it most, as the exams start in a matter of days. We're studying *Tess of the d'Urbervilles*, which suddenly seems rather fitting. I hope this isn't an omen. Things didn't end too well for Tess.

When I woke up this morning, I suddenly knew that I have to break up with Seymour. It's the decent thing to do, and I suppose this whole Jackson situation has only confirmed some things that Seymour and I both already knew. As soon as it hit me, I realized it was obvious. I've never felt this excited about Seymour – and it's taken this to make me see it. More to the point, in all the time we've been going out together, I've never been able to talk to Seymour like I can with Jackson, and he's never made me feel like my best self. Not like this. Even if nothing ends up happening with Jackson, it's made me realize that it's over with Seymour. I just have to tell him.

I've always thought I was a pretty brave person – but I can't bring myself to do it. I've been telling myself all morning that I don't have time – I've been too busy getting dressed and putting on eyeliner and dyeing my hair on the spur of the moment. But really I don't have the guts, not yet. And so, on the most exciting day of my life so far, I feel like the world's most terrible person.

I can't even pretend not to have made an effort this time. For once I thought, Why the hell not? So I am wearing a ridiculous red dress and feeling utterly overdressed to be sitting on another train that is on its way into London. But in a good way – like I have a secret. If only everyone on this train knew where I was going.

I'm just hoping that my absence at college for one more day might go unnoticed – I sent a vague text to Nishi elaborating on my made-up dentist story. As luck would have it, my mum has her first in-person date with Richard Jenkins tonight. So she's been too preoccupied to pay much attention to me for the past day or two, which has helped. It also means that she'll be out for the whole evening. It's not like I'm intending to stay out all night – I'm really, seriously, certainly not – but at least if I get in a bit late because of the trains or something, I won't have to go into some big, awkward fake explanation. This must be the first time I've ever been so genuinely pleased about one of my mum's dates, so at least that's a plus.

I've been fidgeting and jiggling all the way into London, staring out of the window at the whizzing grey scenery as it turns gradually – painfully gradually – from suburban to urban, because I am physically incapable of concentrating on a book, or even a magazine. I can't even listen to my iPod – it would be too weird to listen to Sour

Apple when I am on my way to a secret assignation with Jackson Griffith, but I can't think of anything else I want to listen to right now.

It occurs to me that I still seem to find it impossible to think of him as just 'Jackson'. I mouth the word into the thin air to practise, and it feels foreign in my mouth – not right somehow. I can only think of him as 'Jackson Griffith' – pop star, pin-up, international playboy, not a real person. This surely means that I am way too immature and stupid to be meeting him at a hotel in London.

It's too late to be thinking about any of this, as the train is pulling wheezily into Paddington. As I get off, I see the day has now turned sunny and warm, rays of bright sunshine falling through the grand glass roof of the station. Now that I am an anonymous girl in the big city, I suddenly don't feel so ridiculous in my second-hand red 50s dress. As of this morning, my hair is now a dark red, rather than brassy blonde – more Rita Hayworth than Riot grrrl – and I wanted to dress fittingly. Or so I tell myself. Like I am doing all of this 'for myself'. I hate to admit that I just wanted to try my best to feel pretty for once.

Just for a moment, here where nobody knows me, I imagine that I could be any normal, pretty girl on a sunny day, on my way to an exciting date that might change my life. Maybe passing strangers might think that I am called Sophie or Lucy – something lovely like that – and that I might be the sort of person who has brothers and sisters, or a dad.

It only lasts for a minute, before I get self-conscious and wonder if people who turn their heads are actually looking at me because I'm weird, not pretty, a bit too fat. Uncontrollable Chew. But it's nice while it lasts.

And then here I am, miraculously on the pavement outside his hotel.

It's a perfect day. The sun is still shining down on me. I am standing here in a grand street in the very centre of London, a beautiful white building looming in front of me, a discreet brass plaque confirming that this is the right place. Inside is a hotel that is super-fricking-trendy cool and old-school luxurious in equal measure – apparently it's Jackson's favourite place to stay whenever he's in London. I've never been anywhere like this before in my life.

Outside, amid the few people walking past on their way somewhere else, there are again a couple of men with cameras. It would be pushing it to call them 'a crowd of paparazzi', but it's obvious that is what they are. Either luckily or unflatteringly, I seem to be invisible to them. They are paying absolutely no attention to me; they are just hanging around in the street outside, smoking and laughing, far too deep in conversation even to look up. If they did, I expect they would think that I was a hotel employee, a waitress on my way to work, maybe even a renegade teenage Sour Apple fan. Too ordinary to suspect of anything else.

I'm so self-conscious that I trip over the doorstep as I walk inside, even though I feel as though I'm making every move in slow motion. Thank goodness I don't fully fall over, but I stumble badly and have to grab the door frame to pull myself back up. Cool, Chew – very cool.

It's enough to take away from what I suppose ought to be a moment of triumph. Instead I feel mousy, kind of sheepish – far from the loud, confident and clever girl that everyone thinks I am – as I walk into the hotel and up to the reception desk. I still think this might all be a joke.

'Yes?' the hipster girl behind the desk intones.

She's what I would typically have imagined in all my worst nightmares – sleek black hair, thick black glasses frames, red lipstick, half a sneer. Perfect, probably French. I have to remind myself that I am supposed to be here. I have been invited.

'I'm here to see Jackson Griffith,' I say, practically a whisper. 'He's expecting me. My name's Tuesday Cooper.'

'Sorry, Ruby Cooper?'

'No, *Tuesday* – like Tuesday Weld or, you know, the day of the week.'

'What an, ah, *unusual* name. One moment. I'll just check if he's awake . . .'

She smiles in an unpleasantly proprietary fashion, as if she knows all his domestic habits and I know nothing.

The receptionist discreetly covers her mouth as she murmurs into the phone, half turning away from me so that I can't quite hear what she is saying. If he's asleep, or he's forgotten, or he's changed his mind – I'll die. I swear I will die right here on this beautiful Moroccan rug.

After a moment she turns back to me with a bit more interest, visibly thawing by at least ten degrees, but she still sounds surprised when she speaks.

'He's awake,' she confirms, her pussycat smile spreading across her alabaster face. 'You can go on up. Lift's on the left; Jackson's up on the third floor – his usual, room 316.'

I raise my eyebrows at her just for a split second to show that I know her game. She's jealous that I'm on my way up there – invited – and she's trying to psych me out. I might look like nobody, but obviously – and against the odds – I am *somebody*. People don't like unexpected twists like this.

'Thanks so much for your help,' I say, imagining I'm Courtney Love or Liz Taylor or Kate Moss – anyone but me – as I walk to the lifts.

The lift glides with such expensive precision it doesn't feel like it's moving. It's me who's uncontrollably jiggling on the spot. The carpets are so thick I can't hear my own footsteps. The whole process seems almost too smooth when I find myself outside his door. I have to remind myself: *Jackson Griffith's hotel-room door.*

Then the door opens before I have even raised my hand to knock, while I am still standing there dumbly. I'm staring down at the carpet and the first thing I see is a pair of large, slightly grubby bare feet. I look up slowly until I see that unmistakable face, shaggy dirty-blond hair and dreamy blue eyes – the colours of the sand and the sea. He's seems much taller than I remember, standing over me in the doorway. I don't know where to look, because he is wearing only a pair of battered jeans that are hanging low on his hips. That's it. I don't know where to look, because I want to stare and stare and stare. I have never fancied anyone this much in my entire life – so much so that it's unsettling.

I put up no resistance whatsoever as he pulls me inside and closes the door behind me. Honestly I'm still trying to get my breath back, just from the *look* of him. Just from being near this golden beauty of a man. With no top on. He practically glows. He looks as though he has been carved out of fresh yellow butter. In a good way.

It's so different this time, in a hotel room instead of a crowded cafe, and with none of the excuses of yesterday. This is not as safe as being on the other end of the phone line. I am still just lucid enough to think, I could get myself in so much trouble.

'Hey,' he says with a grin. 'How are you doing this morning?'

I try to reply and just make a strangled noise at the back of my throat.

'You OK?' he asks.

I nod a bit too emphatically. 'Fine,' I croak. 'You?'

'Yeah, I'm cool. Had a pretty good sleep actually. And I have a feeling today's gonna be a great day.'

Thankfully he goes to pull on a stripy T-shirt and my eyes are able to roam far enough to take in the scene inside the room – it's a beautiful hotel room as I expected, all high ceilings and lavish features and white linens; there's a sitting area as well as a bedroom and a bathroom, and a balcony – but it's all a total mess. I can see at least three guitars, a couple of room-service trays, coffee cups, discarded newspapers and overflowing ashtrays, clothes strewn everywhere. The level of carnage is impressive, and I wouldn't consider myself a tidy person. The image conjured up is of a grown man who is used to people picking up after him. Now I've been confronted with him in the flesh like this, I can see why they would.

When I look up, I can see that he is watching me intently, a beautiful smile on his face. All trace of sensible thought is wiped from my brain.

'Hi,' he whispers, leaning down close. 'I'm so glad you came.'

For a second I think he's going to kiss me, but we just keep staring at each other. On the one hand, he seems so much older and worldlier than me, but on the other, it's already very evident that he's just a kid, not much older than I am and appealingly helpless. There's something about him that puts me at ease, even here in a hotel room where we barely know each other.

'I'm sorry about the mess. It's a really bad habit, you know? I got in late – I'll clean up at some point in time, I promise. Stuff just seems to . . . accumulate somehow. Hey, we should get some tea. I know how much you love a nice cup of tea. Maybe a few English muffins or something. Mary Poppins. Queen Elizabeth. Did you eat breakfast yet?'

Actually one unexpected bonus by-product of this clandestine meeting is that I haven't been able to eat much in the way of solid food since yesterday's cake. However, suddenly the knot in my stomach has gone without a trace, and I am starving. Before I can answer out loud, my gut gives off a massive, thunderous rumble. It sometimes does that at the mere mention of food. Jackson laughs in delight before I have time to be mortified.

'You read my mind. Hold that thought,' he says, simultaneously picking up the bedside phone to call room service.

'Breakfast's on its way,' Jackson says, creeping up behind me a minute later. 'I didn't know what you like so I kind of ordered everything.

For want of anything better to do, I sit down in the living area and switch on the massive TV. Jeremy Kyle is on, which kind of kills the exotic, luxurious, forget-about-the-real-world buzz that I've had going on. I don't really know what to do, here in close quarters, so I concentrate on the TV for a few minutes. We became so relaxed with each other by the end of yesterday, and we talked about everything imaginable on the phone last night, but here in this room it suddenly all feels a bit too real. It's sending me into a very quiet panic.

When I next get up the nerve to look around at him again, I see that Jackson is just staring at me, an amused look on his face.

'You look really pretty today by the way,' he says. 'I like your hair.'

We just stare at each other for another long moment, before there is a knock at the door. Even though Jackson ordered breakfast, we both jump.

He disappears and comes back shakily wheeling a huge trolley bearing food and a giant silver teapot. Once he has manoeuvred the trolley into the sitting area, he just stands there next to it, resting his weight on one foot and hovering like he doesn't have a clue what to do. There is silence for a moment, underneath the noise of the TV.

I would have thought that I would be the one feeling awkward, out of place and not knowing what to do with myself. As it turns out, there is no choice but for me to take charge. I stand up and usher Jackson on to the sofa, swapping our positions.

'Shall I be Mother?' I ask.

I kick off my shoes and get stuck in. I know it's not exactly rocket science, but I am so often all clumsy fingers and thumbs that I'm glad I can do something that makes me feel at home – I work as a breakfast waitress in a hotel in all the school holidays and I am a bit of a whizz at juggling crockery.

'How do you take your tea?' I ask him, looking up from the task at hand to find him staring at me again.

'I have literally no idea.' He laughs. 'You're very cute though.'

'Well, then you can have it the same as mine – strong, with a dash of milk and no sugar. I take tea quite seriously.'

'I like my tea like I like my women,' he drawls, picking up one of the many acoustic guitars littered around the place, this one a battered blue beast covered in stickers and leaning against the sofa. 'Strong, with a dash of milk and no sugar . . . Sounds good to me, sugar. Sugar, booger, Zeebrugge . . . That's a place in Belgium, you know. Greatest songwriter of my generation, so they say!'

'Well, genius – eat a muffin. I'm having this chocolate croissant. Probably two.'

I pass him his cup of tea and we curl up next to each other on the sofa, top to tail. His arm is so close to mine that it is almost touching. The funniest thing is that it doesn't feel funny. The close-together feeling we had on the phone last night, at a safe distance, is still there – only it's much more electric and dangerous now.

Although my heart is beating about one-third more frantically than it usually does, it's not in the way I would have anticipated. If I could have predicted any of this craziness, I would fully have expected still to be sitting here inwardly imploding, silently shrieking to myself, 'OMG, it's Jackson Griffith!' I'm not. Not really. I'm sitting on a sofa with a gorgeous boy, who's actually not that much older than me, feeling nothing but happy and surprisingly relaxed. There's something about him that makes him very easy to be around. The fancy hotel room, the china cups, the best *pain au chocolat* I've ever tasted in my entire life – none of it matters all that much; it's just random stuff that makes a weird, special day all the nicer.

'Hey, kiddo.' Jackson pokes me in the shoulder with a dexterous bare toe. 'You make a mean cup of tea.'

'Thanks. Well, there's only one thing that's better than a good cup of tea . . . and that's daytime telly. If I'm skiving off college, we've got to watch *Jeremy Kyle*. I'll talk you through it – the guy is basically like Jerry Springer but really, really mean. Ooh, "Admit You're a Prostitute, Then Prove My Boyfriend's the Dad". This should be a good one.'

'You sure know how to show a guy a great time.'

'If you're lucky, I'll take you to Greggs later. You'll love their cheese-and-onion pasties. Not until after *Cash in the Attic* though.'

'Sounds electric. Where've you been all my life?'

We spend most of the day like this. Watching TV, chatting, giggling a lot, ordering chips and Cokes from room service for our lunch. So slowly, at first I think I must be imagining it, I begin to notice that Jackson is gravitating towards me on the sofa as if we are both magnetic. I feel as if I'm in a dream. When I realize that his hand is resting across my leg I almost stop breathing, frightened that if I move it will break the spell. I look at him out of the corner of my eye, searching for a clue, but his eyes are fixed on the TV. In fact, I notice that he is starting to look a bit glazed – jetlag might finally be setting in. I wonder if he'll want me to go soon, and the idea of this makes me feel sadder than I would have imagined.

Just as I think I can hardly bear it, he turns around and looks at me.

'Hey, Tuesday?' he whispers sleepily. 'This is really nice.'

He leans down and for one crazy moment I think this is really it – he's going to kiss me. Then he nestles his head into my shoulder and closes his eyes.

'I'm really glad you're here,' he mumbles, before

falling straight into a deep sleep.

I have to pause for a second to remind myself that this is real, and then I have to stop myself from bursting out laughing. His mouth is hanging open and he immediately starts snoring, but somehow he looks totally adorable. I lie there, half curled up on the sofa, and try to remain as still as possible so as not to disturb him.

Then, after quite a while, I start to wonder when he might wake up and how difficult it would be to manoeuvre myself out from underneath his lanky sprawl. My right arm has gone completely dead.

I should leave. It's getting late and there is no point hanging around here watching someone sleep. This would be the ideal point for me to slip away, write him a note on that fancy hotel stationery I clocked on the bedside table and get myself on to the next train home. That would be the sensible thing to do.

But, when I think about moving, I find myself mesmerized by the starfish shadows of his eyelashes, unfairly long and thick considering his light hair. It's like he won every possible round of the genetic lottery. He hit the jackpot. In sleep I can get a good look at the perfect lines of his face – his slightly wonky nose, the hollow of his cheekbones, that impossible jawline. For the first time, that hint of 'it's Jackson Griffith!' hysteria is threatening to set in; it just seems so crazy that I am sitting here watching him sleep that I almost have to stop myself from snapping a photo. I have a feeling I might want to remind myself of this strange, dreamy day at some unspecified point in my future life. I don't want to be creepy though, so I force myself to commit the moment to memory the old-fashioned way – by staring like a psycho with barely a blink.

Then he lets out a small puff of a fart in his sleep – and he is just a nice, handsome boy again. I have to suppress a giggle.

I keep telling myself I must leave, but I can't bring myself to. I do my best not to move for what must be a very long time, keeping one eye on the TV and the other on the sunlight moving around the room and beginning to fade. My entire right-hand side has now gone completely dead.

He wakes up eventually, with a start, kicking his legs out and mashing his eyeballs with his fists. He sits bolt upright, every muscle tensed. He was so peaceful only seconds ago.

'Where am I?' he asks in a strange voice.

'Um, in London? In a hotel? I'm Tuesday, remember? Off the Internet.'

He breathes a sigh of relief, and so do I, as he crumples back down into the sofa. He puts both of his arms around me and cuddles into me and I don't have time to think about anything else but how nice and cosy and warm he feels.

'Ruby Tuesday. Of course I remember. I'm so glad you're here. I sometimes get freaked out in new places by myself. I know I'm crazy; don't be mad at me.'

'I'm not cross with you,' I murmur back, stroking his

surprisingly silky hair. 'Of course I'm not. It's OK. I'm here.'

We lie scrunched up on the sofa together like that for ages. I'm not sure how long, but neither of us moves. We barely breathe. He smells inexplicably like bonfires and fresh cake mix. By the time he breaks away and sits up, *Pointless* is on.

'I've got to go,' I say lamely, not moving.

This time I know I've really got to. I've already stayed much later than I should have done.

'Oh, Ruby Tuesday! Don't go. Please.' He sounds genuinely panicked. 'I was hoping you could stay over. We could spend the whole evening together. It's my last night in London before I have to go off and start doing these gigs. I thought you said that we were going to go to Gram's for a cheese pasty.'

'Greggs,' I correct automatically and then pause. 'Are you nervous about going back out there – these public appearances, I mean?'

'Well, when you think about it: imagine being washed up, divorced and in therapy by the age of twenty-three. Having to start out all over again, everyone thinking I've screwed it up for good. It's not a great feeling.'

'But most people at that age are still just starting out,' I argue. 'You've already achieved so much more than any of them – you should feel really proud.'

'I could use you there to hold my hand though. I wish you didn't have to go. Can't you come with me?'

I want to so badly – and know that it's impossible –

that I can't speak. Gathering that I'm not going to say anything – the silence hanging in the air making the room uncomfortable for the first time all day – Jackson picks up yet another guitar and starts strumming aimlessly, lighting a cigarette in his other hand.

For want of anything better to do, I put my sandals back on and gather up my bag and various belongings. Once that's done, there's nothing else I can think of to procrastinate further. I guess this is it.

Inwardly I'm crying out to stay here with him; I don't *want* to go. I keep thinking of all the reasons why I could technically stay – my mum's out for the evening anyway; nobody would ever have to know. But it seems like too big a step, like I'd be selling myself out. I should not let my head be turned by all this. Maybe it's silly, but it seems very important to me somehow.

'Well, thanks for a lovely day,' I call out, the words sounding brittle, breaking the intimate atmosphere that's built up between us. 'Do I owe you anything for all that food we ordered?'

'No, my management are picking up the tab,' he replies, only half turning around. 'It's cool.'

'OK. Bye, then . . .'

'Bye, Ruby Tuesday,' he says quietly, and his voice sounds so sad that I want to weep.

I stand there for a minute, but he still doesn't turn around, and so I close the door softly behind me as I leave. My footsteps on the thick carpet in the hallway are so muffled by luxury that they are completely silent.

To: Tuesday Cooper
From: jackson evan griffith

Ruby Tuesday/ace young writer/pretty girl/lovely tea-pouring internet princess in a red dress . . .

Please forgive me. I had a wonderful day visiting with you. You were and are just as sweet and as smart as I hoped.

You were right to leave when you did. It bores me stupid when people just do what i want all the time and agree with every damn word I say. I know you're different and that's why I like you, but I guess I still sometimes have a ways to go in not being a rockstar ego diva nightmare.

I want to see you again so badly. Right now I'm eating a room-service curry and watching some terrible movie on TV, some crazy morality tale about a nice girl with a terrible boyfriend. If you were here, it might seem funny. You make me laugh like nobody else has for a very long time. Did I mention that you looked really pretty in your red dress?!

I know it sounds weird but I think I miss you. You only left a couple of hours ago – I guess you are home by now. Do you still want to talk to me?

Love, Jack xxx

'So, how was your date?'

'It was . . . perfect!'

I am home now after a miserable train journey back to the suburbs. I've had a shower and I'm in my pyjamas, scrubbing off all the make-up, hope and preparation. Still feeling a bit grubby and not quite right. Guilt is a bit more difficult to eradicate, I suppose – like black London bogeys. I'm eating a tuna sandwich when my mum sails through the front door.

'Eleven out of ten,' she adds for good measure.

I must admit, she is looking beauteous. It's not only her flimsy blue sundress, white jacket and high heels, or her new highlights and matching nails. She has a definite glowy-ness to her, almost invisible but totally unmistakable.

It makes me wonder for a second whether my actions are written as legibly on me. My mum is unmistakably a woman who has just come home from a great date, a woman who has recently been kissed. I remain unkissed, and I can't decide whether to be relieved or disappointed about this state of being; I mean, I didn't expect a man like Jackson Griffith to want to kiss me or anything, but I wonder whether I look like a girl who has spent the day in a hotel room with a notorious rockstar. No – of course I don't. I just look like Tuesday Cooper – a girl with a silly name, wearing pyjamas and eating yet another sandwich. I try my best not to feel grumpy and resentful about my mum and her new boyfriend, who will undoubtedly become the centre of our family universe, whether I like it or not.

'So, tell me all about it then!' I grin, not just to be kind but because I'm glad of the distraction. 'I want to hear all about Richard Jenkins the history teacher. Did you call him "sir"? Bet you did, you strumpet!'

'That's a fine way to talk to your mother, young lady!' she says with a laugh.

We troop upstairs and I loll about on her bed as my mum takes off her 'date dress' and begins her extraordinarily complicated skincare regime. She despairs of me and my 'soap and water when I can be bothered' approach. Maybe I would be a better person if I could make myself care about that sort of stuff. Maybe I'd realize I really *am* 'worth it' after all. Or maybe not.

As she potters about at her dressing table, Mum tells me about her night. Richard Jenkins took her to a French restaurant (her favourite), and he ate oysters and a rare steak (sexy, apparently). My thoughts, of course, stray involuntarily to Jackson – I wonder if I'd think it was sexy if he ate an oyster. Not particularly. But at least he looks like a man who *could* eat an oyster if he wanted to. Seymour's allergic to them. He's allergic to most shellfish and to pineapples and kiwi fruit. He also has mild asthma. Jackson looks like he could, like, fix a car and go surfing and then eat three dozen oysters. And then an ice-cream sundae.

I slap myself down immediately. I need to stop thinking like this; it's not fair on Seymour. It's horrible of me. I am evil. I need to decide what I'm going to do, and soon – it's inexcusable not to. I'm just really dreading having to have any kind of conversation with him.

It's funny though – it wasn't long ago that I felt so lucky that Seymour wanted to go out with me, like he was too good for me or something. I don't want to get above myself, but in the last two days Jackson has made me feel more awesome about myself than Seymour ever has. In fact, it's made me realize that Seymour doesn't make me feel good about myself at all – and, whatever my faults, surely that's not right. Jackson aside, I don't know how I can have gone so long without fully realizing that there might be something not completely great about me and Seymour.

As if this wasn't realization enough, my mum is still talking about exactly what a dream date *ought* to be: 'We drank lots of red wine, and we talked and talked. We didn't even notice that we were the last people in the restaurant and that they were stacking chairs on to tables all around us, we got on so well.'

It hadn't occurred to me that it was so late. Only now do I realize it's gone midnight. I must have got home later than I thought as well. Thank goodness Mum's date went so well – I would have had a lot of explaining to do otherwise.

'He kissed me as I was getting into my taxi; we're going out again on Saturday night,' she confides. 'He's already texted me twice since I got home. He's a very charismatic man.'

I want to be pleased for her; I honestly can't fathom why I feel a tiny bit deflated by the huge juxtaposition in how our respective 'dates' today ended. Was it even a date that I was on? I keep telling myself that it was just a friendly meeting, that Jackson knows I have a boyfriend so I haven't done anything wrong . . . There is a good chance I might just be kidding myself.

I keep telling myself that I didn't even kiss him so it's fine, but I spent the whole day cuddled up on the sofa with him. I didn't tell Seymour where I was going; I stroked Jackson's hair while he lay there with his head in my lap; I have a boyfriend; this behaviour was clearly treacherous and wrong. I'm a much more terrible human being than I ever thought.

So why am I disappointed that he didn't kiss me?

'What did you talk about?' I ask my mum.

'Oh, I don't know – everything!' she exclaims. 'I found out a lot about him actually. He's divorced and he has two sons – the youngest is a couple of years older than you. They're both at university; one's on a study year in America. Richard's originally from north Wales, but he lives quite near here. He went to university in London and lived there for a long time after that . . .'

As she carries on talking it makes me realize that – although I felt so unexpectedly close to him for most of our day together – Jackson and I didn't really talk about anything. Nothing important anyway. Most of our conversations have just been fun and silly. Maybe I've been imagining a hidden meaning behind it all. I just know that I like him more than anyone I have ever met. Maybe I'm being some ridiculous, pathetic fangirl and it's just because he's handsome and famous – but I really don't think that's it.

I know everything about Seymour. I know his family. I know that his favourite colour is green and he's scared of spiders and he used to wet the bed until he was eleven. I saw him cry when his dog Ted had to be put down, and he came with me to the funeral when my favourite auntie Clara died. This is the stuff that is important.

'Are you all right?' my mum says.

'Yes,' I reply decisively. 'Yes, I am.'

'I've been going on about myself for quite long enough,' she goes on. 'You look tired – how was your day?'

'OK, thanks. Actually I am a bit tired. I think I'd better go to bed. I'm really glad your date went well.'

All of this is true. None of it is a lie. It seems important to me, from now on, to make sure that I am completely honest.

Tomorrow I will talk to Seymour and tell him the truth. It's the right thing to do. Jackson Griffith or no Jackson Griffith.

The Last Tuesday
(Jackson Evan Griffith/Sour Apple Music)

She's a face on the screen.
She's a voice in my head.
She writes like a magazine.
She's not too jaded yet.

Day like I've never seen.
Just hang out, watch TV.
She makes me teapots of tea.
Never want her to leave.

Hope this time it might last/Don't knock me off my
path . . .

Ruby Tuesday dream girl.
Can't believe you're real.
Ruby Tuesday dream girl.
Teach a robot to feel.

The only face on my screen.
The loudest voice in my head.
Keep writing your magazine.
Don't get too jaded, not yet . . .

'Hey, Ruby Tuesday. I didn't wake you up, did I?'

'No, I was awake,' I lie, luckily perking up as usual at the sound of Jackson's voice. 'How did the gig go?'

'It was OK. People are expecting me to be such a train wreck I think they're just happy if I show up.'

'Where are you now?'

'Some place up north. Newcastle, then Glasgow tomorrow. It's good, but I wish you were here. Actually I've gotta go – we're driving overnight and they're waiting for me. I just wanted to say hi.'

'I'm really glad it's going well. Thanks for ringing. Speak later, yeah?'

'Definitely. Speak to you later, Ruby Tuesday.'

Have I mentioned that I am the world's worst person? I've been talking on the phone to Jackson constantly and rereading his emails every chance I get, still unable to believe that this is really happening – but it is. It is the best thing that has ever happened to me and it should be perfect.

But I still haven't talked to Seymour. It sounds so lame, but there just hasn't been a good time. I've built it up to be such a big deal in my mind – and it is. I've never had a boyfriend before and I have never broken up with somebody before, so the moment has to be right. It doesn't help that I am absolutely terrified about instigating such a horrible conversation.

I've barely seen him, and I've made it through the week on autopilot. Luckily Seymour doesn't seem particularly to have noticed. This should be a good thing, but it's making me feel wretchedly guilty. Especially when in one of our brief conversations he said that it 'meant a lot' to him that I've stopped blogging lately – he said it really showed that we've both been mature about the situation. I didn't know whether to laugh or cry, honestly.

My first exam is only a few days away; luckily I've been so busy revising and stressing about that that I haven't had much time to think. None of us has. As the exams get closer and closer, I feel like it would be too cruel to dump him just before our A levels start. I'm not saying that I'm, like, so amazing that it would be the worst thing in the world for someone to be deprived of going out with me – but we've known each other for a long time and I owe it to him to do it properly. *I'm* finding the idea of us not being together a bit sad, and it's me making the decision – and, let's face it, I've got the consolation of a gorgeous pop star on the other end of the phone, even if we're technically 'just good friends'. Telling myself that this means I'm not doing anything wrong is starting to sound fraudulent, even to me. I've got to put a stop to this bizarre situation, and as quickly as possible.

In fact, I've been so preoccupied with Jackson – not to mention exhausted at college every day, due to staying up late on the phone or messaging with Jackson every night – that I've been neglecting my real life entirely. I haven't been blogging at all. Nishi is still being a tiny bit weird with me, I think. But that might be all in my head, because I've barely seen her – she's been so busy all of a sudden as well. The exams mean so much to her, she has gone into lockdown. I'm probably just being paranoid. Maybe it's my own guilty conscience at work and I should leave Nish out of it. Anyway, even if she is being weird, that's just Nishi – she's always been moody and we've always been OK in the end.

I was gearing up for breaking up with Seymour this weekend. All set. Then my heart sank when he texted to remind me that I'm going to his house for Sunday lunch. Feeling mean, I've been telling myself that I'll get lunch out of the way and then do it straight after that, as soon as we get the chance to talk on our own.

Now it's Sunday and I've been psyching myself up all morning, feeling so anxious I can barely function. The prospect of lunch with Seymour's parents would have me feeling nervy at the best of times – this has been amplified times a billion now that I have decided today is the day to have The Talk.

I decide to open up my laptop and just check my emails quickly before I go. It is not lost on me that this is probably particularly treacherous – I can't deny that I'm hoping for a quick email from Jackson before I go round to Seymour's.

I see his latest email and I am thrown. Completely thrown. Thrown to the wolves; out on to the motorway. For a loop, a curve ball. *That song.* He has emailed me the lyrics and attached a link to a video of him playing it. It's a song about me; I can't believe it.

Watching it is the most surreal experience of my life. It's Jackson Griffith, singing in that voice I know so well from a million records. The song is beautiful; it's classic Sour Apple, up there with his best – I can imagine hearing it on the radio.

But he is still wearing the same stripy T-shirt he had on that day at the hotel. Some of his things scattered about the messy hotel room in the background look familiar. The fact that I am getting to know him as a real person makes my heart leap. *He is singing my name.*

I'm sitting on the edge of my bed, laptop swaying on my shaking knees. I'm due to leave for Seymour's in ten minutes; I'm even wearing a sensible mid-length skirt and non-holey cardigan in honour of the occasion. I've kept my wonky attempt at cat-flick eyeliner though, and the Sonic Youth T-shirt I'm wearing underneath the cardigan – I can't sell out on my fashion principles entirely.

Jackson Griffith wrote a song for me.

I take a long look at myself in the mirror. I straighten my sensible skirt and give my fringe a last comb so it sits just right. I look myself in the eye, dead on. Then I run out of the room and slam the door behind me, stumbling so hastily down the stairs that my legs nearly fly out from under me. I must get this lunch out of the way and talk to Seymour as soon as possible. I am not a liar by nature; I was not built for a life of intrigue. I must be brave.

Who am I trying to fool with all this 'just good friends' stuff? I might have met him only twice. I might have had a poster of him on my bedroom wall when I was a kid. But I have got to know him – really know him – through his emails and his late-night phone calls, his husky laugh and his easy, sun-drenched accent. Who am I trying to fool, full stop? I have fallen in love with Jackson Griffith. Not the pop star. The lovely, weird, erratic, sweet boy.

Now that I've heard that song – that beautiful song that is all about *me* and has totally nailed this crazy, brilliant situation – I no longer think I'm deluding myself to suspect that he might, just might, feel exactly the same way.

For the first time a feeling of total joyous excitement overtakes the dread in my stomach about what I have to do today.

I almost collide with my mum at the bottom of the stairs and narrowly avoid her full coffee cup ruining my neat and tidy outfit.

'Watch it!' she snaps, taken by surprise.

I know how she feels. I feel as though I've been hit by a freight train this morning too. Mum didn't get back until late last night, and she is still shuffling about in her dressing gown. This is most uncharacteristic, so her second date with Richard Jenkins must have gone well.

'Good night?' I ask her.

'Terrific. We might go away together for the weekend soon. Maybe to Bruges; I've always fancied Bruges, and of course Richard is very interested in the history. I think there's quite a lot of history there. He's a very bright man, you know – a real academic. Anyway, you look nice. Are you going round to Seymour's?'

'Yeah. I'm running late actually; I've got to go. Can't be late for Sunday lunch. Roast beef apparently.'

'Good. Well, have fun. Give Seymour a kiss from me. And say hi to his mum.'

I think of the slightly sour face Elaine makes whenever I mention my mum. I don't think she means any harm, or even realizes she's doing it – but it makes me hug my mum extra hard before I leave to walk round to Seymour's.

'And how's your mum, Chew?'

As she says this, Elaine's nostrils flare by just half a millimetre, and the right-hand side of her top lip curls up to meet it halfway. After a split second her features return to their usual formation, but the slip of her mask is burned into my vision like one of those flick books you make when you're a kid. I should have known that being round at Seymour's, with his parents' disapproving faces and slightly snotty vocal tones, would knock all the fight out of me. If I wasn't so polite, I'd use this as an excuse to rebel, but as usual her icy glare makes me feel too pathetic to say anything out of line.

At least Elaine can bring herself to say my name now without looking literally like she has to chew it. You can still see her secretly wishing for a Lucy or a Charlotte or a Sophie, but she manages to hide it better than she used to – I guess she's got used to me. I know she'll be delighted when I'm off the scene though.

'Mum's brilliant, thanks,' I say, grinning through a mouthful of homemade tiramisu. 'She's got a new boyfriend and she's really happy. It seems to be going well – so, you know, fingers crossed.'

'How nice.'

Of course, if there is one thing this lunch has been, it's 'nice'. We're on our third course; we've already had prawns as a starter and then a full roast dinner. Now there's pudding *and* cheese. There's a tablecloth and flowers on the table. Seymour and I have been allowed a glass of wine each. His younger brothers and sister have finally been excused from the table after a million rounds of 'please *may* I' and 'elbows *off* the table'; I can hear them playing outside in the garden. I kind of wish I could be out there with them, running free. Seymour's younger siblings are the funnest people in this house – they always appreciate my latest hair colours and fashion choices, so I try to sneak them in some Haribo whenever I can.

Yes, it's all been very *nice*. Seymour's family have been so hospitable and perfectly polite to me. I don't know why I have to keep reminding myself of this.

'Actually, I'm glad you're both here.' Elaine smiles at me with her teeth and abruptly changes the subject. 'There's something that Michael and I have been wanting to talk to you both about.'

Seymour's dad looks decidedly uncomfortable, and pours himself another glass of wine. This cannot be a good sign. Seymour and I exchange a quick glance. I notice that he has turned slightly pale. I feel more treacherous than ever. I just want this lunch to be over so that I can do the whole awful 'we need to talk' thing on Seymour.

'Of course, you're both well aware that your exams start very soon,' Elaine goes on. 'Seymour, I know your first sociology paper is on Tuesday morning. Chew, I'm not sure if the same support is available to you at home, but Michael and I are very serious about making sure that Seymour does the absolute best he can in these exams. A levels are so important; they can really alter the whole course of one's life. I don't know what your plans are, Chew – if you'll be going on to higher education – but of course Seymour will be going on to university'

I open my mouth to chip in, but she actually holds up a hand to stop me. I didn't know people even did that in real life – not ones that claim to be so hot on bloody manners anyway. But I know when I'm beaten, so I keep my mouth shut.

So I don't get to say that – actually – I work harder than pretty much anyone else in our year, certainly harder than Seymour. I've already put in the groundwork – and if Seymour hasn't, which I suspect might be the case, then there's not much hope left for him at this point. I get better results than him in every subject. I got the highest mock result in our whole year for English literature, and my teacher said that he has never had the pleasure of teaching someone with such an 'enquiring literary mind' before. Yeah, I know it's not nice to boast, but how often do I get to do it? Besides, this is all news to me, as Seymour has been saying lately that he isn't planning on going to university, because he wants to 'concentrate on his band'.

I got offers from all five of my uni choices and (fingers crossed) I'll be going to London to study English when the results come in. Nishi – that Asian lesbian whom

Elaine pretends not to disapprove of – is even on track to go to Oxford.

Oh, and by the way, my mum has a really good job at a marketing agency, thank you very much – as opposed to Seymour's mum, who seems to think it's a virtue that she has 'never had to work'. Apparently it's still the 1950s in this house. I should probably have worn a girdle, whatever that actually is.

Elaine smiles at me in what she obviously thinks is a very kind fashion, taking my shocked silence for acquiescence. She probably doesn't even know what acquiescence means, I find myself thinking meanly.

'I know that you two have grown very fond of each other. Of course, we're all very fond of you, Chew. But Seymour has his whole life in front of him and he mustn't have any distractions at such a crucial time. I'm sure you'll understand we just want the best for him.'

She looks over at Michael, as if willing her husband to chip in and say something, not leave it all to her. The atmosphere is getting palpably more awkward by the second.

'Of course, it won't be forever,' he mumbles. 'You can always see each other again in the summer, after the exams are over. Then again, I know how quickly these teenage fancies can blow over – who knows what will happen, eh?'

'Exactly.' Elaine claps her hands and smiles around the table as if we should all be glad that this messy little matter is all settled.

Her eyes lock on me for a second to make sure that I'm not going to argue. On principle I know I ought to: challenge her perceptions, make a point, battle in the name of fairness. She doesn't realize that she is actually doing me the biggest favour imaginable. I feel awful for using this to my advantage, but Elaine has just made my life so much easier. Much as he likes to think he's a bit of a badass, Seymour never, ever stands up to his mother. He does exactly what she says, all the time – then complains about it behind her back.

This way I can play along and do what he always does – complain about it loudly – but admit that (sigh) she's probably right and we should just stop seeing each other. I doubt he'll be heartbroken, and this way it's nobody's fault and we can just be friends – which is probably what we should have stayed all along, I realize. It's funny, but it's only since meeting someone who I really, madly fancy that I've realized that things between Seymour and me have never really been right.

Things have worked out so perfectly that I've already got one foot half out the door. All I can think about is Jackson. I can't wait to talk to him when I get home. Once the exams are over, who knows what might happen between us? This seems like a genuine possibility, and now that things are going to be over with Seymour and me – and so amicably – there's not going to be anything to make me feel bad about the best thing that has ever happened to me.

Then I look over at Seymour. He has gone deathly pale,

a muscle clenching in his cheek.

'No!' he shouts suddenly, his voice thundering from nowhere and startling all of us – most of all Seymour himself by the look of it. 'I'm so sick of this. I've had enough; I'm not putting up with it any more.'

For once even Elaine is silent. My heart sinks so fast that it makes me feel sick. My exit window is starting to look a little bit smaller; I can see it shrinking before my eyes. All I can think is, Please shut up, Seymour; don't say anything. Please.

'Mum, I'm sick of you slagging off Chew and calling her a chav. You keep saying she's going to drag me down and stop me going to university – but I don't even *want* to go to university. I can do that any time in the future, but for now I want to concentrate on my band. It's important to me. And actually – you've made me realize it today – so is Chew. Chew is important to me. You're going to have to deal with it.'

Elaine and Michael look so mortified at being called out on saying I'm a chav, they don't even argue. In fact, the expression on their faces almost distracts me from the fact that, in his little speech, Seymour didn't manage to say a single nice thing about me to redress the balance – it was all about him.

Seymour stands up and holds a hand out to me.

'Come on, Chew. We're going. If you're not welcome here, I don't want to hang around.'

For a moment I am frozen. I look at Seymour's parents and an apologetic smile automatically forms on my face.

Ironically, my mum has always drummed such good manners into me that I'm tempted to apologize for the disturbance and thank them for the lovely lunch.

I'm actually embarrassed that they might think Seymour's outburst is anything to do with me, when in reality I don't even agree with him. I'd like to tell them that, nice as he is, my A levels and my future are way more important to me than their precious son is.

All I can do is give them a sympathetic look, which I hope they interpret the right way, and follow Seymour out of the room. I have to stop and pull on my shoes in the hallway, so it's not quite the dramatic exit he hoped for.

By the time I get outside, he is already halfway down their long driveway. I have to trot to catch up with him. He doesn't turn around to look at me; he just keeps walking. All I can see of him is his set, white profile, that same muscle still clenching in his cheek.

I see in a flash that this is nothing to do with me at all. Seymour should have stood up to his parents long ago; this has been brewing for some time. This is about principles, his band, an overdue rebellion against his mother. I am just a convenient excuse. Seymour might have to keep this up to prove a point, but it's certainly not because he's so madly in love with me that he can't bear the idea of not seeing me for a while.

The most treacherous thought ever sneaks into my head before I can stop it: it's not like Seymour's ever even written a song about me . . .

But now this has all gone too far, and him standing up to his mum like that is a very big deal. I know I am going to have to go along with this and be on his side. Whether I really agree with him or not. He doesn't know it, but Seymour has completely derailed my big plan in one fell swoop. There is no way I can have The Talk with him now. It wouldn't be right. I know I have to do it sometime, but the right moment keeps being pushed back further and further. The excitement about today being the day, about being able to go home to tell Jackson and see what happens, has drained away and might as well have never existed. I feel even more weighed down than I did this morning.

When we reach the end of his road, Seymour automatically crosses and turns the corner towards my house and I follow at his heels. At the corner he comes to a sudden stop and swings around to face me. After all the silence and clipped pace, it gives me a bit of a fright. His face is still a set mask, a bit like something you might do in papier-mâché around a balloon in junior school.

'Look, Chew.' His voice comes out louder and more strident than usual, and I'm worried he might start having a go at me – probably my own guilty conscience on overdrive. 'I'm really sorry you had to hear all that. I'm sorry about my parents. I meant what I said. I did. I do.'

He sounds as though he's trying to convince both of us. I have an uncomfortable feeling that he's pulling me on to the wrong train, one it's going to be very hard to get off.

'I mean, I know it's a difficult position for you to be in,' I start in my most diplomatic tone, improvising on the spot, clumsily trying to force that emergency exit back open. 'Your mum may not always put things in the nicest way, but maybe—'

I'm about to argue that Elaine might have a point and we Have To Be Mature About This and Think About Our Future. I'm building up to a rousing speech, but Seymour interrupts me.

'Too right she doesn't. Like I said, I'm not having it any more. I can't keep on putting up with her bullying me like this. I'm eighteen years old; my band is really important to me; most of all, I won't let her talk about my girlfriend like that any more.'

'No, but maybe . . .'

'No, Chew. I'm sorry – it's made me realize I've been really crappy to you lately. All that stuff with your website, and Nishi and me having a go at you . . . It wasn't fair. You were right. You've even stopped doing your blog because of me, so the least I can do is stick up for you against my snobby mum. I'm going to start being a much better boyfriend. You'll see. I promise.'

It's the second time today that a member of the Brown family has taken my silence for acquiescence. In fact, I have a horrible feeling that Seymour thinks I may be overcome with emotion at his little monologue.

He grabs my hand and squeezes it, and we keep walking towards my house. He doesn't even notice that he's kind of dragging me along.

'Do you want to come in?' I ask half-heartedly, cursing my own good manners the second the words exit my mouth.

'Yeah, why not? It's probably better than going home right now. At least *your* mum likes me!'

To my slight mortification, Mum is still in her dressing gown, drinking coffee, eating a bacon sandwich and watching *Here Comes Honey Boo Boo*. Way to prove Elaine right, Mum – thanks a lot. Then I feel ashamed of myself for caring what anyone else might think. Mum and I absolutely love Honey Boo Boo.

'Hi, you two,' she greets us cheerfully and styles it out, even though I know she would really rather Seymour not see her in her dressing gown. 'Did you have a lovely Sunday lunch?'

I'm all set to lie. I have the fake smile already on my face and I'm about to say that yes, it was lovely. I don't want to risk hurting her feelings by revealing the Browns' real view of my family. But, yet again, Seymour interrupts me before I can even get started.

'No, Carrie, we did not,' he says gravely. 'It was awful.'

'It wasn't that bad,' I chip in helpfully.

'Yes, it was,' Seymour ploughs on. 'My parents don't want Chew and I to see each other any more. And they want me to give up my band.'

'Well, A levels *are* starting really soon now . . .' I counter slightly lamely, hoping I might get her on my side.

Then I realize that there is no point. Usually my mum is quite a sensible woman. Obviously she wants me to do well in my exams, just like I do. However, one look at her face right now is enough to confirm that – from my point of view, at least – the timing of this sucks. It's a combination of hangover and new boyfriend that's making her all weird and *sentimental*.

Honestly her eyes actually well up.

'But that's *terrible*, she wails. 'Just terrible. It's so *unfair*.'

'I know,' Seymour agrees a bit too quickly, clearly enjoying this.

'I mean, obviously A levels are important, but you're both sensible kids. She shouldn't underestimate you like that. Relationships are so important too. You two are wonderful together; surely she can see that. We should all be encouraging you, and feeling proud of you, not creating arbitrary rules and holding you back. Well, Seymour – you're always welcome around here, whatever your mum says.'

She's clearly got romance on the brain – herself and Richard Jenkins, rather than me and Seymour. We've caught her in a *Romeo and Juliet* mood.

'Well, thanks, Mum,' I say awkwardly. 'I don't want to prove Seymour's parents right, so I really ought to get on with some revision now. I've got a lot to do.'

'And I suppose I ought to get dressed – can't hang around in my dressing gown all day.' It's already four o'clock. 'I wouldn't want you to think I'm always this sluttish, Seymour!'

I cringe and try to usher Seymour in the direction of the front door as my mum drifts upstairs.

'Good luck with your parents,' I say. 'Don't be too hard on them – they just want what's best for you.'

'You're lucky – your mum's so cool.'

Very uncharacteristically, as my mum is only just upstairs even though she is well out of sight, Seymour kisses me thoroughly there on the doorstep. Full-on tongue. He sneaks it right in there before I have a chance to stop him. It feels like cheating, only I'm not even sure who I'm cheating on.

As I wave him off and close the door behind him, all I can think is that – only a few weeks ago – all of this would have made me really happy.

To: Tuesday Cooper
From: jackson evan griffith

Ruby Tuesday . . .

I'm so happy that you liked the song. I was so nervous to send it to you! What are you doing to me?! Usually I'm pretty cool, you know . . . ?

It sounds so cringey, but I think you inspired me. There's something about you that's kinda like a lucky charm. I know I'm being silly but I don't care.

Anyway, I think i'm doing the best work I have done in a long time.

Sorry I haven't had the chance to chat so much the last couple days. Things have really taken off with this whole secret gig thing, and it's all gone kinda crazy. Like I said, I think it's meeting you that's put a rocket under my ass! It's the first time in a long time that I've been inspired to work like this. So, good news (I hope you think so) . . . My management agree, and I will be staying in the UK for a while so that I can (drum roll, please) play at Glastonbury. I guess you know about my history there (i.e. it's where I once lost my mind and my career!). So it feels like a pretty big deal to me.

I'd love it if you'd come with me. Maybe you're going anyway? I know how popular it is over here. Have you been before?

I know you have your own life and you may have plans for that weekend, but please come with me? I really kind of need you there, if I'm honest. I'll Instagram some falafel, buy you cake, do whatever you want. I'm basically begging you: come to Glastonbury with me. Obviously my management will fix all the details and you'll be on the guest list.

I just like you so much. Let me know.

J xxx

Now that our A levels have started up and stress levels are rising, the temporary love-in between Nishi and Seymour is officially over. In fact, Nishi seems like she's had quite enough of both of us. She's so wound up, even by her own standards, that I'm starting to get a bit worried about her. Only thing is, I haven't had the chance to see her on my own to talk about it properly.

This is partially thanks to Seymour's quest to be A Better Boyfriend, which is kind of making me want to crawl out of my own skin. The only good thing is that we are all so busy with A levels, we haven't seen much of each other.

Which is definitely a good thing, because I have more than enough to deal with at the moment. Thankfully this morning's exam went really well, as have the others I've done so far. I don't mean to sound arrogant; it's just that I can tell that all my revision has paid off. I haven't had any unexpected questions, and although they've been hard, it feels like stuff that I'm prepared for. I'm amazed at how relaxed I've been feeling. I guess I've earned it.

It's no bad thing that Jackson's touring schedule starting up has coincided with my exams. We've still been talking but I've found it quite easy to get my revision in and concentrate on my work. It's like our sort-of relationship has given me this new confidence that's making life a bit better all round. I feel like I'm in a little bubble and, cowardly though it may be, I'm doing my best not to let the rest of the world intrude on that too much.

I haven't told Jackson yet that I can't be at Glastonbury. Mostly because I'm hoping that something might happen to make it possible for me to go. I know it would be total insanity, as I will have my last English exam still to come by the time Glastonbury starts. I know I shouldn't go. But let's just say I still haven't completely ruled it out. I can't bear to shut the door all the way on that one, not yet. I'm hoping to keep my options open as long as possible. As if some miracle is going to fall out of the sky, like A levels are cancelled forever or the college might be hit by a freak earthquake.

Today's exam is over by lunchtime, so I head over to the college canteen and queue up for cheesy chips. When I head over to the usual table, Nishi and Seymour are already there. They clearly have nothing to say to each other.

As I walk closer and pull up a chair, I can see that Seymour looks all awkward and fidgety – he can be very angular when he wants to be – and Nish looks plain old moody. Very moody. It's a look that I should be used to on her, but this one seems worse than any of the usual (political/moral/life in general) snits I have ever seen her in before.

I wait for them to ask me about how my exam went, but they both sit there in silence, so I am obviously expected to do the talking for all of us.

'Hey, guys,' I say with a false cheerfulness, feeling a bit like a children's entertainer in front of a group of juvenile delinquents; I'll be doing jazz hands in a minute if I don't watch it. 'How are my two favourites?'

'Um, I'm not sure . . .' Seymour looks a bit scared.

'Look,' Nishi begins, 'I have something to tell you and I don't want to have to say it twice – so I wanted to wait for you to get here, Chew.'

The look on her face seems to confirm my worst suspicions. My guilty conscience is in full swing yet again as I wonder what bombshell she might be about to drop.

'Nish, whatever it is, it's—' I start to say, and put my hand over hers on the table until she abruptly pulls it away and interrupts me.

'Get off,' she snaps, but I know her and her weird hang-ups so well I don't hold it against her. 'I don't want to get all touchy-feely about this and I don't want any questions. Basically I don't want to cry in public. Me and Anna have broken up.'

This must be really bad if Nishi is saying things like 'me and Anna' – usually she is very particular about grammar and makes sure she gets everything exactly right at all times so that she can hold herself up as a paragon of punctuation. I can't even think of anything to say in response to this news.

Unfortunately Seymour does not share my speechlessness.

'Nishi,' he says in a Special Serious Voice that makes me want to cringe, 'Chew's right: it's OK to want to talk about things and we *are* here for you. This must be really, really hard for you. I mean, I can only imagine, but . . .'

Why can't Seymour just act like a normal crap boy and be awkward and silent, instead of dragging me into some pop psychology emotional soup? Then he looks at me like he's expecting a pat on the head and so I have to feel guilty and sorry for him as well as everything else.

'Seymour, maybe you could –' I say gently, and give him a look that I really hope gets the message across.

Instead, as he seems to be doing so often these days, he just talks over me.

'. . . but it might make you feel better to tell us what happened.'

'We broke up,' Nishi intones stonily. 'This has happened right in the middle of the most important exams of my life, so I just need to forget it before I mess those up as well. What more do you need to know?'

I know Nishi well enough to know that this is her default defence mechanism. I'm not going to force her to bare her soul in the middle of the college canteen if she doesn't want to. Maybe that makes us both emotionally stunted wrecks and the worst best friends ever, but it's worked for us since way before Seymour or Anna came on the scene.

'Seymour,' I say more stridently this time, 'maybe you could leave us alone for a bit . . . ?'

He actually looks put out.

'All right,' he agrees begrudgingly.

Then he visibly has a bright idea that he thinks will save the day.

'Nishi, you've got to come along with Chew to my gig

on Saturday night. The two of you can come together and we can have a proper night out. It'll cheer you up, I promise.'

I know he means well, so I grin at him overenthusiastically to make up for Nishi's glower. Needless to say, she does not look massively cheered up by the prospect of seeing Seymour singing to help her out of her state of heartbreak. I even find myself doing a double thumbs-up at him. Just to get him to go away. Have I mentioned lately that I am the worst? Now I suppose that I can't break up with him until after this gig is over. He seems to be taking it more seriously than his exams anyway – it's a very big deal for him and I don't want to be responsible for ruining it. Despite all else, I just want to make this as easy on everyone as possible – a task that is proving to be impossible despite my very best intentions. I wish I wasn't such a coward, always wanting everyone to be happy and think that I'm a nice person.

As soon as he clears off, I look at Nishi with a half-smile/half-grimace that is supposed to indicate that all's right with the world and we are not going to get all soppy and girlie – even over this.

'You're not going to keep on talking, are you?' she says, forcing herself to laugh. 'If you say another word, I might have to kill you.'

I shake my head and mime zipping my mouth shut. Then I have a better idea and reach into my bag; I fish out a half-eaten Kit Kat and shove it across the table towards her. She should know how lucky she is – it's rare that I ever have a half-eaten anything to hand; usually I inhale the lot in one go. This would never have happened with a Snickers or even a Yorkie. Kit Kats are just so boring. Still, she must be depressed, or she just appreciates the gesture, because she takes it off me.

Then I deliberately look down to my cheesy chips, which have now solidified into one lumpen rubber mass, and concentrate on them intently as I eat them. I don't look back up at Nishi at all, much as I want to.

I don't know how long we sit there for, but it's way longer than it takes me to polish off my big bowl of chips, and then to eat a sachet of salt slowly by licking my finger and dipping it back in there repeatedly. I keep doing it until my finger stings and I can't feel my tongue.

When I finally break the spell and look back over at Nishi, she is sitting perfectly still and staring into the middle distance. Her face is totally expressionless.

'Thanks, mate,' she says to me, and manages half a smile as she gets up and leaves.

Even after she's gone I feel glued to my seat, weighed down so that I can't get up. The room is almost empty by now. I glance over at the clock, which confirms that I'm already late for my afternoon revision workshop, which is obviously a really bad show, what with A levels being in full swing now. But I still can't be bothered.

It's not just Nishi and Anna, although that is obviously way more than enough. It's loads of things. Some of which I can't even put into words, or let myself think about properly.

Your New Favourite Band

Yes, that's right. You heard it here first.

Terminal Ghosts might be a bunch of eighteen-year-olds from a sixth-form college in a small town in the middle of nowhere, but they are greater than the sum of their parts. Besides, haven't some of the greatest bands of our time come from the dreary, rainy, uninspiring English suburbs? If you live somewhere where literally nothing ever happens and there is little in the way of cool things to do (bowling, anyone? no?), then the kids have to get creative and make their own fun.

Terminal Ghosts, as you can probably tell from the name, are nothing if not creative. They might have some classic elements of the teenage band – they are arty student types in skinny jeans and hipster glasses, who practise once a week in the bass player's garage. But they are totally their own creation.

They play a mix of covers and originals, but the covers aren't just the really obvious ones. No cheesy rock classics here. They offer their own takes on slightly more obscure songs by their favourite bands – like the Smashing Pumpkins, Nine Inch Nails and Soundgarden.

They are led by their singer/guitarist, Seymour Brown, who is as talented as he is cute.[1] The rest of the band are just as good at providing a solid wall of talent

---

[1] *Full disclosure: I would be going to their gig tonight even if Seymour Brown was not my boyfriend. Honest.*

for him to bounce off. Catch them live if you can, or if not you can check out their website <u>here</u>. And don't forget to thank me for introducing you to them before they get too famous, so you can look like a cool early adopter in front of all your groovy friends!

Comments
Great post – have fun at the gig!
Carrie_Cougar

Hope you guys all have fun . . . miss you. x
anna_banana

Judging by what I can gather from other, possibly more normal, people, getting ready to go out with your friends is meant to be this really fun process that can take hours, possibly the whole afternoon. Fortunately Nishi and I are not like most people. Making a hobby out of 'getting ready' is an idea that makes me want to cry for the future of mankind. Maybe I'd feel differently if I was any good at doing hair or applying eyeliner straight. If I didn't have such a short attention span, I'd probably be vastly more attractive. Being truly pretty seems like a full-time job to me.

I've talked Nishi into coming with me to Seymour's gig, and invited myself round to her house beforehand to make sure that she actually comes out. It would probably be more sensible for both of us to stay in and revise, but I feel like we both need a break. OK, that's code for: I can't get out of going to Seymour's gig tonight, so I really want some backup. Nishi's working so hard and stressing so much it's starting to get counterproductive. Besides, tonight is really important to Seymour. It's the least I can do.

I'm feeling a tiny bit sick about the blog post I put up before I left the house this evening. I did it in a fit of misguided conscience, but now I'm worried Jackson will see it and comment. Or, worse, that his feelings will be hurt. I wanted to talk to him about it, but he can be really hard to get hold of sometimes – and then it was time for me to leave the house to go out. Yet again, I'm not sure who I'm betraying the most – just that this situation is getting more and more murky.

Nishi and I are just killing time. We don't have to leave for the gig, which is at a pub in town, for another hour, but we don't have much in the way of getting ready to do. Nishi is already in her signature shirt, skinny jeans and trainers, with her hair slicked back to show off the sides of her undercut and her multiple ear piercings, so she's all set.

For some reason when I was getting ready, probably to remind my treacherous self that my boyfriend is actually in this band, I decided to channel a 70s groupie look for the evening, in a tight top and painfully high-waisted jeans that are definitely threatening a camel-toe situation. I look quite tarty, but it's supposed to be kind of a comedy look so I have smeared on some red lipstick and am using an afro comb I found knocking around in Nishi's room to do a bit of crazed backcombing. I'm worried I look way over the top, but I don't have anything else to change into and it's too late to go home and start again from scratch. So instead I have opted for just avoiding looking in the mirror again and forgetting about the whole thing. I hope people realize it's a joke and don't think *I think* I actually look hot.

'You look nice, girls!' Nishi's stepmum exclaims cheerily, not looking as though she means it at all. Bless her.

'Have a good evening,' her dad chimes in. 'Hope the band are rad!'

'Da-ad!' Nishi glowers.

It's actually a shame that Nishi's parents are already heading out for the night, because I really like them. Nishi's dad is a psychologist and her stepmum is a primary-school teacher. They are so new age and touchy-feely it's untrue. This combination is basically the reason why Nishi has become very adept at hiding her emotions.

When Nishi came out to her parents, she told them flatly that she had a girlfriend and that was it. They were pretty delighted and wanted to talk about her feelings for hours on end, but Nishi just yawned and asked what was for dinner. She told her dad that if he was in any way surprised by this news then he must be a really crap psychologist, and she didn't really have time to talk because there was something she wanted to watch on TV. She then phoned me and we both laughed about it for at least ten minutes.

Ever since Nishi got together with Anna, her parents have been so sweet and pleased, trying to make Anna feel welcome and include them both in 'family activities'. For a while Nishi was so happy that she almost forgot to be annoyed by them. She hasn't told them yet that she and Anna have broken up – she doesn't want to talk about it, and even I still don't know exactly what happened between them to cause this, except for Nishi making a few dark mutterings about 'bloody girls and all that bloody talking'.

'Bye, girls!' both her parents chorus. 'Have fun!'

As soon as they're out the door, Nishi immediately starts taking advantage of the situation. In the absence of her overly interested parents, she decides to try to drown her feelings and raids their dining-room cabinet.

This is really unusual and I wonder if I ought to be alarmed by it. It's not like we're deliberate teetotallers, but my little gang and I are definitely not big drinkers in the usual course of things – Nishi in particular is practically straight edge. It's something I've always admired – she does her own thing and won't give in to peer pressure; she generally has loftier things on her mind. She has been heard to say with total seriousness that she wouldn't like to jeopardize a possible future career in politics by indulging in 'clichéd teenage indiscretions' that might come back and haunt her later.

So it's a surprise – and not altogether a good one – to see her this evening. She's blasting Hole's first album out and swigging alternately from dusty bottles of Galliano, amaretto and crème de menthe. I don't even know what those drinks actually are and, judging by the look on Nishi's face, they are not delicious.

'I'll just take whatever looks oldest from the back of the cupboard, so they won't notice anything has gone missing,' she explains with her usual impeccable logic. 'It would make them so happy to see me indulging in such tediously predictable teenage rebellion behaviour that I don't want to give them the satisfaction.'

'So . . . why are you?'

'Don't you want a bit of crème de menthe?' she asks, totally ignoring my question. 'We could be like normal teenagers for once. We can hold each other's hair back while we puke in the bushes or something. Isn't that what we're supposed to do? It might be fun.'

I shake my head while trying to make a non-judgemental face, and stick to my orange squash in a large coffee mug. I feel that if Nishi's going to get drunk, and she seems hell bent on doing exactly that, then I ought to stay in a fit state to look after her if I need to. I quite like the idea of being the sensible one for once.

'No, thanks,' I say brightly. 'It looks seriously rank. Why don't we just go?'

The pub where the gig is being held is only about fifteen minutes' walk away. Where we live, everything is pretty much only a short walk away, which is both a good and a bad thing. It's such a nice warm evening that the fresh air doesn't really sober Nishi up as I had hoped, particularly as she brings the last dregs of the Galliano with her in an empty Coke bottle.

'So, are Seymour's band actually, like, any good?' she asks me, kicking the kerb with unnecessary force as we cross the road into town.

'Yeah, you've heard them – of course they are,' I say automatically, hackles up.

'Well, I haven't seen them live in ages and that blog you wrote about them today was a bit crap. You've got to admit.'

I don't *have to admit* anything. I can tell she's being antagonistic on purpose; she gets this hostile tone that I've learned to recognize and ignore. I think part of the reason why Nishi and I have managed to stay friends for so long is that I've learned not to always take her personally – she can be pretty mean, but it's usually to do with her own insecurities so I don't allow myself to mind too much; this time she's inadvertently hit a very raw nerve and I don't like it one bit.

'Well, I never claimed to be the best writer,' I say, slightly avoiding the issue. 'I just thought it would be nice to get Seymour's band out there. Do my bit, you know. I like to support my friends, that's all.'

'Well, that's the funny thing. I *know* you're not necessarily the best writer, but usually your blog is good because it's about the things you're passionate about. In that post, you didn't even sound as if you *like* Seymour's band that much. I thought it was a bit lukewarm, that's all. I'm not criticizing you, so don't get defensive – I'm just saying it came across as a bit arbitrary.'

Nishi can have such a mean way of putting me down and then making me feel like I'm the one being oversensitive. She claims I can't take criticism, and usually I don't think that's true. I'm determined not to rise, but this time I have a nagging feeling that she might be right. She's too clever for her own good sometimes – she just doesn't realize that what she is saying has a whole world of secrets and meaning behind it. Thank goodness.

Luckily we are outside the pub and so we don't have to continue this discussion, as I don't think any good is likely to come of it. We have the whole distraction of joining the short queue, getting our hands stamped and heading inside.

It's a pretty standard place – just a regular pub with a stage in one corner. It's not packed but there's a decent crowd, and I recognize a few people from college, who I wave and say hi to.

I lose track of Nishi and suspect that she's already disappeared off to the bar. I'm totally on my own and look like a complete loser among a sea of cool people, all in their own little groups. While I wait for her, I look around for Seymour. When I spot him, I find that – rather than relieved – I feel unexpectedly shy. I have met his band before but I don't really know them and am definitely not a part of their little gang – I've always thought it's important for him to have his own thing, and I've never wanted to be the sort of girlfriend who interferes in stuff like that. I know my music history; I've read enough about Yoko and Courtney to make sure I keep a polite distance. Now the wisdom of my policy feels questionable, as he is surrounded by a big group of people I don't know, and I am too embarrassed to approach him. I certainly don't want to be 'that' kind of girlfriend, but the only alternative is to stand around feeling like a total spare part at my own boyfriend's gig.

I try to look preoccupied – like I'm thinking important thoughts. I wish I was better in situations like this – people seem to think I'm so confident, but I'm really not. I don't know why; I know it's stupid to stand around feeling like this, but I can't control it sometimes. As I glance over at Seymour again, for a second I think he sees me, but I'm obviously wrong as he just turns back to his conversation with his band and all their assorted friends. Right now the lesser of the two evils is just standing here on my own with no mates, so I do that.

'What are you doing?' Nishi asks impatiently as she barges her way back to me. 'Seymour's over there, you know.'

I notice she has bought a drink for herself but didn't ask me if I wanted anything, and I resolve not to start getting petty over it.

'Oh, is he?' I say to hide my embarrassment, feeling like even more of a loser. 'I didn't see him. I was just waiting for you.'

Nishi steamrollers straight over to him, me lagging behind.

'Oh, hey,' he greets us coolly and goes back to his conversation.

He is talking to Futoshi, his drummer – whom I have met the grand total of about twice – and some other people that I don't recognize. Everyone shuffles to make room and smiles generally around at Nishi and me, and they all seem pleasant enough, but Seymour doesn't introduce us and nobody involves us in the conversation. This is fine, really – although perhaps mildly embarrassing. I can sense Nishi getting annoyed, although she just carries on drinking her pint and generally looking disgruntled. So rather than talk to her I pretend to be listening intently to the conversation on my other side, even though I am slightly too far away to make out what's going on.

Fortunately it's not long before it's time for Terminal

Ghosts to go onstage. Seymour picks his way out of the group and steps up on to the raised platform. He busies himself fiddling with pedals and his microphone stand.

'Ooh, get you with your rockstar boyfriend!'

Nishi nudges me in the ribs as we position ourselves nearer the stage – although something stops me from elbowing my way right to the front – and I'm not sure if she is being sarcastic or not. Either way, it makes me feel utterly crap.

It's weird to see Seymour in 'band mode'. They don't play in public that often, and I don't always go along if it's not local. So I find it tricky to reconcile this Seymour with the one I'm used to.

He looks different. He's a bit swaggery, which I would have thought in theory might be attractive. I'm not quite sure why it isn't. Maybe if I didn't know him I would think he looked cool – I tell myself that it's only because I know him too well that the unfamiliar expression on his face is making me cringe slightly.

Still, the overhead lights have been dimmed, the crowd has fallen mostly quiet and – in spite of myself, just for a second – I feel a little thrill of excitement in my stomach when Seymour leans in and speaks into the microphone. It's great that he's doing something he's passionate about. The small pub is quite full. People have come out and paid money to see him do the thing he loves. This reminds me of why I liked Seymour in the first place – having amazing and inspiring people around me like him and Nishi, with her fierce intellect and huge ambition, is a great thing and makes me want to be a better person. I'm lucky.

'Hi, we're Terminal Ghosts and this is a new song we wrote called "The Skies Above" . . .'

Once they get going, the room fills up with sound and they begin a set that's about three-quarters covers, with a few songs they've written themselves.

I try to get swept away in the music and enjoy myself – but it just doesn't seem to be happening. There's a thought building in my head, getting bigger with each song, and it won't go away, even though I am trying my absolute hardest to squash it down. I don't want to think it. It would make my life much, much easier if I could ignore it . . .

Seymour's band are simply not all that good. I never, ever want to have to admit this out loud. I am horribly disappointed; I want so badly to be able to mean it when I tell him afterwards – as I have to – that he was great.

I'm not generally a fan of bands doing covers, but I have to admit that in this instance it's preferable to Seymour's songwriting efforts – I'm pretty sure he just rhymed 'sky' with 'high' with 'fly'. All in a weird, fake Cockney accent.

I start to realize what it is that seems off to me about Seymour's new frontman persona. All of the band seem to suffer from the same problem. They are coming across like they are trying a bit too hard. I don't know if anyone else in the room senses this, but I feel embarrassed for them regardless. Generally, in life, I am of the opinion that trying is good. I could probably never be considered truly 'cool' because I am always visibly *trying*. But in a rock band, this is not a virtue. It's supposed to look effortless.

Nishi's watching the stage with an impassive look on her face and I have no idea what she's thinking. Then there is a pause and Seymour starts talking.

'I'd like to dedicate this next song to a girl called Tuesday. Yes, that's her real name. It's a song I know she'll recognize as it's by her biggest fan . . .'

This is so cryptic, or maybe I'm being wilfully ignorant, that for a minute I think he's going to play a song of his own. Like he's saying that he's my biggest fan. Which would be incredibly sweet and lovely of him.

As he plays the opening chords, the song is immediately recognizable. It's not by Seymour. It's by Jackson Griffith.

'If you want me to be someone else/maybe you should be by yourself . . .'

'Be Someone Else' was one of Sour Apple's biggest hits a few years ago and it's not lost on me that the lyrics are a bit weird, at least for a song that you dedicate to your girlfriend. In public. The narrative theme is a bit mean, but I tell myself that this is just coincidence. My guilty conscience again, et cetera. Maybe I should be finding this hilariously funny right now.

Seymour obviously thinks he's being smart, and this is just a well-known song. Then again, he can be a bit passive-aggressive at times.

I'm watching him so closely that I am nearly knocked off my feet when Nishi suddenly pushes past me and through the crowd towards the loo. I'm almost glad of the distraction as I am forced to follow her.

When I burst into the ladies' loos, both of the cubicles are engaged but Nishi is standing by the sinks, leaning against the wall with her arms up by her face. The walls are slightly sweaty and scratched with crap graffiti, and the whole room is damp and smells of wee – she must be really out of it.

'Nish, are you all right?' I ask her soothingly, putting a hand on her shoulder and rubbing slightly – as she's obviously ill, I think this gesture will be appreciated rather than brushed off for once. I like having my back rubbed if I feel like I'm going to puke. 'If it's an emergency, do you want me to see if I can get someone out of the cubicle?'

Her response is so muffled I can barely hear it. To be on the safe side, I prepare to shout through the flimsy doors that someone needs to get out of there quick before my drunk friend vomits in the sink. I give Nishi's shoulder another quick rub for good measure as I do so.

'Didn't you hear me?' she says, more loudly this time. 'I *said* leave me alone. Get out of here.'

As she turns to face me, I realize with agonizing, face-palming slowness that she is not ill but crying. Uncontrollably.

'Go away,' she continues, trying and failing to stop sobbing, and furiously wiping away a thick rivulet of snot. 'I can't stand to be around you at the moment. If it wasn't for you, Anna and I might still be together. Now I've got nothing and you've still got your stupid, good-looking boyfriend. Well, I hope you're happy. I just can't look at your face right now. Leave me alone, OK? I mean it, and not just tonight. I've got to get out of here.'

Nishi flees the room, sending the door swinging after her. I can hear waves of bass rumble flashing in and out. I'm still standing there in the toilets, completely flabbergasted, when one of the stall doors opens and a pretty girl about my age comes out to wash her hands – having heard the full conversation she obviously thinks I've done something heinous to break up my friend and her girlfriend and shoots me a dirty look as she barges past me. Maybe she's actually right – I wish I knew. Maybe if Nishi ever talked to me about anything important, I'd have some idea. If I thought it was worth following Nish, then I would, but I know it would not only be hopeless but probably make things worse.

I feel guilty all over again when I see that Seymour's set has finished. He is standing by the stage talking to a girl I don't recognize. Fortunately he doesn't seem to realize I missed the end, as he looks cheerful enough and waves me over to join them.

'Hey, Chew,' he says with a slightly twisted smile. 'This is Sophie – she's Jack, our bass player's, sister. Sophie, this is, um, Tuesday.'

'Hi.' I smile at her, as they both go awkwardly silent.

'Did you enjoy the set? It went really well, didn't it?' He doesn't wait for me to reply. 'Now of course you can see why I can't just give up on the band like my mum wants me to. What we're doing is really important.'

'Definitely,' Sophie agrees. 'I mean, I totally agree.'

'By the way, Chew?' Seymour goes on, smiling at me in the same weird way. 'I wanted to talk to you about something. You know that blog post you did about Terminal Ghosts?'

'Oh, I'm glad you saw it already. I just thought it would be a cool idea to—'

'Yeah, I'm sure you did – and it *was* a nice thought. It's just, maybe you could ask me in future before you do anything like that. Jack and Futoshi – and me, to be honest – well, we weren't sure you really get what we're trying to do. I mean, we're trying to build up a brand and it's really important that any press reflects the right influences and that kind of thing.'

'Oh. I just thought . . . Never mind. OK. Sorry.'

'I know you probably didn't think, because it's just such a small blog and hardly anyone reads it, but we still need to make sure it sends the right message,' he ploughs on. 'Maybe next time you could do a proper interview with us and we could have copy approval first.'

If Seymour had talked to me about this on my own, then I might have tried to argue. But Sophie is looking at me like I'm a total idiot and she feels sorry for me, which makes me just want to get off the subject as quickly as possible. I wonder if that might be why he chose to bring it up in front of some random girl, and if that's why he's looking so shifty about it.

'Anyway, well done tonight,' I tell him. 'It was great; you were really good. I've got to run though. Nishi's waiting for me outside – we've got to go, and I'm staying round at hers tonight. So I'll probably see you at college on Monday. I've got an English paper in the afternoon.'

Once I've escaped outside into the street I try my best to build up some sort of righteous anger to power my walk home. It doesn't work and I remain slow and heavy; I only quicken my pace through necessity when I come to the end of the brightly lit high street and realize that it was stupid to walk home alone at night just because I'm in a bad mood.

Then, as I reach the safety of my road, a horribly guilty thought hits me and the whole thing seems far, far worse. I've heard Seymour's band before and thought they were good. Maybe the difference isn't them. I mean, it's unlikely that they've suddenly got worse at playing their instruments. Maybe the problem is me. I used to like Seymour's band because *I used to like him*. Once this thought has entered my head, I can't unthink it. I wish I could. I really, really wish I could. My own treachery is making me into a horrible person – here I am picking holes in Seymour's musical ability, when I'm the one who doesn't even want to go out with him any more. I'm the one in the wrong, yet I'm inwardly snarking at him for not being as good a songwriter as Jackson Griffith. I am the worst human being possible.

When I finally make it home, I let myself in quietly, glad that the house is empty and in darkness. My mum's out on another date with Richard Jenkins tonight and it's still pretty early, so I've got the place to myself. I'll probably eat some cereal and watch TV for a while.

As I switch on the sitting-room light, there is an ear-piercing scream and a commotion that gets me all disorientated. My first crazed thought is that it must be burglars, but then I realize that my mum and a man who is presumably Richard Jenkins have sprung up off the sofa.

Thankfully – *thankfully* – they are both fully clothed, but my mum's dress is unbuttoned halfway down the front and Richard Jenkins is hastily wiping lipstick off his face. I stand there and wish that the earth would swallow me whole.

'Oh, Chew!' my mum exclaims in a high-pitched symphony of humiliation. 'I thought you were staying at Nishi's tonight. I mean, of course it's fine that you're home. What I mean is, we were just having a little lie-down. Oh god, this is embarrassing – you're a legal adult, for goodness sake. Sorry. You caught us out there. Tuesday, this is Richard. Richard, this is my daughter, Tuesday.'

'Hello,' Richard says, understandably not quite meeting my eye.

'Hi.'

'Now –' my mum laughs with admirable aplomb – 'after that legendarily awkward introduction, let's all be civilized and sit down and have a drink together.'

She scuttles into the kitchen where, as well as getting us all a drink, she is hopefully going to do up her dress. I'm not exactly desperate to hang around making polite conversation with her new boyfriend after seeing him groping my mum on the sofa, but it would be too rude and immature to run upstairs immediately after that.

'So . . . good evening?' Richard asks me.

'Yes, thanks. I went to see a gig in town.'

I really don't want to elaborate any more than that. Richard seems OK; he's actually not bad-looking – for a middle-aged person, I mean – and he is being perfectly nice. But I've got too much on my mind to want to make small talk with strangers in my own house. Besides, who knows how long he'll hang around? Getting attached to my mum's boyfriends is something that I learned a very long time ago not to do – it never ends well.

'So, you're taking your A levels at the moment, I believe.'

'Yes, that's right.' I smile very tightly.

Fortunately my mum comes in then with three cups of coffee on a tray.

'Good evening, darling?' she asks, and again I nod vaguely.

'You?'

'Fabulous, thanks. We went to that new Spanish bar in town, which was lovely.'

'Great. Listen, it was really nice to meet you, Richard; thanks for the coffee, Mum. But, um, I've got a lot of revision to do and I don't want to cramp your style, so I might just take mine upstairs, if you don't mind.'

'Good idea, darling. Oh, before you go – I just wanted to run something by you. Richard and I were talking tonight, and you remember I said we were thinking of going on a mini-break to Bruges? Well, we've found a great last-minute deal. The only thing is, it's next weekend. I know your last A level isn't until the following Monday – so we'll leave on Thursday and be back on the Sunday night in time for your final exam. Does that sound OK?'

'That sounds great, Mum. I know you've always wanted to go there. Actually, it'll probably be good to have a quiet house for some last-minute revision that weekend.'

'Well, I know how serious you are about English, so I don't mind leaving you alone for the weekend. I know I can trust you to be an adult about it. I'll be around to give you a lift into college on the Monday – you don't want to have to worry about walking or getting the bus when you've got your important exam to think about. That'll work out fine then!'

'Definitely. Thanks, Mum. Night-night.'

As I close the door firmly behind me and walk up the stairs with my cup of coffee, I wonder whether this really is a sign or if I just have an evil mind.

To: Tuesday Cooper
From: jackson evan griffith

I saw your website tonight. i don't wanna get all macho on you and kick up about this. I know it's not my right and the thing I like best about you (actually one of many, to be accurate) is that you are so much your own person.

But I gotta admit . . . it felt like a kick in the teeth. It's my own fault. I've gotten ahead of myself and I know I have a real tendency to think I'm the centre of the universe. I know I'm an egomaniac and I'm sorry.

It's just . . . I was starting to think there was really something between us. I kinda forgot about your 'boyfriend'. I just assumed you weren't together any more. I guess it was wishful thinking . . . ?

I'd still love it if you wanted to come to Glastonbury. You haven't said, so I'm not holding my breath. Please?

Yours,

J xxx

To: jackson evan griffith
From: Tuesday Cooper

One word. Yes.

Glastonbury – let's do it. I'm in.

I'm sorry. The world has become very strange. I'm probably not handling it all in the best way. No excuses, but I'm not used to all this. I'm always doing things because I think it's for the best and I want everyone to be happy, but at the moment I only seem to make things worse.

But the stars have aligned. I am throwing caution to the wind. How can I not?! I don't want to get carried away with myself either, but you're right. There is something between us. I don't know what, but . . . I don't want to embarrass myself here, but it's not like anything I've ever experienced before.

Most of all, I just really want to go. (I would also like, more than anything, to see you again.)

If you'd still like me to, I'd love to come with you. Let's talk and make a plan – ring me when you can, OK?

RT[1] xxx

---

1 *Ruby Tuesday, in case you didn't work it out yourself.*

I feel like I'm on a secret date. All right, like I'm on *another* secret date. This time, there is no grey area: I really do feel as if I'm cheating. That's probably because I am. I intend to, anyway.

I'm sitting in Macari's, watching the door like a particularly paranoid hawk. When she walks in, I'm surprised at how nice it is to see her.

'Anna, I've missed you!'

'Oh, Chew – me too. I'm so glad you texted me.'

I stand up to greet her and we fall into each other's arms. We squeeze each other tight and hang on, not letting go for at least a full ten seconds. Although I'm usually proud of the fact that Nishi and I have (had?) a less typical female friendship, I have to admit that it's lovely just to have a proper squishy hug from a real friend. We're both a bit damp-eyed but also grinning by the time we break apart.

Anna still looks as pretty as ever, but she's not in the best shape I've ever seen her. Her eyes are tired and I suspect she might have lost weight, even though – unlike me – she didn't really have any to lose in the first place.

We order milkshakes and chips and settle into a tucked-away booth at the back. Luckily the place is quiet.

'How are you?' I ask her.

'I've been better, to be honest. And you?'

'Snap. To be honest,' I reply carefully.

'How's Nish?' Anna asks quietly.

'Well, that's the thing. I don't know. We had a big fight last Saturday night; ever since then I've been trying to catch up with her at college, but she's totally avoiding me.'

'*What?*' Anna looks genuinely shocked. 'You two are such best mates! I don't understand it. First she dumps me and then she dumps you. What the hell has gone wrong with that girl?'

'Hang on. What did you say? *She* dumped *you*? She's been acting all crazy and she told me you guys had broken up, but then she refused to talk about it – but she's been so upset I just presumed it was you who broke up with her. Oh, and she blamed me, by the way.'

As I add this last sentence for good measure, I am ashamed to note that I'm pleased to see Anna looking appropriately shocked and furious.

'That girl has got some serious issues,' she says. 'She went bonkers about that night at Moshi Munchers because you and I walked home together, and I told her that she should talk to you about it but she refused. Then basically she dumped me for no good reason, refused to talk to me or tell me why. She's been ignoring my texts and we haven't spoken since. Communication problem, do you reckon?'

'Poor Nish,' I find myself saying. 'She'd hate me saying it, but I think she's more messed up than she even realizes. She really loves you; I know she does. This is like self-sabotage or something. It's practically self-harm.'

'I think you've hit the nail on the head, Chew. That's exactly what it is. She's broken my heart, but I actually feel sorry for her. I'm even more worried after what you've said. The worst bit is that there's nothing we can do. I think it's the stress of exams; she puts herself under so much pressure. But there's no point trying to tell her that – it would just make things worse. There's literally no way we can help her until she wants to be helped. If she ever does.'

We both know she's right. We sit in silence for a minute and munch thoughtfully on our chips.

'So, what's up with you and Seymour?'

'Well, it's kind of a long story. And I haven't told anyone else. Not even Nishi – I know she'd disapprove. And there's a lot going on that I definitely can't talk to Seymour about.'

Anna gets all alert, like a little rabbit; I swear her ears actually prick up. 'OK, I'm all ears and my lips are sealed. I don't have to get home for ages yet. Hit me.'

'Well, you remember those comments on my blog that really were from Jackson Griffith . . . ?'

By the time I make it to the end of the story, Anna's mouth is literally hanging open. Most of her chips remain cold in the bowl in front of her, untouched and forgotten. I hate wasting food; I can't stop looking at them.

'So that brings me around to what I want to ask you,' I finish up eventually. 'What are you doing next weekend?'

'Um, pretty much nothing. Why?'

'Because Jackson has asked me to go to Glastonbury with him. He's playing a secret set there on the Saturday afternoon. I asked him if I could bring a friend with me, and he said that would be cool – he can sort us out with tickets, backstage passes; we can stay with him in the artists' VIP section. We just have to get ourselves there on the Thursday or Friday, as he's already playing a gig in Bridport the night before. What do you say?'

She's too speechless to reply but her eyes are shining with excitement and a smile is beginning to play on her lips. Our expressions are matching, mirror images of each other. I can feel my own excitement building as I suspect that she might say yes.

'I . . . I really, really want to. I so mega want to! But . . . how are you going to swing it? You're in the middle of your bloody A levels!'

'I know. It's ridiculous. I can't believe this has come up now, of all times. But the exams will be practically over by then. I'll only have one left to go, and all the others have gone really well so far. And . . . I don't know why – I just feel like this is something I have to do.'

'I don't blame you. I want to do it too. If we can come up with a plan so that we can do this without getting busted – and it has to be a watertight, foolproof, awesome plan to end all plans – then I'm in.'

We shake hands across the table, unable to suppress our cheesy grins. It's funny, I'm getting this really bizarre feeling that everything is lining up just right – not to sound like a total hippie, but like this is almost meant to be.

'Have you ever been to Glastonbury before?' she asks me.

'No, but I've been to Reading a couple of times, and to

quite a few big one-day events, so it's not like I've never been to a festival before. How about you?'

'Never. I've always wanted to, but none of my friends have been into that sort of thing and I couldn't exactly go on my own. Until I met you and Nishi. I mean, it's not like I have a lot in common with most of the girls at my school. Before I met you guys, to be honest I didn't really have any proper friends. Anyway, I've always wanted to go to a festival. Nish and I had talked about going to some over the summer, but I guess that's out now . . .'

Her eyes fill up with tears. I know I'm being treacherous by meeting up with Anna, but now I know a bit more I have a feeling that the situation is far from hopeless and maybe I can even help. Either way, I really want to stay in touch with Anna and I think that it's the right thing to do.

I'd speak to Nishi and explain this if I could. In fact, I'd genuinely love to. But it's become apparent that she was deadly serious when she said that she can't be around me at the moment. She hasn't replied to my calls or texts, and she has managed to avoid me at college.

With Seymour it's the opposite: I've been kind of been avoiding him. We haven't seen each other in the flesh since the night of his gig and have only exchanged perfunctory texts. I have been citing exam pressure and excessive revision. I know it's childish that I'm hoping this whole situation will somehow magically go away; I just can't handle dealing with him at the moment.

Although it was great at the time when the four of us

were a gang and everything was hunky-dory, it's a relief to hang out with Anna and escape from the double stress of Nishi and Seymour. Anna and I stay out longer than we expected to, just because it's so nice to see each other – we share an ice-cream sundae and chat for ages, hatching plans and going off on festival flights of fancy.

'Stay in touch, OK?' she says as we're leaving, hugging me outside the cafe before we part ways. 'I honestly think we can do this.'

I agree. I go home with the feeling that this really could happen. I don't know if that's actually a good thing, but right now I don't care.

So, I am deep in the very depths of my A levels. I really shouldn't be blogging. However, my brain is about to explode and I thought a little distraction might be a good way of staying sane.

Here I am, up to my ears in set texts, marking up books with a neon rainbow of highlighters and trying to stick to all those overambitious revision tables I made weeks ago.

However, I am still a human being who loves music and ridiculousness, and this got me to thinking . . . Maybe it would actually be helpful if I could give my English lit characters their own theme tunes!

King Lear would be into Neil Young (his favourite song is 'A Man Needs a Maid' – look it up if you're not a sad old granddad in an eighteen-year-old girl's body, like me!), but Goneril and Regan are always like, 'Dad, turn this crap off!!' and they make him listen to Radio 1 when they're all in the car together. They like to do sexy dances to Rihanna and think that 'Blurred Lines' isn't really sexist cos they're, like, so empowered. Cordelia, on the other hand, loves Mumford & Sons and is all smug and wholesome about it.

The Bennett sisters in Pride and Prejudice like to listen to retro Spice Girls and argue over which one they are. Lydia (my favourite) can't decide if she wants to be cute like Baby Spice or naughty like Ginger. When all the sisters are at home together, they like nothing more than to drag the Lucky Voice karaoke machine out. Mr Bennett stays out of the way with mortification, but they can't get their mum off the mic once she starts up with her renditions of Katy Perry . . .

Lady Macbeth is obsessed with Bruce Springsteen. She's got a massive crush on him (who hasn't?) and listens to *Darkness on the Edge of Town* all the time. She likes his work ethic and his muscles. Her husband doesn't dare to argue.

Procrastinate, me? Wish me luck . . .

Comments

Hope you're not going barmy locked away up there – researching the 'madwoman in the attic' theory in action . . . I'll bring you a cup of tea!
Carrie_Cougar

Yes, please! And a biscuit if we've got any. I need the sugar!
Tuesday-yes-that-is-my-real-name-Cooper

'How are you getting on?'

I am propped up in bed with my laptop, surrounded by books and papers. My phone and a bumper pack of highlighter pens are next to me on the bedside table. My crazy revision timetable – made up of four A4 sheets taped together and colour-coded so it looks like the London tube map redrawn by a serial killer – is pinned up on the wall next to me.

My mum finds a space to sit down by my feet and she deposits a cup of tea and a Penguin on the bedside table.

'Thanks, Mum. It's going OK. I think. I don't really know by this point. I'm losing all perspective.'

'It's great that you're working so hard, but don't be too tough on yourself. You can only do what you can do.'

'I know. It's just really important to me that I can at least feel like I did my best.'

It's true. I'm not just laying it on thick to hide the fact that I have so many other things on my mind. I was starting to feel pretty relaxed – after all, I'm on the home straight now – but the idea of missing my entire last weekend's revision before the final exam is enough to scare me into overdrive. I have to compensate for it somehow, and not mess everything up by falling at the final hurdle. I could never forgive myself if I let that happen.

I've got a lot going on at the moment, but I am still determined to do well in these exams and get my place at university. I'm not thinking too far into the future, just sticking with Plan A. I just have to do a lot more juggling than I anticipated.

The A levels were already a big deal, even when I had a cosy, easy-going gang with my boyfriend and my best friends, and Jackson Griffith was still just a name in my record collection.

Now I just have to make sure I can deal with it all – it's too important to mess up. So many things at the moment feel like a chance I have to grab right now, before I lose the opportunity forever.

For four days when my revision and preparation should be at their absolute maximum, I will be hanging out in a field, miles away in the West Country, watching some of my favourite bands and hanging out with Jackson Griffith. This is really happening. This is my life.

'I'm proud of you, Chew,' my mum says, standing up. 'I'll leave you to get on with it, but don't push yourself too hard. I know you've done your best all year, so you'll do well. And whatever happens, you've worked your hardest – I'm proud of you no matter what.'

A massive lump comes to my throat as my mum ruffles my hair and walks out of the room with a last backwards smile over her shoulder, closing the door behind her. Particularly when, before the door is even halfway closed, my phone beeps.

I put down my copy of *King Lear*, careful to keep the page, and read the text from Anna. She's booked our train tickets for Thursday. We've turned out to be a pretty good team – I have the ideas and she is way more organized than I could ever dream of being. We're both excited to an epic level now, probably intensified by the fact that we can't express this to anyone except each other.

I haven't even been in touch with Jackson much, as his latest run of secret gigs is coinciding with him staying with an old friend and his family out in the countryside, as he works his way closer to Glastonbury. I had to try to be cool when I found out that said 'old friend', one of Jackson's musical mentors, and his wife and children are a famous family – rockstar and fashion designer, their eldest daughter a top model – who I have read about in magazines.

Even Jackson has started to feel a little less real to me, now that he is edging back into the public eye. It seems like the music world is welcoming him back with open arms – his new solo material has been really well received and he's had some lovely reviews for the secret gigs in unlikely locations. Anticipation is building for his hotly rumoured Glastonbury appearance, and it is being touted as either the greatest comeback or the must-see disaster of the weekend. Reading about this in the *Guardian* online, with a photo of him that I can tell is at least a couple of years old and that makes him look like a proper rockstar, I can scarcely believe that this is the same boy who sends me emails, writes me songs and has been known to sprawl on hotel-room sofas watching daytime telly. I can't wait to see him again.

Anyway, Anna and I basically have a plan. On Thursday morning my mum goes to Bruges. On Thursday afternoon Anna and I will take the train, the tube, and a three and a half hour coach journey to the festival, which is not even in the actual town of Glastonbury and appears to be in precisely the middle of nowhere.

Jackson has sorted out our tickets. When we arrive I just have to call his manager, Sadie Steinbeck – Jackson has given me her UK 'cellphone' number – and she will come to the gates and meet us with our passes. Not just that, but they will be the coveted 'AAA' – access all areas – so that we can go backstage with Jackson and stay in the artists' section, rather than camping out with the masses. It'll be nice to go to a festival and not have to lug a tent with me, I must admit.

Still, I can't think too much about all that now. I've worked so bloody hard for the last two years – and before that – that the idea of messing up my very last exam is something that I just can't let happen.

I turn determinedly back to *King Lear*, orange highlighter in hand. I don't even look up from the book as I feel for my cup of tea and the Penguin next to me. I consume both of them without even noticing, engrossed in the text and trying to decipher my own scribbled notes in the margins. I curse my past self, as is so often the case – why I scrawled 'POETIC FALLACY???' across an entire page is now beyond me. Why the three question marks, Chew – what was your point???

My phone beeps again and I am glad of the interruption. Until I see that it's Seymour, asking if he can come over after he finishes Sunday lunch with his family. Obviously he's having a hard time at home since the awkward argument with his parents. I am hit by a renewed wave of helpless guilt, knowing it's my own fault and I still haven't done anything to help the situation.

I text back a vague reply saying that I'm really busy revising, nicking my mum's madwoman in the attic joke and reusing it. Not cool, I know. Only a few days of this to go.

I put my phone down and try to go back to Shakespeare, but my concentration is shot. I stand and stretch, picking up my empty mug and Penguin wrapper. I might just see what's on telly while I take them downstairs. I really hate myself sometimes.

Ones to watch: Jackson Griffith

An unexpected addition to the list. The Sour Apple frontman made a well-publicized fall from grace way back in the annals of pop-music history (i.e. a couple of years ago). He's fulfilled every rockstar cliché going – from marrying a French model to allegedly drinking himself through the inevitable divorce. Throughout it all, his deceptively jaunty, nostalgia-tinted brand of retro Californian pop has remained popular with a certain type of young lady, helped along by his poster-boy good looks. Derivative, sure – he's famously enamoured with all the classic troubadours of the peace 'n' love generation, from Gram Parsons to James Taylor – but young Jackson is certainly easy on the ears as well as the eyes. So expect a female-heavy audience this weekend if the rumours are true and he chooses this year's Glastonbury to return from the wilderness. Early reports on his new solo material are unexpectedly positive – so, gents, if your girlfriend drags you along to the acoustic stage to watch his set on Saturday afternoon, you might find yourself pleasantly surprised. Especially if the sun is shining and you have a pint of local cider in your hand. Stranger things have happened.

'Do we think this is a Bruges outfit?'

'Definitely. You look great.'

My mum does look unquestionably great, but she has been trying on slightly different variations of white jeans and sexy T-shirts for the past two hours, and the little wheelie suitcase sitting on her bed is still almost empty. In the bottom of it is her sponge bag – actually enormous as it's stuffed full of every variety of make-up and beauty product imaginable – plus one silky grey nightie and, in full view, the ridiculously sexy Elle McPherson underwear she has bought especially for the occasion, with the tags still attached. Mum has been obsessing over whether sensible trainers for walking around Bruges might make her legs look short, but I have a feeling that they are not going to be doing a massive amount of sightseeing outside of their hotel room. I should probably be more disgusted than I am, but I'm so used to this sort of thing by now that it's only medium-gross. I'm sure some future therapist will have something to say about this when I'm a middle-aged wreck, but for now it's easiest just to go along with it.

'It's June so I should be OK with just my denim jacket, do you think?' She puts on said garment and looks again in the mirror. 'But then what if it rains and my hair goes frizzy? Perhaps I ought to take something with a hood . . .'

'You can borrow my red American Apparel hoodie, if you like,' I suggest. 'It's quite warm as well, but it wouldn't take up too much room in your bag.'

'Ha ha, very funny. If you're not going to offer any serious suggestions, do you fancy making us another cup of coffee while I try to figure out what on earth I can wear to dinner in the evenings?'

Her sarcastic response is a bit wounding, as I was genuinely trying to be helpful. In fact, I was being pretty selfless as I really want to take it with me to Glastonbury, although obviously she can't possibly know that. What the hell is wrong with my red American Apparel hoodie? It's cool. I think my mum is against unisex clothes on principle; American Apparel confuses her.

I head to the kitchen to make yet another cup of coffee as instructed. While the kettle's boiling I take my phone out of the pocket of my pyjama bottoms and check my texts. There are, unsurprisingly, an excitable two from Anna already this morning. I text her back quickly to say that my mum is mucking about and taking *bloody ages* but Richard Jenkins is due to pick her up in a taxi to St Pancras in an hour, so I'll call as soon as the coast is clear. We need to be on our way by midday, on pain of death, in order to make all of our many, complicated transport connections.

When I come back up the stairs, I'm pleased to see that the white jeans and various T-shirts have been added to the suitcase, along with a big gold necklace that sits on the top. However, my mum is now wearing a small sparkly dress and high heels and looking at herself critically from the back in the mirror. Tendons are straining in her neck as she tries to examine her own bottom.

'Do we think this is possibly a *little* excessive?' she asks.

'Yes. What about that nice wrap dress you wear for work sometimes?'

'Really, Chew – *really*? You want me to look like a middle-aged mum going to the office on my first dirty weekend in at least five years. Thanks a lot.'

'Mum, you couldn't look like a middle-aged mum if you tried,' I reply truthfully.

This seems to placate her, and she actually throws a black jersey dress into the case.

'Now, if I wear my skinny jeans and black boots on the Eurostar . . .'

'Yes, that sounds a very good plan,' I say decisively. 'Richard's coming to collect you at eleven, right? You should probably try to be totally ready by then; you don't want him to think you're a flake, or neurotic, or something.'

'Thanks for that extremely helpful advice, Tuesday,' she snaps. 'Please remind me why you're hanging around while I'm *trying* to get ready. And why don't you get dressed? I would really rather Richard didn't see you still slopping about in your pyjamas at this time of the morning.'

'Well, I'm not planning on leaving the house for the next four days, so this is as good an outfit for my self-imposed hardcore revision boot camp as any.'

Yes, I am evil. It's official.

'I'm proud of you, darling,' she replies in a softer voice this time, stopping and smiling at me for a second. 'Sorry,

I don't know why I'm so stressed; I just really want this to go well.'

I know the feeling. I know it better than she could ever imagine right now. I hug her as she throws a pair of high heels into her case, and squeeze tight. It suddenly hits me that so much will have happened by the time I next see her, and everything could be completely different by then.

'Don't worry, you're going to have a great time – I know it,' I murmur into her shoulder. 'And don't worry about me for a second.'

By some miracle, by eleven o'clock she is packed and in yet another pair of skinny jeans, if somewhat over-caffeinated. She is waiting by the front door when Richard arrives bang on time in a taxi. He grins when he sees her and helps her with her case; he even holds the car door open for her. My mum inspires men to do some very strange things.

'Don't work too hard, darling – see you on Sunday night, about eight o'clock!'

I wave them off until they are out of sight, and then I spring into manic action. In my haste I trip up the stairs and stub my toe while texting Anna. I limp into my bedroom, open my wardrobe and pull out the rucksack I've got stashed away in the bottom of it. It's already full of the things I might need at Glastonbury – a couple of summer dresses, a jumper and my American Apparel hoodie; knickers and socks and two clean T-shirts; my swimsuit just in case; all the usual things like dry shampoo, wet wipes and metric craploads of eyeliner. That's pretty much it. I've got my festival routine pretty much sorted now that I've been to Reading a couple of times; I know what I'm doing. This time round, of course, my festival experience is going to be exponentially more awesome, but I guess the general set-up will be exactly the same.

With lightning speed, I strip off my pyjamas and pull on the outfit that I've had secretly ready for days. Vintage denim shorts, my favourite T-shirt with a picture of John Peel on it, granddad cardigan and a parka that I know from previous experience can double up as a sleeping bag if necessary. I lace up my Converse – high-tops as I've heard the terrain can be pretty rough at Glastonbury, especially if it rains – and I perch my biggest sunglasses on top of my head. My very few valuables – phone and a bit of scraped-together cash – go in a perfectly hideous 80s bumbag that I fortuitously found at the charity shop for just such an occasion as this. My outfit is actually pretty practical, I think.

I'm all set, but as I wait impatiently for Anna I become paranoid that I might have missed something. I know that if I am to avoid getting caught, I've got to have planned for every eventuality. I've watched enough *CSI* to know how these things work. I need to get forensic.

I've told my mum that I'll text her at regular intervals, which should be easily done – both to save her phone bill in calling from a foreign country and so that she doesn't risk disturbing me at any crucial points in my 'revision timetable'. I've even stacked up my blog with a few auto-timed posts that will show up on the site while I'm away. Mum went to the supermarket before she left and filled up the fridge with food to keep me going throughout my 'revision weekend' – I've shoved most of it into my bag, which serves the double purpose of making it look like I was here eating regularly and providing us with snacks for our adventure. Festival food can be really expensive – although I wonder if there'll be catering backstage . . . Backstage! Back-bloody-stage!

I'm all ready – as ready as I will ever be – so I lock the door behind me and lug my rucksack outside, sitting on it while I wait for Anna to come and call for me en route to the station. I take out my phone to write the text to Seymour that I've been dreading sending. *Seymour, I'm sorry but I've been thinking and your mum's right: I know it's a bit late now, but I don't think we should see each other again until after the exams have finished . . . especially as we haven't been getting on that well anyway. I've *got* to concentrate on final revision and I can't think about anything else right now. Good luck and we'll catch up soon – not long to go now. Love, Chew xxx*

I know it's half-hearted and I'm not saying I'm proud of myself. I couldn't in good conscience go to Glastonbury to meet Jackson without having said *something* to Seymour. I can't pretend that I'm going to meet Jackson to 'interview' him or for any perfectly innocent reason any more – and I can't pretend not to know that he feels the same, whatever that does or doesn't turn into.

But at the same time – and I am well aware that this is awful and self-serving of me – I can't risk incurring such wrath from Seymour that he comes tearing round here, wondering where I am and making this situation even more potentially complicated. I had to be just ambiguous enough not to cause any extra fuss. I know it's pointless, but I can't stop cursing myself for not doing this sooner, and properly. What a mess. But this will have to do for now.

If I know Seymour, and I think I do, then he will go straight into sulk mode and not contact me for a while out of principle. Not for at least four days.

Luckily I don't have long to dwell on my own treachery, as Anna appears round the corner, so I stand up and wave madly while stashing my phone away in the hideous bumbag.

Anna is dressed ridiculously impractically, in a long floaty dress and gladiator sandals, with fake flowers in her hair. It's immediately obvious she's never been to a festival before – she looks great and it's sunny outside now, but it gets cold at night and it might rain. She's only got a medium-sized handbag with her. I have a feeling there might at least be one person who won't turn her nose up at the idea of borrowing my red American Apparel hoodie at some point this weekend.

We squeak and jump up and down a little bit as we hug and then rush off down the street to the station. We're both a little on edge, which only adds to our mania and speeds us up. Bumping into anyone we know would be a disaster; one glance at us would make it pretty obvious exactly where we are going today.

For me, although I'm technically on study leave now, obviously it's still a college day and I am supposed to be at home revising. Anna has it a bit easier – she has told her parents that she's got a school trip to London for the weekend, to see a few plays for drama. The other bonus of this – and I suppose I should be unsurprised because Anna lives in a posh house near Seymour's and goes to the girls' private school – is that she told her parents they had to pay for the school trip, and they just *gave* her £150, plus spending money. No questions asked. This is obviously crazy, but I'm not arguing as it definitely works in our favour on this occasion.

'And it's not a *total* lie,' Anna explains optimistically. 'I mean, there's a theatre tent at Glastonbury, isn't there? This weekend is going to be *educational*.'

This glass-half-full attitude is not the only reason why I'm glad Anna is here. She's pre-booked our tickets, so we can nip straight on to the train without too much messing about. Which is a very good thing as we're both getting a bit twitchy in the small, crowded station.

Once we have dashed on to a train for Paddington, we throw ourselves into a double seat with a table. We both watch, practically holding our breath, as the train pulls out of the station. We are moving. We are on our way. From this point on, nobody knows where we are.

I can't believe we are really doing this. In a few hours' time, we will be at Glastonbury festival.

To: Tuesday Cooper
From: jackson evan griffith

Ruby Tuesday,

I'm supposed to be soundchecking right now, but I had to write you a quick note. It feels like we haven't spoken for a while – I'm sorry I've been so busy, but I guess you have been too. How did that exam you had this week go? Hope everything is good. I have faith in you – you'll do great!

I hope I don't sound crazy, but I really miss you! I'm getting so nervous now about Glastonbury – I'm seriously having nightmares about it. The only thing keeping me going is that you'll be there.

Don't mean to get heavy . . . I thought of a record you might like yesterday. Maybe you've already heard it? 'He's a Rebel' by the Crystals. I love those 60s girl groups!

Anyway . . . Can't wait to see you . . .

J xxx

It is dark. The coach has dropped us in a muddy car park and I can't get my bearings. After all my misplaced confidence, one thing is obvious: Glastonbury is absolutely nothing like Reading festival.

It's immediately apparent that this is a very different set-up. For one thing, it's about ten times the size. I always thought people were just showing off when they said that Glastonbury kicked Reading's arse – like, 'Look at me, I've been to all the festivals!' – but it turns out they were telling the truth. Glastonbury is like a giant mythical city.

But we are yet to discover the inner workings of this magical kingdom. We are stuck on the outside. After our triumphant escape from suburban tedium, our day has not gone according to plan. It has taken us much longer to get here than we expected; we thought we'd be arriving to enjoy the sunny afternoon, not rocking up tired and lost in the dark.

We follow the other people getting off the bus, but they all have their tickets and ID at the ready for the complicated entry system and head through heavily guarded turnstiles. Still hanging around in the muddy car park, I call Jackson's UK mobile number. I'm not even surprised when the annoying plastic voice tells me that his phone may be switched off – I tell myself not to panic just yet. He doesn't even have voicemail set up. I hang up and dial the number that he gave me for Sadie Steinbeck.

Before I even finish dialling, this plan – which seemed so simple and straightforward when I was planning the whole thing out at home – is starting to look somewhat flawed. The sheer size of the place indicates that it might not be as easy as I thought to meet a total stranger at a vaguely specified meeting point.

I can tell that Anna is thinking the exact same thing. I'm trying not to let on that I am starting to feel slightly panicked. My phone reception is sketchy – presumably because there are so many people here, another factor that hadn't occurred to me – and it takes me a few tries before I can even get the call to connect.

The line at the other end rings, and rings. And rings. Interminably. Until it goes to answerphone. I had half expected this by now, but the disappointment is still crushing.

'Um, hi. Sadie, this is Tuesday Cooper. I'm a friend of Jackson's. I hope he told you . . . He said to call you when I get here – I'm at Glastonbury – to get passes from you. For me and my friend. Well, we're here. Waiting in the car parking field. So, could you please possibly call me back on this number . . . ?'

As I hang up it dawns on me that it was incredibly stupid just to turn up here, in the middle of nowhere, on practically the other side of the country, with vague contact details from a man I barely know. A man who is famously flaky, who has been in all the papers because he is known as an unpredictable mess. It doesn't matter that he doesn't seem like that to me; it doesn't matter that I don't want to believe everything I've read. For all those hours on the phone, the dozens of emails and photos passed back and forth, there is no disputing the fact that

I have met this man only twice. I have schlepped all the way out here on a whim and a very shaky promise, and I have dragged Anna with me.

When I turn back towards her, tucking the phone into my coat pocket where I can get to it easily if it miraculously starts to ring, I am dismayed when I catch the look on Anna's face, just for a split second. It disappears in a flash, but I know I saw it there. I don't blame her. She is wondering if I'm crazy, if I've made this whole thing up. Of course, beyond what I've told her, she has no concrete proof that any of this is real.

'I've left a message,' I say, looking around and seeing not much but field and cars and fences. 'Hopefully she'll call me back really soon.'

We smile at each other tightly. Neither of us wants to admit defeat and ruin the spirit of fun and adventure. At least I'm lucky to be here with Anna, rather than Seymour or Nishi. Anna and I at least share the same combined sense of optimism and politeness, which means we want to keep things cool in the face of adversity. Nishi and Seymour would be blaming me, bitching and complaining by now. Plus, we know each other too well so we don't feel any great need to be nice to each other – which is probably the wrong way around with your best friends, when you think about it.

'Shall we try walking around the edge a bit?' Anna suggests. 'Maybe there's a way in somewhere.'

I'm pretty sure that, like me, she's just trying to think of something – anything – to do, but I agree gratefully.

We walk around, me almost buckling under the weight of my rucksack and Anna shivering as it gets colder, but we see nothing to do, nowhere to go and, crucially, no way in.

'Would you like to borrow my red American Apparel hoodie?' I say eventually, glad to think of at least one thing I can do to be helpful.

'No, thanks,' she replies.

She's trying to make her voice sound as calm and nice as possible, but that's how I know she's actually, secretly, really annoyed with me. I understand – I wish more than anything that I was at home in bed with *King Lear* and a packet of Jaffa Cakes, and this was all *my* idea. Jackson Griffith is starting to feel like a very shaky mirage, even to me – and I've met him.

'Look,' I say, 'I know this is the most rubbish Glastonbury arrival ever, and it's probably my fault for not planning better, but we've got four days for things to get way more awesome than this. On the coach here I noticed there was a 24-hour service station a couple of miles back. I'm hoping this Sadie woman will call me back, but maybe in the meantime we should walk that way – just in case?'

'Yeah, why not? Maybe I will borrow that hoodie after all, if it's OK . . .'

As we walk back along the main road, it's like everything about it is designed to make life as awkward as possible for renegade pedestrians like us – it's dark and feels impossibly remote; when cars come past they roar at monstrous speeds. I keep one hand on my phone the entire time we're walking, just in case, but it may as well be a stone in my pocket.

Then it starts to rain, a thin drizzle that turns into a downpour as we stumble along the muddy grass verge in the dark.

I actually want to cry. If I let go for a split second and allow myself to give in, I will dissolve into tears of disappointment and frustration and anger and shame. I will fall down and I might not get back up any time soon.

Instead I force myself to burst out laughing – manic, starting out as fake and then veering into hysterical – until Anna joins in. The two of us laugh and laugh. I know without seeing myself that I look like absolute crap. The flowers in Anna's elaborately braided hair are kind of dissolving.

We link arms and power on.

'Can you imagine if Nishi was here?' Anna giggles.

'Oh my god!' I exclaim. 'Thank goodness she isn't. I'd never hear the bloody end of it. She'd be bitching and complaining and refusing to walk because she hates walking. She hates most things, but especially anything involving physical activity.'

'Yeah, but you know what she's like – she'd have located us to exact latitude and longitude, and probably come up with some amazing idea by now . . .'

'You're right,' I am forced to admit. 'She's gobby and annoying, but she's got a brain the size of a planet. And she can be pretty funny when she wants to be.'

'I really, really miss her.'

'Oh, Anna . . .'

We fall silent for a moment.

'Sorry.' Anna sniffs. 'I'm not going to get all maudlin and silly. Hey, we're here at Glastonbury having an awesome time, right?' At this point she breaks off into an appropriately ironic laugh. 'I'm not going to dwell on it. What about you and Seymour?'

'Oh, I just don't know . . . Can we make a pact not to talk, or even think, about either of them? Just for this weekend. Would that be really bad?'

'That's probably a good idea. You've got a deal. But just before we start, I have to say – it's so weird, isn't it? I actually used to think you and Seymour were so perfect for each other. Then again, I thought me and Nishi were too. It's just all so . . . weird.'

We walk in silence for a while until – thankfully – after walking for literally miles, we come to the bright lights of the service station.

It's lovely to be out of the rain, but it's depressing at the same time. We are in a rubbish, generic service station on a main road through the countryside. The lights are artificial and unflatteringly fluorescent, and the air is just a bit sad. Obviously it is not where we were supposed to be tonight. This is most definitely not VIP.

Walking past the newsagent's kiosk, I spot a picture of Jackson on the cover of the *Independent*'s arts section. I don't mention it.

We stroll slowly and dispiritedly through the food

court and decide that we at least need something hot to eat. My phone still isn't ringing, so we make a conscious, tacit decision to eat our all-day breakfasts – very all-day since it's now after midnight – as slowly as we possibly can. Like, literally a baked bean at a time. Somehow I still manage to finish mine in about half the time it takes Anna to pick at hers.

Rather than admit defeat, we keep on chatting inanely, and order two more rounds of coffee after we've finished our late-night meal. I glance at my watch and see that it's gone two in the morning. A wave of sadness engulfs me – as I try to imagine what everyone else in my life is doing right now. I can't believe that nobody in the world knows where Anna and I are. It's scary, as well as depressing. Thank goodness we've got each other.

I take another gulp of coffee to try to perk myself up, and start privately making plans for how we can get home as soon as daylight returns. I'm sure we will feel a bit flat about having to head back to London again so quickly, but we can make the best of it. We could catch the first coach back and have an entire day hanging out in Camden Market or the big Topshop or Portobello or something, and I could still get home in time for a full weekend's revision. Anna could even stay at mine, and we can hole up for the whole weekend watching films and eating our way through the remainder of my mum's grocery shopping. Actually, that doesn't sound too bad at all.

Maybe this whole stupid, doomed affair has all been intended to teach me a lesson, in order to learn that my boring little life is actually pretty great. Isn't it . . . ?

'Oh my god, Anna – look!' I shriek. Out of nowhere, all these pure-hearted and well-intentioned thoughts instantly fall out of my head. 'It's Mad Reggie!'

As she doesn't go to college with the rest of us, there is no reason why Anna should know who Mad Reggie is. I spring up from our plastic table, finding out in the process that I am practically welded to the seat and my legs have gone dead.

'Hey, Reggie!'

He's in the KFC queue, with a small group of friends who all look as dreadlocked and mildly drugged-out as he is. Reggie is a bit of an urban legend at college – I see him strolling around the hallways and in the canteen a lot but never in classes, and nobody is actually sure what he is studying or if he is supposed to be there at all; he's rumoured to have been hanging around the place for years, but I'm sure that can't be true. Anyway, we've had some quite pleasant chats in the common room and always at least nod to each other in passing. In this setting, surely that means we're long-lost best friends.

'Tuesday!' He gives me a cross between a high five and a hug, then addresses his nearest friend. 'Dude, this chick is called Tuesday. That's her *actual* name. No joke.'

I smile modestly, as he looks so delighted with himself it's like he's telling them I'm a celebrity or something. I feel like I should be doing jazz hands, or at least looking a bit nicer than I do.

'This is the craziest coincidence, man! It's actually

blowing my mind. You got to be here for Glasto, yeah?'

'Um, yeah. Actually, it's a long story. My friend Anna and me were supposed to meet, um, someone I know who has our tickets, but she hasn't turned up. So, we're kind of stuck . . .'

One of Reggie's friends looks over to our table, where I vaguely indicated. Anna is sitting staring out of the window, still looking undeniably winsome even after a long day of schlepping and getting rained on. I suspect that I haven't come off quite as well.

Anyway, there is really no point in telling this group that Anna is my best female friend's ex-girlfriend. Although we are both damsels in distress, Anna looks much more damsel-esque than I do.

'Well, then you're in luck – we're here to save the day!' Reggie announces with a crooked grin, touchingly pleased with himself. 'We've got a camper van because we're helping out on a stall for some of our mates who are already in there. You two can bunk down in the back if you like. There's not loads of room, but it'll be all right. If you're stuck?'

'Yes! Yes, please!' I practically launch myself at Mad Reggie. 'Anna!'

It has to be said that Anna doesn't look completely jazzed at the idea of sleeping in a camper van with a bunch of crusties she's never seen before in her life. I can't blame her, but it's the best offer I've had all day and there is no way I'm saying no to it. Further proof that nothing – *nothing* – is turning out even slightly like I imagined.

The Perfect Mix Tape

I know I waste my life being full of nostalgia for a time I can't even remember. Everyone's always telling me it's pointless. They're probably right.

I just want . . . the perfect mix tape. That's all. I want a laptop and an iPod too – I don't see what's wrong with that. We're living in the future, so why wouldn't we shamelessly cherry-pick the best bits of the past and use them for our own ends?

I like old photographs found in junk shops, where you don't know who any of the people are and you can make up stories about them. I like old VHS video tapes, full of pointless things that people recorded off the telly and labelled with funny sticky strips and biro.

Most of all I love mix tapes. You can hardly even find them in charity shops any more. They're a dying species. I hunt them out where I can, obsessively. I buy blank cassettes on Fleabay and make my own on my mum's old plastic ghetto blaster from a million years ago. I even have some old mix tapes that were my mum's – made for her by friends, old boyfriends: favourite songs and stuff taped off the radio herself. They're full of Prince, early Madonna, cheesy 90s soft-rock bands that I can't identify and would never have heard of. They're better than a time capsule. Best of all, someone actually made them. To make a friend smile, to impress a girl, to remember . . .

All I want in life is the perfect mix tape. That's not too much to ask, is it?

Comments
[No comments.]

I wake up in the cramped and crowded van, and everything feels different.

Having spent the night shoehorned into the back of a van that smells of diesel and manages to be cold and sweaty all at once, I am desperate to stretch my legs and go for a pee. Everyone else is still asleep and I can sense it's crazily early, but it's already light outside and I know there's no chance of me going back to sleep or even settling down again. It's not only that I'm wide awake, but my bladder is really not going back to sleep either. I'm going to have to try to find some spot by the side of the road where I can go to the loo while hopefully retaining some small shred of dignity.

I manoeuvre myself out as carefully as possible. Anna and I slept crammed into a tiny space right at the back and over the rear left wheel – which we were lucky to have and extremely grateful for, obviously – and both huddled under my parka, and most of the other clothes from my rucksack, for as much warmth as possible. I shift myself slowly out so that Anna doesn't stir and has the whole coat over her, and slip through the back doors.

As soon as I'm outside, I feel weirdly better about things. It's not sunny and it's still damp, but it's bright and the fresh air is lovely. I feel free. Even if we end up going home today, as I breathe in the cold green morning air, I'm glad I'm here.

But as my eyes slowly wake up and take in my surroundings, I actually laugh out loud. We climbed into the van in the dead of night, and I expected to wake up still in the service-station car park. At some point in the night, or this morning, the van must have moved while I was asleep.

We are in. The van is parked in a vast green field, surrounded by other vans and people setting up stalls. It's already a bustling hive of activity, a shanty-town shopping centre. By hook or by crook, and I'm not sure which, we have got into Glastonbury festival. We are here. I am here.

My first reflex thought is to go and wake Anna up immediately, but then I decide to explore by myself for a bit. This is kind of a unique opportunity.

Stumbling around in my denim shorts and my Converse, which are still wet from yesterday's epic walk in the rain, I pull the sleeves of my cardigan down so that they cover my hands and the fact that I don't actually have a wristband. Although, now that I've made it through the impenetrable fence, everything seems pretty relaxed.

Loads of the stallholders nod and say hello to me as I pass, interesting-looking people busy doing cool things. I walk the length of the market field and find myself turning down a narrower green path. I still don't know what time it is, but I know it must be early because even though there are people around, it is definitely not crowded yet. I've a feeling that will change very soon.

The path opens out, and before me is a huge view of Glastonbury. I feel as though I am standing on top of the world. My breath actually catches in my throat. There are tents as far as the eye can see, higgledy-piggledy but with a strange sort of order to the whole picture, stretching far away into the distance. Bigger and grander than anything else, dominating the skyline, is the famous Pyramid Stage. (It really is a pyramid!) From here I can see a couple of the smaller stages too, although I know from obsessively reading the line-up online that there are more tucked away all over the place. I can see a fairground, with a Ferris wheel and a big top.

I feel a massive thrill of excitement as I look out over it all. I think of all the exploring I can do, the amazing experiences to be had out there. All new, things that could never happen at home. I don't want to go back yet.

After I finish admiring the view, I find a compost toilet that isn't actually too bad; this is *nothing* like the awful chemical toilets I've experienced at festivals before. Even better, next I come upon a tent that is strung with fairy lights and decorated inside like a cross between a cafe and a cosy sitting room – complete with rocking chairs, rugs, and paintings hanging on the canvas walls. I buy myself a cup of tea and settle in a rocking chair that peeks outside the door – a cup of tea always somehow tastes better outside, and it certainly seems fitting this morning.

As well as the expected hipsters, crusties, the odd ageing punk, I'm quite delighted to see families with tiny children running about and even a very old couple in full evening dress.

'Now *that*,' says the dapper elderly gent as he walks past me and clocks my appreciative grin in his direction, 'is how to make an old man's day.'

On my walk back to the stallholders' field, I buy a bag of hot doughnuts, like the kind you get at the seaside, from a stall painted up like a gypsy caravan. A breakfast present for Anna and the rest of the gang, and to say thanks to Reggie and his friends.

By the time I get back, not only are they all up and about, but they are helping to construct Reggie's friends' stall. Anna is standing on tiptoe holding up a corner of tarpaulin as high as she can, while men with dreadlocks whisk about her with ropes and poles. Still in her floaty dress and with the now ruined flowers in her hair, she looks like she is at the centre of some sort of pagan maypole ritual. The scene is straight out of *Tess of the d'Urbervilles*, despite the camper van right behind them.

'Hey!' Anna yells, collapsing in giggles as the tent falls all around her.

The others get a whiff of the hot doughnuts and come running, leaving Anna holding up her pole.

Most of the stall is already set up – Reggie is apparently just helping out his mate Joules, who has been here since Monday and already seems as if he has lived here forever. They are running a stall selling fancy-dress costumes; they've got loads of dressing-up boxes and fairground mirrors, and dozens of outfits from vintage finery to homemade tutus to crazy full-body dinosaur suits.

After breakfast we help with the remainder of the preparations, and the stall is already beginning to get busy.

'Thanks for helping, you two,' Mad Reggie says,

grinning down at us, with a jester's hat flopping over his eyes. 'You should go off and have some fun, see some bands or something.'

'We can't just ditch you! Not after you got us in and put us up for the night,' Anna instantly protests.

'Well, it would be great if you girls could help out, if you don't mind . . .' says Joules, who is dressed as a penguin. 'Stick on some costumes, if you like, and get stuck in.'

And so it is that Anna and I find ourselves working at Glastonbury festival, dressed up as a mermaid (me) and Supergirl (Anna). We are soon rushed off our feet with people who, upon walking past, suddenly decide that a ridiculous costume is a life essential. Despite the fact that we're working hard, the atmosphere on the stall is incredibly relaxed and it feels like one big party – we've got music blasting out and everyone's in a carnival mood.

'Roll up, roll up!' Anna calls out into the passing crowd, adding a top hat to her super-heroine outfit. 'Costumes for all!'

I sell a feather boa to a man with a beard and a pair of massive sparkly sunglasses to a tiny girl, then stop for a quick dance-in-the-sunshine break. We've got Bob Marley blaring out; the sun is boiling by now and I'm pretty sure I must be catching the sun, if not burning. My mermaid costume – my absolute favourite of the whole selection – is basically like an extended sparkly swimsuit, so I'm probably going to get some weird tan lines. I'll have to tell my mum I've been revising in the garden all weekend.

'Hey, Tuesday!' Reggie shouts out suddenly, while I am up to my elbows in fairy wings. 'I've just been having a sneaky kip in the van and your mobile's been ringing off the hook.'

He chucks my parka at me, which I left hanging on the van door with my phone in the pocket. Immediately it starts to ring again. I don't even glance at the screen.

'Hello?'

'Tuesday Cooper? Where the *hell* have you been?'

Crap. It's my mum. Nobody else talks to me in that tone of voice. She's supposed to be in Bruges; how on earth does she know I'm not at home?

'Um—'

'This is Sadie Steinbeck,' the voice continues. 'We've been trying to get a hold of you for hours. Jack's going out of his mind over here.'

I'm an idiot. Of course it is not my mother on the other end of the line. My mother does not have a clipped New York accent, and she actually sounds a bit nicer than this woman, even when she's at her most cross with me.

'Well, I *did* try and call you. Then we couldn't get in, so we walked for miles to the nearest service station and thankfully we bumped into Mad Reggie from college, so—'

'Right. I need you to come and meet us right now. Jack has interviews and appearances all lined up, and this has really thrown a monkey wrench in the works. Seriously. Hurry.'

I look over to Anna, who is talking to a group of girls

213

and animating a full-length Chinese dragon with both hands and a lot of roaring. They are all laughing as the three girls pile in and form the complete dragon, each holding the attached sticks and with red fabric flapping over their heads.

I falter. 'Actually I'm right in the middle of—'

'Look, if you want these passes you have to come and get them *now*. Jeez. Some girls would be more grateful. No wonder Jack's been gabbing about you and how effing "different" you are for days now.'

She says this sourly, like it's a bad thing. But I can't help swelling up with joy slightly. Any disgruntlement at being dragged away, ignored and then summoned at a whim vanishes into thin air.

'OK. Where are you?'

'VIP section, between the Pyramid Stage and the Other Stage. Be there *now*.'

Having imparted all of the important information in a way that is both unpleasant and makes no sense, she hangs up.

'Anna? We've still got those VIP passes, but we've got to get going . . .'

'Funny.' She laughs. 'I'd forgotten all about them.'

So had I. Kind of.

Everyone hugs us goodbye, and Joules lets us keep the costumes. Strolling through the fields and drinking our beers, hearing chilled-out reggae coming from the Other Stage as we skirt the periphery of the crowd, it would be really nice just to hang out, and wander around, and dance in the sun. But the idea of the VIP section is even more exciting – I've never been a VIP before. Actually I'm not sure I've ever been any kind of an IP.

As we get closer to the Pyramid Stage, the crowds thicken and the reggae gradually turns into an anthemic indie singalong. It's one of those blokeish bands I've never really been into, the kind of music that you hear on mobile-phone adverts, but once we are in the thick of it, I have to admit that the whole scene is surprisingly moving. People are holding their arms in the air, singing along unselfconsciously. There are so many of them that the sound is like one big wave; everyone is united by it in this brief instant. I am swept away by the beauty of a communal live experience and the power of a perfect two-minute pop song.

'Where *is* this VIP section?' Anna asks eventually, after we've done a lap of the whole area.

I'm thinking the same thing. Either Sadie Steinbeck got it wrong – which seems unlikely, given her tone of terrifying efficiency – or the VIP section is really hard to find. I don't know what I expected – a red carpet, a pearly gate. Maybe it's more like a secret Narnia-type thing.

'Why don't we try here?' I sort of suggest.

There is a gap in a boarded-up chain-link fence with a few people milling about outside it. There is something about a couple of the men hanging around that reminds me of the paparazzi outside Jackson's hotel last time.

As Anna and I approach, I become aware of a definite force field, a weird energy surrounding the area. Even though it is just a gap in the fencing, and it is essentially unguarded, nobody goes near it. A few surrounding people are looking on in inexplicable fascination, even though there doesn't appear to be anything much going on.

As I stride through the gap, with Anna in tow, all eyes are upon us. It's like there is a collective intake of breath, as if everyone there expects us to be turned away, surprised that we are even daring to chance it. One of the cluster of photographers raises his camera for a split second, then lowers it again without bothering to take a picture.

I see the crowd of people watching me, and I hate myself for how much I enjoy it. The fact that I am so smug to be On The List makes me question all my values and everything I have ever believed about myself, just for a second. They can finally see how special I must secretly be. I hate myself just a tiny bit for letting this make me feel important – but mostly I just really, really enjoy the attention.

Within seconds of us setting foot on the other side of the divide, a security guard appears as if from nowhere. The crowd senses blood.

'I'm Tuesday Cooper and this is Anna Russell – we should be on the list . . .' I say.

I'm aiming for 'quiet authority' and 'I do this sort of thing all the time', but I'm not sure that I quite pull it off.

'Tuesday! Get your ass back here now!'

I recognize Sadie Steinbeck's shrill voice straight away,

and I am entirely unsurprised when a woman who looks like Kate Moss's older, more raddled sister appears. She is clearly aiming for the bucolic English look, with her Barbour and Hunters, but still she somehow comes across as pure Manhattan. This only increases the collective interest, which is probably more confusion by now. Sadie Steinbeck and the security guard have a quick confab; Anna and I are both given wristbands and lanyards and ushered quickly inside.

I can't resist a last look back over my shoulder – at the gathered proletariat – before I disappear into the coveted enclosure. I should probably be insulted by the evident bafflement on each and every one of the faces I see. The thought process is transparent: she certainly can't be a model or a TV presenter, she isn't even good-looking enough to be an old rocker's daughter, so who the hell is she? Anna could maybe pass for a minor pop star in the Lykke Li mould, but I'm not fetching enough even for that.

I don't care. The knowledge that it's me who is here to see Jackson Griffith makes me feel not only defiant but officially vindicated against any opinion that has ever been formed of me. *I win.*

However, as Sadie Steinbeck hauls me through the fence, I notice how quickly they all turn away. Not much to see here.

To my total surprise, there's not much to see on the other side either. Again I wonder what it was that I was expecting – fountains, marble or gold compost loos?

The VIP compound looks like a car park. With a few wooden flowers dotted about in a lame attempt to make it look as if we are actually at a festival. It's depressing. Until I start to notice details like the free bar and the luxurious Winnebago area beyond.

'Here she is,' Sadie Steinbeck announces.

When I see Jackson, everything else becomes irrelevant. He looks even more golden and sun-bleached in the summer outdoors. He is still barefoot, with feet looking decidedly filthy, and wearing only a pair of ratty denim shorts that pretty much match mine. If anything, his are probably a few sizes smaller.

He looks supernaturally magnificent – I hear Anna next to me take in a quick, sharp breath – but for some reason he is lying flat out on the grass.

'Jack! I *said* she's here,' Sadie Steinbeck repeats, more loudly this time. 'Finally.'

He springs up and does a double take, as if he needs a moment to believe it's really me. Then he hugs me for a very long time. It's a full minute before he lets me go.

'I'm so glad you're here,' he breathes into my ear, barely audible.

Just like last time, he smells of bonfires and cake mix; it's a smell that makes me feel all floppy. He holds my face in his hands and presses his forehead down to mine. It's finally going to happen, I think.

'Why are you a mermaid?' he asks me, suddenly and earnestly, breaking away and holding me at arm's length. 'Am I dreaming?'

I had seriously forgotten that both Anna and I are still in fancy dress, and I burst out laughing. I am brought back down to earth – we are in a field and there are loads of people around. This whole situation is just too ridiculous. Lovely, but ridiculous.

I turn to Anna and see the look of total incredulity on her face – and I realize that this is the first time anyone has seen that this exists, this is real. Until this point, it has just been the two of us – alone in a room, or in private emails or just talking on the phone for hours. Suddenly, out in the open, exposed, what we have feels so fragile. Jackson keeps an arm around me, and Anna and I exchange an *I know, right?* glance. This feels beyond strange.

As if I could forget, I am soon reminded that Sadie Steinbeck is here as well.

'Whatever you do,' she whispers in my ear – a harsh whisper, not a soft one, 'do not leave this fenced area, and *do not* let him out of your sight. OK?'

She eyeballs me until I nod like a nodding dog.

'Right, Jack,' she adds much more gently, 'does this mean we can get some work done now? We've got BBC6 Music, MTV2 and that documentary crew waiting for you . . .'

For a second he looks very young and surprisingly frail, but he looks at me and manages a smile, squeezing my hand before letting himself be led away. I find myself wondering when we will ever be alone long enough again that he might kiss me – I might have to be brave and take

219

matters into my own hands soon, before I spontaneously combust on the spot.

'Oh my actual effing . . .' Anna exhales, watching the two of them as we follow them towards the adjoining press enclosure at a small distance. 'I can't believe this.'

'I know . . .'

We stand back a few steps as Jackson is engulfed by the festival's media, watching as Sadie manoeuvres him around.

'Oh my god, Chew!' Anna exclaims again, watching the whole spectacle. 'This is, like, a real thing.'

'Admit it – were you starting to think I had made it all up?'

'Well . . . I wouldn't go *that* far. Maybe just that you had exaggerated – a bit. Got overexcited, maybe. I don't know. Anyway, I was *so* wrong.'

'Seriously. I can hardly believe it myself . . .' I say, in the understatement of the century. 'I know this whole thing has been completely crazy. But, now you can see – here it is.'

Just then Jackson turns and looks at me while he is being interviewed, points in my direction and suddenly grins.

'I understand now,' Anna says, reading my mind. 'I sort of did before. But now I *really* do. I get it. I mean, look at him looking at you. And even I can see that he's – well – he's . . . *Jackson Griffith*!'

'But even if he wasn't, he's . . .'

I want to say 'special' and that 'he really gets me', but

it's just too cheesy, so I stop talking.

'Anyway,' Anna goes on, checking out her lanyard and the magic 'AAA' pass, 'we're here! That bit was real too. This is awesome! So, what shall we do?'

'Well,' I reply, looking towards the Pyramid Stage, out beyond the divide, 'Sadie said I'm not allowed to leave the backstage area. I have to stay here with her and Jackson.'

The sound of any music from here is indistinct, being between the two main stages, and the restricted view – due to the high fences and panelling to keep the prying eyes of the crowds out – means that we can't see much of anything.

'Well, I suppose this is cool too . . .' Anna says.

Careful to keep Jackson in sight, even though he is preoccupied with work and surrounded by people, we do our best to explore the hallowed VIP area. The weird thing is that it doesn't look especially hallowed, once you're actually in it. There's not much to it that we haven't already seen. We find the free bar, which is pretty cool but not exactly amazing as far as I'm concerned – I mean, there's free drink but that's it.

Someone, presumably a model of some sort, suddenly comes barrelling out of a Winnebago on endless bare legs, pouting and covering her face at once, flicking blonde hair in every direction.

'Not now!' she snaps for no good reason and shoves me out of the way as she passes.

'Charming,' Anna comments.

We get ourselves a free beer from the bar – I don't even

like beer, but it just feels like we might as well. We sit on the grass and chat while Jackson gets on with it, but after a while – to be honest – it feels as though we might as well be anywhere. We might as well be at Macari's. I have to keep reminding myself that we are actually at Glastonbury, and looking over at Jackson to tell myself that he is real.

'Hey! What in *the hell* do you think you're doing, man?'

Our little pocket of calm is broken when I hear shouting coming from Jackson's direction. It's a second before I realize that it's him shouting, not until I see him standing up to his full lanky height and shoving the small Italian journalist who has been interviewing him in the chest. It's hard to know who said what to him, and who started it, but now Jackson is the only one making any noise. The kerfuffle grows pretty quickly as the whole press tent starts to watch with an air of glee.

'Seriously, man – that's out of line. I'm not gonna talk to you if you're being like this. No, seriously. Back off. I *said*, "Back off!"'

He pushes his way out, Sadie Steinbeck instantly springing to his side. I'm not sure what to do, and I hang back for a moment before my instincts take over and I have to see if he's OK.

'Just leave me alone,' he snaps, as if he hasn't even realized it's me.

Sadie glares at me as if this is all my fault, and then takes Jackson off into a quiet corner of the enclosure.

'Blimey,' Anna says, wide-eyed.

I feel disproportionately embarrassed and kind of wounded that Jackson brushed me off like that – I thought I was here to save the day. There is an awkward silence.

'Hey,' Anna says, eyes gleaming with a new idea, 'why don't we get out of here?'

'I can't – I said I'd stay here.'

'Well, we're not much use hanging around here, and you have to admit that the VIP experience isn't exactly thrilling. Bat for Lashes and Tied to the Mast are playing on the Other Stage tonight, and I'd really like to see them. Come on – we could go now, while Jackson's busy doing . . . whatever it is he's doing. I bet Sadie won't even notice if we sneak off for a while and she's got your number if she wants you.'

It sounds really tempting. It's my first time at Glastonbury and I haven't been up to the Green Fields, been on the fairground or even seen a whole set by a band yet.

'You should go without me. Honestly, Anna – I know how much you love Bat for Lashes. Go off and have some fun, OK?'

Anna tries to convince me, but in the end she goes off on her own. I'm glad in a way – I don't want to have to feel responsible for keeping her here when it's really not that great. How funny that the VIP area isn't anything like it's cracked up to be.

But even if I could go with her, I'd still want to stay here with Jackson.

The Comeback Kid?

Noted hellraiser and former heart-throb Jackson Griffith is reportedly up to his old tricks again. Amid speculation that he is to make his 'big comeback' live at Glastonbury today, he has allegedly been spied staggering around the site looking more than a little worse for wear and brawling with the press. Having split with his obligatory French model wife Célia Le Masurier, rumours are rife that he now has an anonymous English schoolgirl in tow. Watch this space – a leopard doesn't change its spots, so there is bound to be more controversy from Mr Griffith before the end of the weekend . . .

Comments

Has-been!
Anonymous

Still hot.
Anonymous

I still would.
Anonymous

You don't know where it's been.
Anonymous

OK, I have to admit that the tepee is pretty cool. It's safe to say it might be the coolest tent I have ever been in. It's definitely the fanciest; it's fancier than most hotels I've ever stayed in. Waking up in the tepee – even in its equivalent to an entrance hall (yes, it has actual rooms and is approximately the size of my mum's entire house) – feels positively luxurious.

However, I begin to register that I have woken up due to the sound of Anna's bag zipping up, and that she is standing in front of me fully dressed. She has a purposeful air that I'm not sure I like the look of.

'What's going on?' I whisper, stretching my legs and uncoiling myself stiffly from my curled up sleeping position in a sort of deckchair.

I cast a panicked look at the canvas door of the tepee 'bedroom', where Jackson has been holed up for the last few hours. In fact, I feel as if I have been either silent or whispering for approximately the past few years.

I was really excited to find out that Jackson has a tepee in the special tepee field – this really is coveted and way better than the boring VIP enclosure. These are actual, massive, awesome tepees. They are for the famous and the seriously rich – who still want to feel like they're living the hippie festival dream, but with all the luxuries of a five-star resort.

Last night, Jackson disappeared into the depths of the tepee and Sadie Steinbeck quickly made her escape, instructing me on pain of death not to leave my sentry position for so much as a second. To let him out of the tepee and risk him potentially doing a runner would seriously be more than my life is worth.

Once we were alone in the vast tent, I ventured into the bedroom to try to talk to Jackson and discover what was the matter. I found him fast asleep, and I didn't like to wake him up when he's got his big performance tomorrow and is in obvious need of the rest.

I was feeling too awake and fidgety to try to go to sleep in there with him, so I sat outside the bedroom by myself, trying my best not to disturb him. I've been too scared even to go to the loo. I went for a wee round the side of the tepee so that I could still see the entrance, although I will not be telling Sadie Steinbeck that.

There hasn't been the slightest movement from in there since. So I've spent half the night sitting in the same deckchair, waiting quietly for Anna to come back. Eventually I must have fallen asleep in the chair.

Anna and I make universal pointing gestures at each other for a few seconds before we come to a silent agreement to hold this conversation outside. As we step out of the tepee, I am surprised to see that the field is vastly muddier than it was a few hours ago. It's pretty grim. I wish I had some wellies; my Converse are already on their last legs and I'm in danger of developing trench foot.

'It rained,' I say stupidly.

'Yeah, it was pretty gnarly out there last night. I stayed out to see Queens of the Stone Age, but it was pelting it down; everyone was soaking. Hang on, have you just been inside the whole time? You were already asleep when I got in, but I thought you must have gone out and done *something*. Were you just in this fancy tent all evening?'

'Yeah. Well, pretty much. It's a tepee actually.'

'How's Jackson Griffith doing?'

I'm kind of embarrassed to admit that I don't know, so I just shrug in what I hope seems like a casual, knowing fashion.

'Well . . . Look, Chew, I'm going to go home. I don't want to leave you here alone, so I really think you should come with me.'

'What? Go home now? Why?'

'Because I'm not having that much fun,' she explains, in a matter-of-fact tone. 'I can now say I've tried Glastonbury and it's not for me. I don't think I'm the festival type. I've been to see some bands, and that was OK but I got rained on and couldn't see that much – I'd rather have watched it on TV with a nice cup of tea frankly. The VIP area is like some kind of grim prison with free alcohol – and I barely even drink! I just want to go home and have a hot bath and a good sleep in my own bed. This is supposed to be fun, not an endurance test; I honestly think that half the people here have forgotten that and they just want to be able to say they were here.'

I want to argue with her, but I know it's pointless. In fact, I really admire her for knowing her own mind and having the conviction to act on it. Seriously, for people of our age and general type, admitting to not loving festivals is like saying you don't like kittens or vintage dresses or something – it just isn't the done thing.

But maybe Anna is more mature than I am, because I'm not ready to give up yet. I'm not even willing to admit that I'm not having a brilliant time, even though I'm really not.

'So soon?' I protest feebly.

'Well, it took us about twenty times as long to get here as we thought it would – if I leave now, I reckon I might get lucky and make it home in time for *Antiques Roadshow* tomorrow night. That's more my speed anyway . . . But seriously, Chew – it took us so long to get here, and everyone I spoke to last night said it's crazy trying to get out of here on a Sunday. I am a bit worried about getting back in time, to tell you the truth – so I thought I'd rather just hit the road than be worrying about it. I just want to get out of here. And *I* don't even have an exam on Monday.'

'Thanks for thinking about me. Honestly. But I'm going to stay. I'll be fine.'

Anna's forehead screws up in concern, but it's pretty obvious to both of us that our minds are definitely made up.

'I really wish you would come with me,' she says. 'But I do understand. I'd probably stay for Jackson Griffith too – and I like girls. Just be careful, OK? I want you to solemnly swear that you will take care of yourself. And just remember you're awesome, OK? You truly are. I really think you need to keep that in mind right now.'

She passes over my bus and train tickets and refuses

my offer to at least walk her to the front gates. We hug for a long, long time and I actually have to look away as I watch her disappear among the tepees, for fear I might start crying.

I can't just keep sitting in silence in that bloody deckchair. There are absolutely no signs of life from inside, so I decide it's safe to bend Sadie Steinbeck's strict rules just for a bit, and stretch my legs in the muddy field. I'm certainly not going to the loo behind the tepee again.

Besides, the tepee field is the good bit of the VIP experience, and I want to enjoy it. I find a little stall with free coffee and pastries, which is my biggest coup yet – a billion times more exciting to me than a free bar. Even the few people I pass in this field seem more friendly and chilled out than in the VIP bullring.

I am almost beside myself with delight when I discover that not only are there luxury lavatories, but also hot fire-powered showers and even a sauna. This is seriously amazing – this is exactly what I thought the backstage experience should be.

I return to the tepee after longer than I meant to, but feeling like a new woman. I even stock up on some extra pastries on the way. My heart sinks when I see a load of commotion outside the tepee. I bowl up in time to receive a withering glare from Sadie Steinbeck, who is surrounded by a whole crowd of people I mostly don't recognize, and I find myself being bundled into the back of a tiny van.

Jackson is pale grey under his usual golden suntan,

shaking like he's in need of an exorcist. Nobody in the van speaks, so I try my best to keep my mouth shut. He grabs my hand and clutches it tightly, but doesn't say a word.

We are deposited around the back of what I guess must be the Acoustic Field – the stage is a bit smaller than the main stages, but it's much prettier around here. I hang about like a bit of a spare part while equipment is sorted out and commands barked and the countdown to Jackson's set begins in earnest.

Before he's due to start, the stage is populated by a few fey little bands with dreamy retro vocals and a disproportionate number of fiddle players, fedoras, accordians and hippie dresses.

Jackson's going to blow them all away – he's got to. I think of the video he sent me of him playing his new song – *my* song, as I like to think of it – and I practically get goosebumps just at the memory.

Then again, the pressure is truly on. He's so nervous he's practically climbing the walls.

'Good luck,' is all I can think of to say. 'You'll be brilliant.'

He looks so scared; I just want to make everything OK for him. I wish there was something more I could do.

'But last time I played here, I was terrible,' he whispers. 'What if . . . ?'

I grab him and hug him before he has finished his sentence – it's all I can think of to do. And then it's time. He is bundled away from me and into the wings of the stage before either of us can say another word.

I feel so sick with nerves that I can't even imagine how he must feel. I can only watch as he is ushered towards the stage and I hear him being announced. He seems so far away suddenly, on his own.

But then something truly miraculous happens. His body language changes even as he walks out on to the stage – he becomes taller and wider in the shoulder before our eyes, losing the hunched and fierce look. A grin slowly spreads across his face as he takes in the sea of faces and the roar of applause that hits him. He silently salutes the crowd before he hoists his guitar. We all hold our breath.

The second he starts singing, I realize that none of us need ever have worried. Even the beauty of his voice on record has not prepared me for this. All the usual clichés about honey and molten gold and melted chocolate spring to mind, but they don t even begin to do it justice. It's not only that his voice is technically great, even though it is; it's more that there is something incredibly charming about its tone. He sounds friendly, even – or maybe especially – when he's singing a sad song. There's a bruised, vulnerable quality to it that makes tears spring to my eyes.

He sounds perfect. This is what everybody here dreamed of hearing. This is a triumph. I'm so happy I am here to see it. Whatever happens now, the risk has been worth it.

He meanders through a few of his best-known songs

before he addresses the audience or even pauses for breath.

'My name's Jackson Griffith. It's good to be back, but I'm a little rusty,' he says. 'Thanks for coming out to see me today. And for humouring me.'

Then he steams through another batch of classics, with only his acoustic guitar to accompany him, and the entire audience is spellbound. When he starts a quiet, sad song – 'I Told You I Can't Talk About It' – it's as if the whole of Glastonbury is quiet with him.

'Sorry,' he says sheepishly when the rapt crowd have barely recovered. 'That was a bit of a downer. Now, I know it's even more of a downer when you come out to see some has-been like me and you hear the words nobody wants to hear: "This is a new song." But you seem a nice bunch and I only want to do one . . . so stick with me, OK? This is a little song I wrote about a swell girl named Tuesday.'

There in the wings, very quietly, I swear I nearly die. Here, today, it's the most beautiful thing I have ever heard in my life.

So it is only when he has finished that it occurs to me that there are thousands of people here, including the world's press. Highlights are going out on TV and radio, for goodness sake. I've been identified to the world. I can't help but wonder for the billionth time why my mum couldn't have just made me a Katie or a Rebecca.

'Thank you. Thank you so much. I think I could do just one more, but I'd better quit while I'm ahead. Besides,

I wanna hang out with my girl Tuesday. Thank you all – I mean it. Have a good one. But not too good. Take it from me. See ya.'

I have only a second to panic, because then Jackson bounds off the stage and comes straight for me, a look of total triumph and delight on his perfect face. It's all for me – it's like there's nobody else there. We can't stop grinning at each other like a couple of total idiots. Then he's not grinning any more; he's looking at me seriously and holding my face in his hands and bending down towards me. I can hardly believe that it's finally going to happen. And then it does.

Without any hesitation, he kisses me in front of everyone there. Our first kiss, and it's so public – but I hardly even notice. It's too lovely. Even here, and with his guitar still slung around his neck and squashed up in between us, it's the best kiss of my life. It feels like the only kiss that has ever mattered.

We are both a bit wobbly when we pull away, processing what has just happened and remembering where we are. We burst out laughing and kiss each other again. It's so exciting but such a relief, all at the same time. I've been waiting so long for this moment; it's like now we've started, we can't stop. We kiss until my head is spinning.

'I'm sorry I've been such an asshole ever since you got here,' he says eventually. 'I've been uptight and so nervous about this gig. Everything's OK now. I'm so happy you came.'

I kind of have to cling on to him so I don't fall over.

Amid all the people here, I have only one thought: to get out of here and on our own.

'I'm starving,' I say. 'Do you still have work to do or can we go and get some food, maybe from *outside* the VIP prison?'

We both automatically look over to Sadie Steinbeck, as if for permission. Unexpectedly, she is smiling.

'Well done, champ. You're done, so I'm out of here – thank god. You can do whatever the hell you like. You're officially the comeback kid. My work here is done. Good luck with him, Tuesday.'

And, just like that, we are free. We scamper off like a couple of schoolkids. It takes us a while to make it out past the stage, as people keep recognizing and greeting Jackson, but everyone is sweet and he doesn't seem to mind in the least.

'You must be Tuesday!' a couple of people even say to me. 'What an unusual name!'

We find a quiet corner of the Green Fields; I give him my (huge, ridiculous, sparkly) sunglasses to hide behind, while I buy us burgers and proper chip-van chips. The mud is drying out and it's turned into a beautiful afternoon.

We sit at the back and watch Cat Power as the sun goes down, and I swear this is the best moment of my life. All is right with the world. We listen to her sing my favourite song and Jackson has his arm around me, and he kisses me in front of the whole of Glastonbury and it feels nothing but completely right.

We spend the entire evening strolling around the site

and exploring everything that takes our fancy. There are interactive sculptures and there is crazy performance art and weird sideshows to be discovered all over the place. We talk non-stop, and laugh at everything, and the whole night passes in a lovely, happy blur. Jackson's previous mood is now a distant memory – he's having fun, and he's everything I dreamed about since before I even met him. I never thought it would be possible to have such a relaxed good time with him.

We go to visit Mad Reggie and his friends at the fancy-dress stall. It occurs to me marginally too late that this might not be a great idea – but I'm having too much fun to particularly care. Back home might as well be another universe by now.

'Hey, Chew! How's it going?'

When he hears that Mad Reggie looked after me on our first night here, Jackson is soon thanking him profusely for taking care of 'his girl'. He starts trying to give Reggie all of his cash, the rest of his chips and even the T-shirt he is wearing. We settle on buying an 80s David Bowie wig for Jackson as 'disguise', and Reggie waves us off dazedly.

'Ground control to Major Tom!' Jackson keeps saying in a terrible cod-English accent – the worst David Bowie impression I have ever heard.

'You sound like Dick van Dyke in Mary Poppins!' I tell him.

'Oi! Chim chim cheroo. Didn't they say in that movie that it's good luck to kiss a chimney sweep . . . ?'

Running over to the fairground, I even manage to

force Jackson into going on the Cage, something he has apparently never seen before.

'Hey, if I puke, will the centrifugal force make it stick to the sides?' he yells while we're spinning at roughly a thousand miles an hour.

When we stagger back on to solid ground, he promptly falls over on the grass. Then he pulls me down with him and we're laughing too hard to get up. It's dark now and the fairground lights are twinkling all around us. The world has never been more beautiful and it feels like it's all ours.

'My inner ear ain't what it used to be, babe. Come on – let's go find out where we can go dancing around here. I don't ever want to go to bed!' Jackson declares.

This whole place is like some kind of amazing labyrinth. We stumble into a field lit by old-fashioned lanterns with all sorts of crazy vaudeville entertainers. We find ourselves in an old converted train carriage; inside it is decked out like it's the 1920s – it looks like something out of *Murder on the Orient Express*. There are even moving images projected on to the carriage windows so that it looks like scenery going past, as if we really are on a train. It feels like a proper secret – other than the people who work here, who are more like performance artists than 'staff' – we are the only ones here.

'Good evening,' says a man in a conductor's hat, who has an extravagant moustache and a totally straight face.

Jackson not only plays along but sits down on one of the train seats like this is totally normal. He has this easy-going quality that makes everyone warm to him. Soon, he and the train conductor are chatting like they're old friends.

'Hey, this reminds me of a place I went to once back in the old motherland,' Jackson says conversationally. 'Hemingway was there. That was one crazy night.'

'Oh yeah,' I join in, as he winks at me. 'Was that the night when Zelda Fitzgerald and I went skinny-dipping?'

'Attagirl. The very same. And Dorothy Parker wrote a story about it – I was so mad at her when she laughed at me for falling in my soup.'

'Oh, those were the days,' I sigh, almost convincing myself that it's true, his play-acting is so contagious. 'Dorothy Parker was my favourite.'

'Hey, she'd have loved your blog, I bet. Good old Dotty.'

By the time we get out of there, we both pretty much believe that we were society figures in 1920s Paris. We are still in full-flight fantasy mode when we head into what looks like a church building next door.

As we push through the doors, we are hit by a palpable wave of loud music and crowds of people. It's like we have crashed a party that's in full swing. A preposterously tall man who is dressed as a cross between Elvis and a vicar greets us as we step inside. It's then that I notice the giant neon sign proclaiming this 'The Little Glastonbury Chapel of Love'.

'Do I have my next willing volunteers here?' he asks in a booming voice as everyone else cheers.

'Sure, why not?' Jackson replies like it's an automatic reflex, although I'm not convinced he knows what's going on – he looks even more confused than I do.

I'm similarly discombobulated when I find myself wearing an enormous wedding veil that trails on the grubby floor behind me and someone shoves an ugly bunch of purple plastic flowers into my hands. A top hat goes on over Jackson's now crooked comedy Bowie wig.

Suddenly we are walking down the aisle to a crazed rock 'n' roll version of 'Here Comes the Bride', we're both saying 'I do' and Jackson is lifting me up and kissing me in a most un-wedding-like fashion. It's only when I come up for air that I realize quite how many people are staring at us. I'm not sure who starts it, but within seconds the place is chaos.

'Hey, isn't that Jackson Griffith?' someone shouts.

'No, it can't be.'

'It is!'

As the ensuing pandemonium really kicks off, Jackson seems to sober up in an instant. He has a presence of mind I never would have predicted. He grabs my hand and gets me out of there as quickly as humanly possible, given that there are dozens of people in our way, all trying to get near him.

We make it unscathed and flee into the Green Fields. Slowing down and falling silent, we walk hand in hand for ages. At first I think that the stars are especially bright tonight, until I realize that people are sending paper lanterns up into the air. They are hovering all around us like a swarm of fireflies.

By the time we make it back to the tepee, it's getting light outside. We fall into the ground-level bed inside, which is surprisingly comfy and piled up with cushions and throws. It's blissful.

As we lie down, still with all our clothes on, it's like the full events of the day only just begin to sink in. We both take a deep breath and close our eyes for a moment, before turning to each other and laughing.

'I really shouldn't go to sleep,' I say, knowing that I'm going to any second. 'I've got to leave really early to get home tomorrow. Today, I mean.'

'It's OK. Don't go. I'll make sure you get home in time. I've got to head back to London anyway; we can go together. This doesn't have to end.'

The idea of this makes us both feel much better.

'We should probably have sex now,' he mumbles. 'I really want to. But I'm way too sleepy. N'night, Ruby Tuesday.'

He cuddles into me, like a little kid or a kitten, before he falls straight to sleep and starts snoring his head off.

An Ending

I suppose it's the lingering scent of exams hanging in the air, but I can't shake off this sense of an ending. It feels exactly like an 80s pop song. The 80s are unfairly maligned, in my humble opinion – that was a decade that did bittersweet really, really well.

Echo & the Bunnymen. Talk Talk. 'Bette Davis Eyes'. Early REM. Late Fleetwood Mac.

But there is no denying (to me, at least) that the king of the bittersweet pop song is 'The Boys of Summer' by Don Henley. Endings and new beginnings, all at once. Love that may or may not last into the autumn. TV-inspired fake memories of driving around in convertible cars that I've never seen in real life.

I'm listening to it on a loop as I attempt to revise in the garden for my final exam. I can't get it out of my head and the feeling is hanging over me as I walk around the quiet house.

This time I'm nostalgic for a summer that's hardly even got started yet.

Comments
'Revising in the garden'. Yeah, right . . . I think that ship has sailed, if anyone else has seen the papers this morning.
Nishi_S

I'm surprised you've even got time to listen to music (or write your own blog) any more, now that you've got the notoriously flaky, divorced mentalist Jackson Griffith to personally serenade you. Yes, in case you were wondering – I found out my girlfriend was cheating on me when I saw a photo of her in the Sunday papers 'getting married' to a fading pop star. My mum woke me up to show me the article in the Telegraph, *which was particularly nice. Stay classy, Tuesday Cooper.*
seymour_brown

Are you the same 'Tuesday' from the song? Think you must be. It's an unusual name. Lucky girl!!
MusicLover97

No, she can't be! I've looked at all the pictures on her Facebook page and this girl is NO WAY good enough for Jackson. She's fat and she doesn't even have a pretty face! If it is her then Jackson just feels sorry for her or he really is taking drugs or something, ha ha. She thinks she is so clever, but she seems really fake. He had a model for a wife and he could get anyone, so why would he want some unknown girl who is fat and not even that pretty? Tuesday is a well stupid name. She is probably just using him to get people to look at her blog. By the way, this blog is crap!!
jacksongriffithfan4eva

Wow, what an articulate reply. You really come across as an intelligent person. Nobody asked you to look at this blog. In fact, to have found it at all you must be some kind of a stalker. You know nothing about my friend Tuesday or this situation. Tuesday did not invite any of this and you are not qualified to comment. I will not sink to your level by getting into a ridiculous argument, but please be warned that I will not tolerate any lies or abuse of my best friend. This is her website and you chose to look at it – have some respect.
Nishi_S

I've been reading all the old comments on this crap website and you are not exactly her real mate – you are constantly hating on her! If she is so great then let 'Tuesday' (if that is even her real name) stand up for herself. Jackson knows who his real fans are.
jacksongriffithfan4eva

Seriously, mind your own business. Whatever our differences, Tuesday is my best friend. A true friend is someone who is like a sister to you – who you would stand up for no matter what, even if you have disagreements among yourselves. This is the last comment I will make, as I have no need to defend myself to you. But I would like anyone who is reading this to know that Tuesday Cooper is kind and clever. She is a girl who has found herself in an extraordinary and public situation, and she has enough to deal with behind closed doors without

strangers interfering and casting untrue judgements. She has not encouraged this attention in any way and she doesn't deserve public condemnation. Trust me, she's going to have enough to deal with at home.
Nishi_S

She's also a cheat and a liar who dumps her boyfriend at the slightest sniff of a rich pop star giving her a free ticket to Glastonbury. Never mind that she's letting her friends and family down and messing up her precious A levels. Jackson Griffith is well known for being totally flaky, a disgusting womanizer and, most importantly, an untalented idiot. They deserve each other.
seymour_brown

Nice, Seymour. Just get judgemental in public, why don't you? Talk about 'classy'.
anna_banana

Anna, I agree with you (although I can totally understand why Seymour would be so upset) – but I don't see what this has to do with you. I don't really know why Chew isn't on here speaking up for herself.
Nishi_S

Thanks for that, Nish. Helpful. I thought you said you weren't going to make any more comments on here? Well, I'm certainly not going to get in a public slanging match so I'll say now that I'm not going to make any

more comments (and I'm going to stick with that). Over and out.
anna_banana

She's not on here 'speaking up for herself', Nishi, because she's too busy shagging Jackson Griffith. This was obviously an automatic timed post, scheduled to show up on her blog now so that we wouldn't know she had sneaked off to Glastonbury with him. Clever – go to that much effort and then blow it by getting your picture in all the papers. I suppose she couldn't resist the attention. The websites I've been looking at have even identified her and tracked her down – that's why this post has got so many views.
seymour_brown

die bitch die!!! leave jackson alone.
Anonymous

This has got on Twitter so you had better watch out. The true jackson fans will get you, bitch!
Anonymous

The Jackson fandom is an ARMY, so you need to watch your back. Sleep with one eye open from now on, slut!
Anonymous

Seriously – pipe down now or I'm calling the police.
Nishi_S

I wake up in the tepee and, as the events of last night come back to me, the first thing I realize is that I am alone. Jackson is not here.

If he's gone, I think irrationally, then I wish we'd had sex last night. Maybe he's gone for good and I will never see him again. If we'd had sex, then at least I could have something concrete to remember him by – everyone has to carry the story of their lost virginity around with them for the rest of their lives. Mine would have been a really good one if we had done it; I would have proof that I didn't make him up.

I am still fully dressed, down to my now completely ruined Converse, and I feel unpleasantly clammy. With a jolt of utter panic I realize that the intense heat can only mean one thing. I've overslept. This is potentially disastrous. I have no idea what crazy hour of the morning it was by the time we got to bed, or what time it is now.

I try to check my phone but it's out of battery – I meant to charge it in the VIP phone-charging area, but I seem to have forgotten to do anything at all useful about this. It's totally dead. I am not winning this morning.

There's still no sign of Jackson, so I stagger outside still half asleep and head through to the VIP bar to check if he's there. I so want to be cool and nonchalant, but I have got to get myself home. And *soon*.

I find Jackson sitting in a deckchair next to the free bar, with a drink in his hand.

'Tuesday!' he exclaims. 'Hey, this is my girl Tuesday, the one I was telling you about.'

He's with a couple of guys who I dimly recognize. Through my sleep-bleared eyes, there's a slight time delay before I twig. They are the singer and bass player from Bucket Tree – a band who are pretty famous and who I actually really like. Even they are looking at Jackson like he is the coolest man in the world, which he kind of is.

'Like I said, Tuesday's a terrific writer. She's probably going to be a famous novelist or something one day.' He grins up at me.

'Wow, that's great,' says Simon, the bass player. 'I really admire anyone who's a real writer. Hats off. That's a proper talent – beats anything in this corrupt music industry.'

I really, really wish I'd bothered to have a shower, brush my hair or, best of all, clean my teeth before I came out to find Jackson. Of course, being in such a sorry state, *this* would be when I get to meet actual celebrities.

Well, at least Jackson doesn't appear to have washed all weekend; he's wearing those crazed denim shorts again and he definitely hasn't brushed his teeth. I wonder how long he's been out here already today, while I was conked out in the tepee for hours. It doesn't seem to be worrying him or anyone else in the least. Styling it out is the only option. I'm a writer, I tell myself – they're practically *supposed* to be scruffy.

'Get yourself a drink, babe. I'd recommend a Bloody Mary, after the night that we had. That'll fix you up; it worked on me.'

'Good idea,' I agree in a small voice.

I go and get myself a tomato juice and sit down next to Jackson.

'Jackson,' I whisper to him, trying not to draw attention to myself, 'do you know what time it is?'

'No idea, sweetheart,' he mutters with literally zero concern. 'Hey, Si – I wanted to talk to you about that Thunderbird bass I saw you with yesterday, man . . .'

I feel mildly ashamed of myself for every minute that I just sit there quietly, not saying anything – but I can't bring myself to break the spell by speaking up.

Eventually, when I've been sitting still for so long that my bum has gone completely numb and I have to either get myself another drink or do *something*, I stand up and ask if I can get anyone anything from the bar. They all smile at me like I'm really awesome.

'You might just be the holy grail of girls,' Jackson comments.

I smile vaguely, thinking that this is quite reductive and probably bordering on offensive – I think Jackson's just kind of wasted and feeling lazy; at least I hope he doesn't really want a girlfriend who stays quiet and brings him drinks. For the very first time, I wonder properly about his French model ex-wife. All I've ever thought before is that she quite possibly needs to have her head examined – how could you possibly let go of such a sweet, handsome, clever man, whatever the circumstances? But then again now, also for the first time, Jackson is resembling the mythical creature that I've read about in the tabloids.

'That's a lot of pressure,' is all I say out loud.

'OK, we'll downgrade you if it makes you feel better,' he suggests. 'We'll call you the Turin shroud of girls. No pressure.'

I don't quite know what to make of that, so I go to the bar with my list of everyone's drinks .

'Excuse me,' I ask the man behind the bar. 'You don't know what time it is, do you?'

'Yep, it's coming up for half past one.'

This is much, much worse than I feared. I'm a dick. A total, total dick. I have always known that, but I have never before been so acutely aware of it as in this exact second.

Conversely, a cheer goes up as I come back with the swaying tray of drinks. As I dole them out, I try to talk quietly to Jackson out of the corner of my mouth.

'Jackson, do you remember last night you said we could go back to London together this morning?'

'Not really.' He shrugs.

'Well, I've really got to get back. I've missed my bus and I absolutely have to be home by seven this evening.'

'Seven? That's hours and hours away.'

'Well, it's a long way and it took us ages on the way here . . .'

'Seriously, man – calm down. It'll work itself out. These things always do. Trust me.'

I wish I could. I take a deep breath. If Jackson really cares about me, and I think he does, then I don't have to do everything he says. I know I can't get carried away by this, but it suddenly seems like a very big leap of faith.

The perfection of last night seems like a very long time ago – this morning everything is different. I'm silently willing him to go back to his amiable, easy-going – and sober – self that he was last night, but it's not working.

'Look, Jackson,' I say, loudly and decisively, 'I have to go. I've got to be back in time. I'm going to leave now and see if I can get a bus.'

Simon and Robin from Bucket Tree make polite, token groaning noises.

'Tuesday, you can't go,' Jackson states. 'You can't. Not after . . . everything.'

He's so shocked and panicky, it's as if he didn't hear a word of what I said before.

'Jackson, seriously. I have to.' I don't want to get into the whole saga in front of half of Bucket Tree – I'm aware that I sound like a tragic child. 'You know my mum gets back this evening, and I have a really important exam tomorrow. I absolutely have to go home.'

'We can go together – later or tomorrow, or whatever. You said you'd stay here with me. You *said*.'

His eyes are opaque. He practically stamps his foot. I'm suddenly very conscious of having an audience. Jackson doesn't seem to care.

'Do you want to come with me back to the tepee?' I suggest. 'Maybe we can have a chat there.'

'If this is how it's gonna be, then you can forget it – *sweetheart*. Man, this is why I said I'd never get married again . . . I end up in some fake Elvis wedding, and next thing I know you're acting like my damn wife. You can forget that. I'm staying right here. Someone bring me another drink.'

'Well, I'm off then.' I might be dying inside, but I feel more than ever that it is morally vital to stand my ground. 'See ya.'

I force myself to walk away. Otherwise I know I never will.

At first I'm absolutely, one-hundred-per-cent convinced that he is going to come after me. With every step it becomes harder not to turn round and check out what's going on.

By the time I make it back to the tepee field, it is very obvious that he is not coming after me at all. I gather up my things and force myself to get on with it and *not* cry. I try my best to channel the spirit of Nishi and make myself get angry instead.

It doesn't really work but I do manage not to crumple in a heap. Rucksack on, I traipse across the site, out of the VIP zone and to the market field.

I find the fancy-dress stall sadly depleted. There are hardly any costumes left, and the ones that are seem to be completely ruined by mud, rain and things that I probably don't even want to know about. The structure has been dismantled back down to its metal bones. Only Joules is left, flogging the remains. His penguin suit has seen better days – crucially, it is missing the entire left arm/flipper.

'You're looking for Mad Reggie?' he says. 'Sorry, love – he and the boys headed off early this morning in the van.

Reggie's still at sixth-form college, you see, believe it or not. He said something about having to head back early because he has some big exam tomorrow.'

As if I could feel any worse. It's official: Mad Reggie cares about college more than I do. He is safely on his way home while I have completely screwed up my entire life as I know it. Probably he'll get my A grade in English, while I will be condemned to doing retakes and hanging around college forever. I might even grow dreadlocks and develop a low-level weed habit. 'Mad Chewie' – that's what they'll call me.

All because I backed the wrong horse. What made me think that I knew so much better than everybody else? I suddenly feel incredibly stupid.

I'm in a daze as I head out against the crowds, towards the exit. Being here has been such a bonkers experience. I wish I could commit all these amazing sights to memory one last time – but I'm too upset to be able to take any of it in. I keep hoping he'll find me. All the way back through the gates and to the car park where it all started.

On flashing my ticket and hoping for the best, I am informed that my bus has already left.

'The next bus to London isn't for, ooh, over two hours now – and you'd have to buy a new ticket,' the bus man adds.

It's then I realize that I don't have any money for a new ticket. I don't even have to force it; I start sobbing, right there at the bus stop.

'I'm sorry,' I snivel. 'I'm not doing this on purpose. It's

just that my friends have left me and my boyfriend and I had a fight, and I really have to get home. I'm going to be in so much trouble.'

There is a pause and the man literally rolls his eyes at me. I guess working at a festival he must see this kind of thing a lot. But I doubt many people can have been as desperate as I am right now.

'Well,' he sighs eventually, 'you *do* have a ticket, so I suppose I could swap it. Of course you'll still have to wait for the next bus though.'

Even if everything goes according to plan once this next bus turns up, I'll be cutting it fine. I might just make it. I'm going to have to sit here helplessly worrying about it for the next two hours, but I am not going to go back into the festival. There's no point.

I sit down on a patch of grass at the edge of the car park and remember that I've still got most of a bag of mini Snickers bars at the bottom of my rucksack. They are warm and squashed, but I eat the lot, at least eight of them in a row. They make me feel heavily sick. I'm glad I won't starve to death here, but I'd rather have a working phone.

Without it, or a watch, I keep having to ask the man what time it is and when the bus is coming. By the time the bus eventually turns up – seven minutes late, which has me completely wigging out – we kind of hate each other and I get the impression he wishes he had screwed me over on the technically timed-out ticket.

I've never seen someone so glad to see the back of

me, except maybe Jackson – who knows? Thankfully there aren't many losers like me who are leaving before the Sunday headliners, so the bus isn't crowded. I have a double seat to myself – and I'm relieved not to have to talk to anyone. I just want to get home as quickly as humanly possible.

Once we start moving, it's so interminably slow that I start to worry I'm literally going to drive myself mental. I can't even sit still – as if my own kinetic energy and force of will can somehow power the bus more quickly along the motorway. It's hours before we'll arrive in London and I have absolutely nothing to distract me in the meantime. I wish more than anything, for the zillionth time, that my phone was working. I am such an idiot.

I try my best to spread out across the seats, my rucksack under my head. It's uncomfortable but it's better than nothing. I close my eyes just to avoid having to keep staring at the same slow-moving scenery. Even though I'm bone tired, I'm sure I won't be able to go to sleep. I'll just close my eyes for a minute . . .

At first I think maybe we're there. I wake up with a start and realize that we have come to a standstill. My heart begins to sink. The driver is standing up to say something to us, which can't be a great sign.

'We're having a few, ah, technical problems,' he announces awkwardly. 'It appears the engine has overheated. I've called for assistance, so I'm afraid we're just going to have to wait.'

His words slice into me like tiny knives and I have to

hold in an audible sob. I am shaking all over.

It's official. It's over. Any chance of making it back before my mum is now officially out the window. Even though there is still some time to go, I am stuck and all I can do is sit here helplessly and wait for this ticking time bomb that is my life to explode all over me. I have a feeling the mess is going to be beyond horrible.

Of course, worst of all is the certain knowledge that this disaster is solely and entirely of my own making and I deserve every scrap of what is coming to me.

By the time the bus gets moving again – which takes, quite literally, hours – I've given up all hope. I'm past caring. There's nothing I can do now. I can't even cry any more. I just feel tired and heavy and so, so sad.

There's no point even trying to find out what time it is. It's late. It's too late. It's been dark a long time by the time we get to London.

At Victoria station, I instantly register that it's a lot quieter – worryingly quieter – than when I was last here. The departure boards are almost blank. Of course – it's Sunday night, and it's even later than I thought. I head to the Tube entrance to find it gated up, and this time I really do want to cry. I thought my despair levels had reached maximum capacity but it turns out that's not quite true. To stop myself from bursting into self-pitying public tears, I kick the metal gate instead. Which obviously doesn't help.

Even if I could get to Paddington tonight, the last train has already gone without me. My mum will be home and wondering where I am, probably freaking out to an unprecedented degree. I would be, if I was her.

There is not only my mum to think about now – obviously I'm going to be in trouble, but it's not only that by this point. My whole future is at stake. All day, I've been worrying about getting home before my mum, but the most important thing is that I have my final English paper tomorrow, first thing in the morning. Now it's starting to look like even that is in danger.

I'd call my mum and confess all, if only I could. That's how frightened I am. She could come and pick me up and I would at least get home tonight – I could deal with everything else later. But I don't have a working phone and I have no money; I'm like one of those pathetic modern kids that people talk about, who live their whole lives through the Internet and have no idea how to survive in the real world.

There's nothing I can do. I'm going to have to hang out in Victoria station until the morning. It's chilly at this time of night, but at least it's undercover. I wrap myself in my parka and sit on a cold metal chair, preparing for the longest night of my life.

'Excuse me, miss?' a man in a uniform says eventually. 'You can't stay here. You need to go.'

'Sorry – what?'

'The station is locked at one o'clock – it will be opened again in the morning.'

'But . . .' I have never felt so desperate in my whole life, but at least this is the opportunity for some sort of human contact. 'Do you possibly just have a phone I can use, please? This is seriously an emergency.'

He shakes his head and ushers me outside. There are a few people sitting or sleeping against the walls of the station, but I don't feel safe here by myself. Let alone as if I can ask any of them if they have a phone I could quickly use. Besides, I can't sit still all night – I will go out of my mind.

I have no idea where I am going, but it's better to keep moving. I vaguely consult a map outside the station (there's a reason I dropped geography straight after GCSEs) and stride off in the general direction of Paddington. I think.

But even the getting-lost bits don't matter, because it's hours until the next train anyway. On the plus side, when I make it there, I discover that Paddington stays open at night, unlike stupid Victoria. Even though nothing useful is open, at least it's quite warm. The wait for my first train of the morning would probably not be that unpleasant if it didn't feel like awaiting my execution. If this were not the worst night of my entire life.

For a second I wonder if Jackson really has come back to London like he said he was going to. Maybe right now he's comfortably asleep in his hotel. In that hotel room of which I remember every single detail. I know there's no point thinking about it. I carry on not thinking about it all night, my eyes glued open until dawn breaks.

It's only when I eventually go to board my train that I realize my ticket – bought for travelling yesterday – has expired, and I don't have the money to buy a new one. Thankfully the barriers are still open at this time of the morning, and I sneak on to the train and hope that no one will notice me.

When the train starts moving, I feel sick.

Sight

The ability to 'see' the truth plays a major part in the play. Both Lear and Gloucester act blindly and foolishly. Lear orders Kent to flee 'out of my sight', while Kent tells Lear that he must 'see better'. Lear's fool mocks his folly by chanting 'out went the candle and we were left darkling'. Of course, the most striking image is portrayed by the blinding of Gloucester in Act III.

Trace the imagery of light and darkness, tears, sight and eyes throughout the play.

There's no time even to go home. I have to get off the train and run straight into college for the exam.

I still have my rucksack on my back and ruined, mud-soaked Converse on my feet. I am wearing shorts, for goodness sake. I would only ever wear shorts on holiday or with very thick tights. Or at a festival.

As I go into the exam hall, my hopes start to drain away. My worst nightmare has come true and I have fallen at the final hurdle. I have technically made it back in time, but I might as well have not bothered.

I haven't been to sleep. I don't have the books with me – the same ones I so carefully marked up and highlighted and which are right now sitting on my bedside table at home. We've been saying for months how lucky it is that we can at least take our books in with us to the literature exam for reference, so that we don't have to spend hours memorizing quotes – I felt smug at how well prepared I was. I don't even have a pen; I have to ask someone I don't know if I can borrow a biro. The end has been chewed and it barely even works.

Although I'm friendly with a few people from my English course, I'm so glad that neither Nishi nor Seymour takes English. If they were here, I couldn't stand the shame. I know I'm being openly stared at – but I can't shake the weird feeling that it's not only because of my unwashed and completely inappropriate appearance. I'm probably just getting paranoid because I'm so tired. All I can do is ignore everyone.

I inwardly tell myself that now I am here, I might as

well try to make the best of it. I must be able to salvage something. I take a deep breath.

As I open up the exam paper, get as far as writing my name at the top and very quickly realize that this pointless. I begin to sob, silently and trying my best not to distract everyone else. Keeping my weeping silent as my chest heaves and a glob of snot drips on to the table feels like a superhuman effort. After everything, the desolation and despair are just too much. Worst of all is the utter finality.

There is nothing I can do. There is no 'best' to be made. This is my only chance, and I've blown it. Oblivious to all the eyes on me, I walk out of the exam hall and out of college, still crying about all the things that have been lost forever and maybe for nothing.

I head automatically in the direction of home, and I don't even bother to slow down to prolong my last walk of freedom. There's no more dread, only resignation – nobody can tell me anything I don't already know, or make me feel worse than I do right now.

I'd assumed my mum would be at work, but then I see her car parked outside – of course she's not at work; she came home to an empty house and she still doesn't know where I am.

I let myself in on autopilot.

'Hi . . .' I say, finding Mum sitting in the silent kitchen, drinking coffee and staring at the walls. 'Look, I'm so sorry. I can explain everything.'

I can't. There's nothing to explain. I start crying again and I can't even keep it quiet this time. I want to crumple up into nothing, here on the kitchen floor. I want my mum to tell me that everything is going to be OK – but why should she? It's not and it's all my fault.

'I don't see what there is to explain,' she says, sounding very, very tired. 'Obviously we all know where you've been. I think I can fill in the blanks fairly easily myself, without hearing all of the gory details, thank you very much.'

'I . . . I don't understand. I'm sorry, but while you were away I went to Glastonbury. You know, the festival. I thought I could get back in time and it would all be OK, but . . .'

'Tuesday, I don't know if you're a better actress than I thought, or if you really haven't seen a newspaper in the last twenty-four hours.'

My genuinely blank face must be enough of an answer, because Mum grimly slides a stack of newspapers across the table towards me. I am actually sick in my mouth when I see the first picture – on page four of the *Telegraph*. I look startled and shiny-faced, definitely not at my best angle, wearing the ratty veil that was shoved on to my head; in one hand I am clutching those ugly purple plastic flowers, and the other hand is entwined with Jackson's. There's no point even reading the words. There are a couple of other newspapers, all turned down to a page with a similar photograph – me and Jackson. A smaller version of the same picture is on the cover of the *Mail on Sunday*.

'Mum?' I begin.

I want to say I'm sorry. That I am a million times sorry.

'Don't, Chew. Just don't. Trust me, there is nothing that could come out of your mouth right now that would make this any better. Nothing.'

She slams her coffee cup down and busies herself washing it up in the sink. I turn away and walk slowly up the stairs. I sit down on the edge of my bed and try to stop crying. My bedroom looks different; I already turned eighteen a couple of months ago but this feels like the official end of my childhood.

A few minutes later I hear the front door slam and my mum's car starting up. Now she knows I'm not lying in a ditch somewhere, I guess she might just as well be angry from the office.

I haul my rucksack down to the kitchen and transfer my disgustingly dirty clothes – including the ones I am wearing – into the washing machine. As I get to the bottom, a shoal of shimmering green sequins comes cascading out. It's like a reminder of when things were still shiny and hopeful and good.

The mermaid costume is beyond repair – practically falling to bits in my bag and raining sparkles everywhere. It's like it's bleeding to death. I chuck it in the bin.

I head upstairs to have a bath; when I get in, the water turns slightly mud-coloured and a few green sequins rise to float on the surface. I keep running the water out and running more hot in until every trace is washed away.

I have to admit, it's lovely to feel clean and wrapped in my old dressing gown. Even after so few days away, I feel almost like I am coming back to civilization again after a spell in the wilderness.

I bite the bullet and take the final step back to the real world – plugging in my phone. It takes a minute for it to light up into action, so I open up my laptop while I am waiting. Everything then instantly goes mental.

My phone starts beeping and won't stop. I have a gazillion messages and emails. I let my phone keep beeping itself into a frenzy while I sit down at the laptop. I daren't even look at my Facebook, but I log into my blog and my jaw almost clangs to the floor. Since Sunday, it's had over thirty thousand page views. Thirty thousand.

It doesn't take a rocket scientist to gather from this that people have seen the newspapers and figured out who I am. So I do what any sane person would do in a situation like this – and Google myself.

Most of it is pretty vague. That same picture of Jackson and me that I saw in the paper. My name, but – thankfully – very few other details. I am described by one music website as 'an amateur blogger', and then as 'a promising young writer' by another. Grossly, the tabloids are all referring to me as a 'teenager', which I think is pushing it as I am technically an adult, and even 'schoolgirl', which is inaccurate as I go to college. Not only am I an eighteen-year-old virgin, overnight it's like I've become the world's most rubbish Lolita.

Then amid all the jokey articles about my 'burgeoning

festival romance' and my fake wedding, I see a line that throws me into blackness. Of course I've been wondering what's happened to Jackson since I left Glastonbury – now I know. It's worst-case scenario. I just hope it's been exaggerated by the press.

I ignore the fact that my phone is still going crazy and, with shaking hands, I call Sadie Steinbeck.

'Sadie, it's Tuesday.'

'Hi, Tuesday – I meant to call you. As you can imagine, things have been insane around here.'

'But what's going on? Is he OK? I only just heard.'

'I'm afraid the stories are true – Jackson got himself into a really bad state after you left. He collapsed and had to be airlifted to hospital from the festival last night.'

'Is . . .' I can hardly get the words out I'm so frightened. 'Is he OK?'

She sighs at length. 'That's a tough question. He should be. He's off the danger list. He's conscious again. But he doesn't seem to be making much sense. I haven't seen him – I flew back to LA on Saturday after I left you. We're having Jack flown back right now; he should be here in a few hours. I've got rehab lined up for him the second he steps off the plane. I think we need to make sure he does more than the thirty-day programme this time, gets himself well.'

'Is there anything I can do?'

'I don't think so,' says Sadie. 'And Tuesday? This isn't your fault, OK? Don't blame yourself. I know I came on pretty tough back at Glastonbury, but that's just how it has to be with him. Jack's been like this for a long time before he met you. Please don't go thinking you can save him. I made that mistake a long time ago. We can only do what we can do. Right?'

This blog Is Closed (for now).

Um, I'm more than a little freaked out. I'm sure you can all understand.

So I've decided I'm not going to blog here for a while. I've also closed the comments section for all of my past posts.

Things are tricky at the moment, to say the least, so I'm not going to comment further on anything that's happened.

Thank you to those of you who have been kind — I really appreciate it. To the rest of you, I genuinely wish you all the best in your lives. I still can't believe that I have created such dramas; I honestly never meant to. Obviously I take responsibility for my actions and I am sorry for any upset I have caused.

So long and thanks for all the fish (I don't even know what that means but I heard it somewhere once and it feels right).

Yours sincerely,

Tuesday Cooper/Chew/Ruby Tuesday . . . The Last Tuesday

x

I freeze as I hear a knock at the door. I can't take any more drama today. I am wrung out.

I go to the door in my dressing gown, and it's Nishi. She looks furious and I cower in the hallway, bracing myself for the onslaught.

'You bloody moron,' she snarls. 'You dickhead.'

I couldn't speak if I tried and I worry that I am going to start weeping yet again, as Nishi grabs me and hugs me tighter than I would have believed humanly possible.

'Don't you dare start blubbing, Tuesday Cooper. And let me in before anyone sees us being soppy idiots all over the place. The least you can do is make me a cup of tea.'

I can't help but grin, despite it all, at the thought of having my best friend back. More importantly, she seems back to her old self.

'Nish, I saw all those comments on my blog,' I say, once we are settled in our usual positions on the sofa. 'Thanks for sticking up for me. Seriously. It means a lot.'

She waves a hand in the air like it's nothing. 'That's what friends do. I know the exams made me go a bit crazy, but that doesn't mean we're not best mates.'

'How did your exams go?' I ask.

'All right.' She shrugs, which I guess means she knows she's done brilliantly but doesn't want to tempt fate. 'I obviously heard about your English exam, by the way.'

'Yeah?'

'Yeah. Everyone did. Like I said, you're a dick. But if anyone can find a way around it, it's probably you.'

Strangely this makes me feel much better, even if it

does mean getting called a dick. Coming from Nish, that's almost high praise. According to her rules, it also means we probably don't have to talk about it ever again, which is a blessed relief.

'Have you been in touch with Seymour?' I ask her.

'Are you joking?' she counters. 'After what he said about you on your own blog? I know I've sided with him in the past, but I'm not having that. Line crossed. Unacceptable. That's it, I'm afraid.'

I wish I had morals as strong as Nishi's. Everything must be so much easier if it all looks black and white.

'Well, I'm really grateful that you stuck up for me, but in a way I don't blame him. I think it's fair to say that he had some provocation.'

'No excuse. It was quite spectacular provocation though, Chew. I can't believe all that Jackson Griffith stuff turned out to be true. I should probably apologize to you for not believing you in the first place, but I'm not going to – the whole thing is so ridiculously off the scale, bonkers, I'm *still* not sure I believe it.'

Nishi has hit the nail on the head as usual. I've been back home for less than a whole day, and not only Glastonbury, but the whole Jackson Griffith affair, feels like a distant memory. Not even that – more like a dream, or something I made up.

'I just wish I could tell Anna about it,' Nish says, in a wistful tone I have never heard before. 'She loves Sour Apple; she'd go crazy if she knew it was all true. But I messed that one up, didn't I? I didn't even tell you,

Chew – the whole thing was my fault. I'm even more of an idiot than you are.'

My stomach lurches and I nearly choke on my tea. It should have occurred to me sooner that this was too good to last. Nishi is being so lovely that I almost forgot that I am the worst friend ever.

'Look,' I whisper, 'there's something I need to talk to you about. Something else.'

Nishi's face instantly shuts down into the defensive mask that I have seen so many times before.

'It's about Anna,' I go on. 'I'm so sorry. I shouldn't have gone behind your back, but you were being mental and taking Seymour's side, and . . .'

'Spit it out, Chew.' Her voice is stone cold.

'That night that Anna and I walked home together from Moshi Munchers . . . She was the only one who believed me about Jackson Griffith. She was the only one I could talk to about it. Jackson said I could bring a friend with me to Glastonbury . . .'

'So Anna was with you,' Nishi states. 'You and Anna went to Glastonbury together. She was in on it the whole time. You went behind my back and you didn't even bother to tell me until now.'

'Yeah, but . . .' I protest feebly. 'You said yourself that friends can do stupid things and still stick up for each other, no matter what. I can see now that it was a really stupid thing to do.'

'It wasn't just *stupid*, Chew. You know, that's always been your problem – you do these things and then you go, "Oh poor me – I'm just so stupid. Isn't it funny?" Well, it's not funny and it's not *just stupid*. It's *wrong*. You went behind my back. You lied to me. I know I'm not perfect, but I have never, ever lied to you. *Never*.'

She's right. I know there is nothing that I can say as she walks out of the door and slams it behind her.

By the time my mum gets home from work, I have cleaned the house and put all my washing away. I have made dinner; the table is set, optimistically. I am dreading more of the cold-shoulder treatment, but I am also counting on the fact that both my mum and I are really crap at staying cross. I know I've done a terrible thing – well, probably quite a few, if I really think about it in detail – but, throughout everything, my mum and I have never really fallen out before. I can't bear the idea that we're going to start now.

I know that none of this is going to fix what I have done, but I hope it will help a little bit – it can't hurt to try to make an effort. Besides, I had to do something to keep myself busy all day.

'Mum.'

'Oh, Tuesday . . .'

I was determined not to start crying again, but her tone of voice instantly makes me well up.

'I've made dinner, and cleaned up and . . . Well, I know that there's nothing I can do to make this better, but I am so sorry. *So* sorry. You have no idea how sorry. Can we sit down and talk about this?' I ask. 'Please?'

My mum and I are also both crap at talking about things. We're much better at just getting on with it. Keep on keeping on. Thankfully Mum sits down at the kitchen table.

'So did you have a good time?' she asks me directly.

'It was . . . up and down,' I reply as honestly as I can.

'Was it worth it?'

'I don't know. No, I don't think it was. It was stupid. I mean, it was *wrong*.'

Laid out like this, the whole thing just sounds incredibly sad.

'Did you go to your exam this morning?'

'Yes.' I pause as I realize that it would be even more stupid to try to bluff my way through this. 'But I might as well have not done. I wasn't prepared. I didn't even have the books with me. I *did* try to come back yesterday, but it all went . . .'

The look on my mum's face tells me that there's really no point in trying to justify any of this now. I know she's right.

'So,' she asks with a sigh, 'Jackson Griffith is your boyfriend?'

'Yeah. Kind of. I don't know.'

'Are you in love with him?'

'I . . . I don't know.'

If I could answer the last two questions with a bit more certainty, maybe the whole thing wouldn't sound so bad. None of the hundreds of messages I've got since I've been home was from him. I don't even know if he's

OK; I so want to speak to him. I can't explain to my mum how small and stupid I feel. That I was so sure there was something really special between us I was prepared to stake my whole future on it. For nothing.

'Did I ruin your whole weekend?' I ask.

'Not the whole weekend. It was fine until Sunday morning; it was great. Then I woke up to about twenty text messages informing me that my daughter is in the papers because she's got married to a quote-unquote *rockstar* at Glastonbury.'

'Oh my god. I am so sorry.'

'Well, the thing is – then I realized it's probably all my fault. I mean, you haven't had it easy. I know I haven't been able to give you the most stable family, or any sort of father figure. I gave you more credit than I should have. I can't believe that I went away before your exams had finished. If I had been here, none of this would have happened.'

'Mum, no,' I protest, panicking. 'It's not like that. It's not. Please.'

'Stop. Just stop, Chew. Things have got to change around here. I need to stop treating you as an equal and start acting like a mother. You're still a teenager after all. I'm going to start keeping a much closer eye on you. Richard and I have broken up, so—'

I know I should keep my mouth shut, but I just can't do it. 'Well, I'm sorry, but if he broke up with you over this, then he's a loser anyway.'

'Actually it was the other way around. This has made

me realize that I can't pursue a new relationship right now. It's as simple as that.'

'But, Mum—'

'No buts, Chew. We can talk about this later. I've got a terrible headache; I'm going to bed.'

I sit alone at the table after she has gone. My mum might be wrong this time, but Nishi was right. Her words are still echoing around my brain.

I have been crashing through life thinking I am this nice person who sometimes makes mistakes and messes things up. Oh, that's just me – a bit fat, a bit of a loudmouth; I don't think before I speak. Poor me.

I've hurt not just myself this time, but the people around me. The people I love. Something's got to change.

To: jackson evan griffith
From: Tuesday Cooper

Jackson,
Where are you? Are you OK?
RT x

In the morning my mum heads out to work while I cower in bed, not wanting to talk to her after last night.

I'm biding my time, but I can't just lie around thinking about my sad, sad life all day. As soon as I hear her car pull away, I spring into action. When she gets home tonight, this time I will be ready for her. I have a long list of things to do.

I don't stop all day. When I hear her key in the door, I'm wearing my most mature outfit (it's not even from a charity shop) and I hand her a glass of wine immediately. She looks confused as she walks into the kitchen.

'Wine? Flowers on the table?' she says. 'Chew, I feel like I'm on a date. This really isn't necessary. I think you've missed the—'

'Well, actually,' I interrupt, 'you are kind of on a date. Or you will be soon. Richard's coming round for dinner.'

'What?'

'I rang him at lunchtime. We had quite a good chat. I thought I'd better apologize to him myself for wrecking his romantic weekend away in such catastrophic style. Not to mention getting him unfairly dumped. He's quite a nice bloke, isn't he?'

Mum's mouthing like a goldfish.

'You look nice as you are,' I continue, smiling at her hopefully. 'But if you did want to get changed out of your work clothes, you'd better hurry up because he's going to be here in twenty minutes. Excuse me, I'm just going to go and stick the lasagne in the oven.'

My mum is so shocked that she doesn't move, and she

just stays in her work clothes; all she does is put on a bit more lipstick. She looks really nice in her smart dress, but it's quite unlike her – usually she would never want a man to see her in an outfit she'd been wearing all day. I think this might be a good sign actually.

I'm feeling much more kindly disposed to Richard Jenkins all round since our chat earlier. I thought he was boring, and he is, but he's sensible – and maybe sensible's what we need around here. He's also prepared to forgive me *and* my mum.

When he arrives at the door he's wearing glasses that I think are the same as the ones Seymour wears, although in a less ironic fashion, plus a short-sleeved shirt with a tie, which is kind of one of my pet hates in life. But I decide that I can let it slide. There are worse crimes, it must be said.

'Glad to see the prodigal daughter back in one piece,' he whispers to me on the doorstep, in something of a conspiratorial tone.

I don't know what he says to my mum, as I hang back for a minute and leave them alone in the kitchen. But whatever it is, it seems to work. They look so crazy about each other that I'm sure they would have got back together eventually even if I hadn't interfered. Luckily for me, my mum doesn't even look too unhappy that I did. She tries for a minute, I can see, but she can't keep it up.

'Tuesday Cooper, you are going to be the death of me,' is all she says out loud.

'Well, I for one was rather pleased that she got in touch,' Richard tells her. 'And I hope you might be as well, secretly.'

He's really good company throughout dinner. Most of all, he obviously thinks that my mum is the bee's knees, or the cat's pyjamas, or some other nonsensical cliché – as he rightly should. I can forgive him the summer-shirt-and-tie combo just for that.

'Oh, Chew – what are we going to do with you?' my mum groans, apropos of nothing, as she finishes her second glass of wine.

Fair enough, I suppose – I'm prepared to take this sort of thing on the chin for a while. She's earned it. But I can't help thinking it's not exactly helpful. Fortunately for me, Richard Jenkins seems to agree with me.

'Well, Carrie,' he says, managing not to sound too pompous, 'I think the more productive question is: what does Tuesday *want* to do?'

I am slightly dumbfounded that anyone is actually asking me this right now.

'Tuesday . . . ?' he prompts.

'Well . . . I want to go to university and I want to be a writer.'

'Right. So you're holding some conditional offers – after yesterday's disaster, do you think you'll have got the grades?'

I look apprehensively over at my mother before I have to shake my head, no.

'I got A's on all my coursework, but – I'm really sorry

to say – I didn't write anything at all in that last paper, except my own name, and then I walked out. I knew there was no point. I'm well aware it's my own fault.'

'It doesn't matter whose fault it is,' Richard says. 'It's happened. It would have been better if it hadn't, but there's nothing you can do about it now. The point is how you deal with it.'

'So what should we do?' my mum asks, hanging on his every word.

Richard laughs. 'That's up to Tuesday, not us.'

'What should *I* do then?' I ask back, only half joking.

'First of all, talk to your tutor as soon as possible about what you might get overall, as you've done so well on all your coursework and you think the other papers went well too. If you really haven't got the grades, of course there are always retakes. You know what they say: "there's no such thing as no, just not yet". I'm not sure if that's strictly true, but it's a good saying nonetheless.'

I can't bear the thought of my life grinding to a halt for another year. If these past few days have taught me anything, it's that I really am ready for a bigger world. My thoughts on the matter must be written all over my face.

He had better not even get me started on 'travelling'. I have spent at least the past six months of my life being completely irritated by anyone who even mentions the word. If anyone at college plans to do it, and insists upon calling it 'travelling' rather than 'going on quite a long holiday', then I know we could never be friends. You can guarantee it just means they want their mum and dad to pay for them to have yet another year of getting drunk with other eighteen-year-olds from England. Maybe a few from Australia. Then they will call it 'a cultural experience' and bore everyone stupid about it when they get home. Even if I could afford it, I like to think that I would never want to 'go travelling'. If I was still doing that sort of thing, maybe I'd write a blog post about it.

'Otherwise,' Richard goes on, 'my only advice is this: be proactive. It doesn't have to be a foregone conclusion. Do whatever you can do; don't just sit there and wait. It's your life. There's clearing, and don't forget there's also just plain old talking to people. See what you can do.'

A smile comes to my face for the first time in a while as I think about this. Meanwhile, my mum takes the opportunity to voice the words that have obviously been playing on her mind.

'So you're not going to forget all about university and elope to America with Jackson Griffith?'

'No,' I say very levelly, looking her in the eye, 'I'm not. We don't know each other that well, and I really have no idea what's going to happen. If he really likes me, I don't have to go running halfway around the world for him, right? He's the one who chased me.'

'Bravo,' says Richard, and my mum looks mildly surprised.

'Now,' I announce, 'I'm going to leave you two cats to it. After I thoroughly disrupted your romantic weekend, it's the least I can do. Don't worry – I'm not eloping. I'm just going to meet Nishi and Anna for a coffee and I'll be back in hour. So behave.'

This is not strictly true. I don't want to worry them with the truth while things are going so well here. I've gone behind Nishi's back again today, and I'm about to find out if she's going to thank me for it this time.

Unfortunately our favourite haunt Macari's doesn't stay open in the evenings – so I have to go to a rubbish generic cafe on the high street. The sort of place where a coffee costs twice as much and you know the atmosphere has been focus-grouped.

But that's the least of my worries. I hang around outside, looking like some kind of weirdo stalker, until I can make them out at a table tucked away in the corner. I wave until they spot me. Nishi rolls her eyes and turns away, but Anna does a tentative thumbs-up behind her head.

I open the door and step inside, but my feeling of dread does not go away. Not even when Anna gets up and hugs me. I can see Nishi glowering behind her.

'I should have known you were behind this, Tuesday,' she says darkly.

'Nishi,' Anna snaps, 'stop underestimating me! *I* was behind this. It was my idea. I told Chew to come and meet us.'

'Look, I'm sorry,' I interject. 'Thanks, Anna, but this was obviously a bad idea. Nishi, you were right and I'm really sorry. I'll leave you both alone.'

'Tuesday, *sit down*,' Anna thunders.

Nishi and I look at each other in utter disbelief. I cannot believe that this sound has actually come out of Anna's body.

'Nobody is leaving until you two are friends again. Do you understand? We've all been idiots. You two are the best friends I've ever met in my life. So deal with it. We're not going anywhere.'

I'm almost afraid to look at Nishi for fear of her reaction. Then I realize that she is laughing.

'Blimey! I kind of like it when you're strict. Who'd have thought it?' She looks at me – only sideways, but it's a start. 'Seriously, Chew – this cinnamon vanilla spice mocha hot chocolate is insane. I've never tasted anything so bloody delicious in my life. We're going to start hanging out here. Get used to it. I suggest you go up to the counter and get yourself one immediately.'

She's right, as always. It tastes like heaven in a branded mug. And, just like that, we're friends again.

'I can't believe you two went to Glastonbury without me!' Nishi exclaims. 'I've always wanted to go and I missed out. How about we all go to Reading in August to make up for it?'

'No way,' I reply emphatically. 'It turns out Anna hates festivals. And I've had enough of them to last me for years. I wouldn't go again even for Jackson Griffith.'

'And you're lucky,' Anna says to Nishi, 'because if Tuesday hadn't seen him first, I swear even I would consider turning for Jackson Griffith. The man is a golden god, a higher species of man. Total weirdo, mind – but bloody gorgeous. I can totally understand why Chew went a bit loopy about the whole thing.'

'Well, thanks for that, but it doesn't matter any more,' Nishi says piously. 'Chew and I are cool. Right, Chew?'

'Yes, thank goodness. So now that's cleared up, I really should leave you two alone. You *are* back together, aren't you?'

'Yes, so leave us alone – not all of us are fans of snogging in public and getting on the front page of the tabloids!' Nishi cackles.

I can still hear them both laughing as I leave.

To: Tuesday Cooper
From: jackson evan griffith

Ruby Tuesday,

I'm so sorry about how I left things with you. I should never have let you go off on your own like that. Straight away I wished I had gone back to London with you. I had such a great day (and night) with you before that.

I don't know why I always have to wreck everything. It's a sick kind of self-harm, I'm not even kidding. I'm so bad at being happy. I like the idea of a simple life, I really do. Girlfriend, house, dog. The whole package. But I can't seem to live it.

Anyway. Enough of my own personal pity party. I guess you heard what happened. I even gave myself a scare when I woke up in that hospital, and I don't scare so easy. I dunno yet if I can call it my very own 'rock bottom moment'. Seems like I've had a few of those already in my time.

So, here I am in rehab again. I'm gonna try and do it properly this time. Maybe it's even for the best – who knows?

I have my guitar here, and some books I've been meaning to read since forever, but mostly I'm doing a lot of sleeping, to tell you the truth. I'm a binge sleeper (I'm a binge everything-er) and maybe I needed to catch up. I'm eating like a fiend as well. The food here's pretty good. I'm gonna come out of here lazy and fat. Hope so, anyway. Sounds good to me right now.

As you can probably tell, I have a lot of time on my hands, so please excuse my rambling. Having computer privileges is kind of a big deal here. It's taken me a week to be allowed on my email. Then nearly that long to remember the password! My brain is fried!

I'd have been in touch sooner otherwise. Actually that might be a lie – I've been pretty self-involved. Who knows? Who knows what might have happened if I'd just come back to London with you? I know it's the road to madness, man! Thinking like that, I mean.

This may not be news to anyone except for me, but it turns out I have a lot of problems.

I think you are an awesome girl. I'm sounding cheesy now, but you've been a little window of sunshine in my life. I don't often meet girls like you any more. You have a very unique style and you are one hell of a writer (as they say). Keep writing! If you do one thing, keep writing. I am not much of an advice giver but that one's a no-brainer. You don't need me to tell you anything. I wish I had more to offer you.

I hope our paths will cross again. I wonder if we will keep in touch. Let me know what you think, if you are so inclined. I hope you will keep writing to me.

Hey, I also want to add that I really wish we'd had sex in the tepee! That would have made my perfect night even better. Although I am very bad at sex – and the way you're supposed to treat people after you've had sex with them – so if we had it might mean that you would hate me more than you already maybe do.

Glastonbury seems to be a bad place for me. I'm sorry that you had to be around for some of it, and I'm not proud of myself. But while you were there, those were probably the best times I've ever had in that place. Seriously. I had a great time with you. What a fun night. Hey, I guess what happened in that crazy Elvis tent (from what I can remember of it?!) means that we are 'Glastonbury-married' – if we ever get there again, I'm totally holding you to it, Glastonbury Wife!

Well, Ruby Tuesday – seriously, whatever else, we'll always have Glastonbury. I'm glad. I hope you are too – but for me you came along at just the right time, when I needed a friend around who wasn't part of the bullshit world I always seem to get myself mixed up in.

Oh, and Jeremy Kyle – I'll never forget it was you who did me the great favour of introducing me to Jeremy Kyle and Greggs cheese 'n' onion pasties.

I might look him up on YouTube. Like I said, I've got a lot of time on my hands.

I hope all was OK for you when you got back home. I know being associated with me is not always the best. I hope you considered it worth the hassle.

Love, Jack xx

PS Sadie says hi – she comes in to see me on a Sunday and brings me grapes, if you can believe it!

To: jackson evan griffith
From: Tuesday Cooper

Dear Jackson,

I'm just glad you're OK. And you will be really OK. I think you're a truly beautiful human being – who sounds cheesy now, eh?

While we're on 'what ifs' . . . I wonder what if you were just some nice normal (but gorgeous and insanely talented, obviously) boy who I met at college and really got on with. In some strange time machine that could never exist, I'd like to make us the same age and to be full of potential together. What if we could just hang out in Macari's (that's an accidentally retro cafe I like to go to in the dull small town where I live) and you could come round to my mum's house for dinner. I think it would be really lovely actually.

I wonder this because I don't think I'm destined to be a pop star's girlfriend . . . If there's one thing you've done for me (and in fact there are quite a few things), I think you've made me realize that I want to be the VIP, not the tag-along who goes to my boyfriend's gigs and sits on the sidelines. Even if I never become a VIP in my own right, I want to try to be a writer and do cool stuff myself.

I was so ridiculously flattered when you got in touch with me on my blog and then carried on paying attention to me. I mean, to an unhealthy degree. I really shouldn't need that kind of validation! I didn't even know you (not then), but I projected all sorts of importance on to it. Like if someone as 'special' and important (i.e. famous – let's face it!) was interested in me, then I must be 'special' too. Ego, man!!

I hope we can stay in touch, like you said. Probably not all the time, but I am glad that we will both think of each other fondly. By the way, I think it's a very good thing that we did not have sex in the tepee, no matter what you say! Although I did a few things I'm not necessarily proud of in retrospect, I feel really good about that night.

I think we will be far-off friends, and (in my ideal dream world) hopefully you can always be a tiny bit in love with me but we will never have sex, and even when we are 90 I will be going, 'Phew – thank god we just stayed friends and he didn't ever mess me up!' Then I will bore my grandchildren stupid by playing them (again!) the beautiful song that a famous pop star with a kind heart and a rare talent wrote for me when I was eighteen years old.

And I'll tell them about the time we went to Glastonbury and in a weird sort of way it was kind of perfect. And it taught me a lot. Etc., etc. . . .

I will keep writing if you promise me that you will do your very best to look after yourself and your voice. I mean it when I say that you have a rare talent. There is something about you that changes the temperature of the room. You don't need me to tell you that, but I think you need to remember that you are a good human with a beautiful voice. You are.

With love from your friend and once-upon-a-time fake wife,

Ruby Tuesday XXX

PS – Say hi to Sadie from me. I've grown weirdly fond of her.

It's almost, but not quite, as if nothing happened. My mum and I are getting on fine again. Nishi and I are closer than we've ever been; she and I plus Anna are back to all of our old routines of hanging out constantly together in charity shops and weird cafes, especially now exams are over and we have blissful time on our hands. Jackson and I email each other, sporadically but sometimes for pages at a time, and I even get the occasional message from Sadie Steinbeck.

Then I remember that I've ruined my whole life all by myself. I'm dreading the results; I know there is no way they're going to be good.

Still, after weeks of texting him and asking if we can at least meet up and talk, Seymour has finally relented and said I can come over to his house this afternoon. I'm pretty sure he just wants to get me to shut up and leave him alone, but I'll take it. I totally understand why he wouldn't want to speak to me, but it's really important to me that I see him and at least try to explain.

Weirdly, as I walk up the gravel driveway to his house, I don't feel as nervous as I used to when I would go round there for Sunday lunch and it was all supposed to be so friendly and civilized.

Seymour barely says hello to me when he answers the door, but I am mostly just relieved that nobody else seems to be at home. Perhaps he had to wait until everybody else was out as Elaine wouldn't let me over the threshold.

'Thanks for letting me come over,' I say.

Seymour shrugs in reply. We stand in the hallway

and don't look at each other.

'Shall I make us a cup of tea?' I suggest.

This is probably against the etiquette of the house, but one of us has to do something. He shrugs again, so I take this as a green light to lead the way into the kitchen and fill up the kettle. It's one of those fancy but annoying Brita filter ones, so I have to stand there for about five minutes while the water trickles through. I wanted to wait until we were sitting down with a cup of tea before I launched into my lengthy apology-slash-explanation, but the silence is getting a bit awkward.

Seymour beats me to it.

'You're not going to try to get back together, are you?' he blurts out, seemingly from nowhere. 'Because I don't know why else you're here and it's not going to work. The answer's no.'

'What? I don't think we *should* get back together,' I reply, trying to hide my total shock. 'That's not why I'm here at all. But we were friends before we ever started going out. It seems a real shame for it to end without us ever even talking to each other again. It just wouldn't be right somehow.'

Again the shrug. Usually Seymour is so articulate he runs rings around me when he wants to; even under the circumstances, I don't understand why he is being monosyllabic to the point of sulky. It's kind of more disconcerting than the tongue-lashing I expected. Maybe he just wants to make this as difficult for me as he can. Who could blame him?

I automatically make Seymour's tea as weak as possible, barely squeezing the bag, and with two sugars – just how he likes it. As I leave mine to stew for as long as possible and beat the living daylights out of it with a teaspoon, I reflect that I should have known we were always ill-suited.

'Mostly,' I continue, 'I wanted to apologize, face to face. I owe you that at least. I'm sorry. I really, truly am. I did a crap thing. I got carried away and I did a lot of really crap things. So . . . I'm sorry.'

'Does your new boyfriend know you're here?' he sneers.

'Jackson knows I'm here, but he's not my boyfriend any more.'

'He *did* dump you then. I knew it.' Seymour laughs with no humour whatsoever.

'Well, it's a bit more complicated than that. It turns out we're better as friends.'

'Funny that, what with him being a total nutcase and all.'

'Look, Seymour – that's not the point. You're entitled to your opinion, but I just want you to know I'm sorry . . . Anyway –' even now I can't resist trying to make a feeble joke – 'your mum must be happy about how things have turned out at least!'

'Actually she was too worried about me to be as petty as that,' Seymour says sanctimoniously, in what I suspect is a whopping great lie. 'Although I must admit, it's given me a great excuse over these A levels – if I fail, I can blame you and the fact that you broke my heart and ruined my life.'

'Seymour . . . I mean, fine, it's my fault, whatever – but I have to say, I did get the feeling even before all this that things weren't exactly great between us any more. I felt like, well, like you'd kind of gone off me anyway?'

Maybe I'm trying to make myself feel better, but I honestly don't believe that Seymour's broken-hearted over me at all. It seems like something else.

He doesn't reply and manages to look even more awkward.

'Seymour . . .' I try again, and then I decide to be brave and voice the question that's been nagging at the back of my head for a long time now, 'are you gay?'

'No! For god's sake, Chew. Do you think *everyone* is gay? Why would you even ask me that?'

'Because you never wanted to have sex with me and it always felt more like we were just mates really.'

I actually feel better for having said this out loud. Finally. This issue has secretly been eating away at me for so long. When we were going out together I kept trying to think of subtle ways to bring it up, but I always chickened out.

'It's not me, it's *you*,' he says. 'I'm sorry, but if you're going to make me say it . . . I'm not gay, but I just never really fancied you. I thought you were really cool and I liked hanging out with you. It was easy, I suppose. You're good fun, but you've got to admit you're not exactly a sexy girlfriend type.'

'Thank goodness,' I can't help snapping. 'And I thought you were so enlightened.'

'It's just . . . Don't let this go to your head or anything, but I thought that going out with you would make people take me more seriously. I mean, you're so *different* and you do your blog and everything. Everyone thinks I'm just this good-looking idiot and they don't really take my band seriously. And you and I had a laugh together, so I thought—'

'Really, Seymour,' I cut in, 'you can stop talking now. I'm kind of sorry I asked. You're basically saying that going out with a non-hottie made you look cleverer. Well, hopefully you can dine out on the story of getting dumped for Jackson Griffith for years now, so everyone's a winner.'

'Look, Chew . . .' Seymour's practically twitching; I swear he's turning into Woody Allen before my eyes, 'it's been easy just to blame this on you, but I have a confession as well. That night at my gig when you left early, something happened with me and Sophie – you remember, my bass player's sister? So it wasn't all your fault. You might as well know that now.'

Not so long ago, this news would have convinced me that every bad thing I have ever thought about myself is true – I'm too fat, not pretty enough, a total idiot. Now I'm actually relieved in a way – at least it explains why he's been behaving like such an arse. Well, even more of an arse than usual – as I am only now fully realizing. I'm surprised at the wave of relief I feel.

'Well, she seemed very nice. She's awfully pretty,' I say. 'Is she your girlfriend now?'

'No way.' He shudders at the very thought. 'I don't think I want another of those for a while. I mean, who knows what's going to happen once we leave college? I might have way too much other stuff going on to want to be tied down.'

'Have you and your mum come to any agreement about what you're going to do?'

'Well, the compromise is I've said I'll try and get a place through clearing at one of the unis this side of London, so I can live at home and commute – that way I can keep the band going. But I don't know if I'll get the grades to be honest. The exams have made me realize I didn't work hard enough – they were a lot tougher than I expected.'

'Oh,' I say. 'I'm sorry to hear that. Hopefully you'll get the grades to go where you want to go.'

He brightens right up. 'It doesn't really matter – my parents are paying for me to go to Thailand for a month in August, so I'm not thinking about it yet. I've always fancied going travelling. And even if I don't get in anywhere, I'll probably be able to get a job working for my dad. Either way I can still concentrate on the band. That's the important thing.'

I don't know what to say to any of this. I kind of want to laugh.

He clears his throat ostentatiously. 'Actually, I was thinking, maybe you can hit up Jackson Griffith for a support slot or something? He's could at least listen to our demo. He *does* owe me one, after all. What with him stealing my girlfriend and everything.'

I can't control it any longer. At this I burst out laughing, and I cannot stop. Even though Seymour is looking at me like it's really not funny. In fact, I think he might actually hate me and I don't care even a tiny bit. How either of us managed to go out with the other for as long as we did is utterly beyond me.

'Well, thanks for the tea,' I say, as soon as I have stopped snorting through my nose and regained the power of speech. 'I guess I'll see you around. Good luck for your results.'

He doesn't move as I stand up to leave.

'I'd say, "You too",' he informs me, 'but there's probably not much point, as I heard you didn't even do the last English exam. So . . . see you around, I suppose.'

I can't help but wonder if Seymour has always been like this and I never noticed, or if it's just everything that's been going on lately that's making him behave like a sulky, spoiled arsehole.

Something that Nishi said to me once springs into my head – you can't ever tell what someone's really like until things go wrong. Some wise old cliché about not being able to tell how strong a teabag is until you put it in hot water.

I have to let it go. It's none of my business what he thinks of me; that's the point. At least I can say I tried.

Never Complain, Never Explain? Nice Idea But Not for Me

All I ever wanted was to be a writer. I've had my eyes on that particular prize for as long as I can remember.

I have always loved books; I have always written everything down; I never had any other ideas or future career plans. It's been my one focus for as long as I can remember.

Luckily for me, all the other stuff – family, friends, having a life – didn't take up too much extra room. My family was only my mum. The only friend who ever mattered was Nishi, who I have known since I was tiny, so we have a shorthand that makes everything easy. In fact, for a girl who loves drama on the page, I even managed to get my first boyfriend in the most non-dramatic, non-hysteric fashion imaginable. Writing was the thing.

Until about two months ago, when everything went just a little bit off track . . .

It all started with writing – this blog you're reading now. It's a throwaway medium, maybe, and I don't write anything groundbreaking on here; but I find it's a good discipline. Besides, as we live in the future these days and the technology is there to make it happen, why not get my writing theoretically out there into the world? Even if in practice it is only on a small scale.

My only readers were my mum, my best friend, her girlfriend and my boyfriend. Other than an occasional accidental tourist who had typed in an obscure Google search such as 'foo fighters are rubbish' or 'weird teenage girl who hates radio 1 and loves leonard cohen'. It goes without saying that they usually left as soon as they'd arrived.

Until the day that Jackson Griffith – pop star, noted hellraiser, possibly the sweetest boy I've ever met, some kind of a cross between a prince, a madman and a puppy – became my newest reader. Turns out he had time on his hands after going through rehab the first time; plus he has an ego on him and isn't averse to a little self-googling.[1]

I should admit right now that I used to have posters of Jackson Griffith on my bedroom wall when I was an immature yet precocious thirteen-year-old, so perhaps that goes some way to explaining my brief spell of madness. In the beginning at least: once I met him, I'd have done the same whether he was the singer in a band or the shelf-stacker in a supermarket – some people are just sort of shiny and special in a way that can't be adequately explained. In my new and limited experience of pop stars, I'd say it's a 'chicken and egg' question, and it would be pretty much impossible to speculate on which comes first.

---

1 *Hi, Jackson! Don't worry, reader, he gave me his permission to write about him. I offered to send this to him first – for 'copy approval', as the stars call it – but he said he trusted me and would be happy with whatever I wanted to write. I don't think anyone has ever paid me a nicer compliment actually.*

I don't need to tell you the gory details of what happened. It's all out there if you do want to know. Even if you're not a tabloid reader, it is of course all preserved on the Internet, for better or worse. The important bits you may not know are that: I fell out with my best friend; I totally let down my mum and ruined her romantic weekend away with her nice new boyfriend; I completely messed up my English A level exam.

Of course, there's always a plus side. Jackson has become a proper friend (albeit a long-distance one, which I think we can all agree is probably for the best). I have become closer to my real friends. My mum and I are cool and it's back on with her new man. My adventure had a point, even though it took me a while to see it.

I don't regret any of it in the end, although it will probably be a source of sadness and embarrassment to me for evermore that I did not do as well as I could have on my English A level – the one where I was Most Likely To Succeed, MY subject, the most important one.

However, I have to tell myself that the writing, the doing, is more important. I have more to write about than I ever have before. I feel so much older than I did only a couple of months ago. If, despite my own folly, I am lucky[1] enough to get the university place I have

---

1 I say 'lucky', but maybe what I actually mean is 'prepared to work hard and be proactive'.

always wanted – well, then I feel better prepared for it than I would have been otherwise. Maybe this is ironic, given that it might mean I miss my chance, but it's a risk worth taking. I know I can do it.

I now know that, whatever happens, I am a writer. I have always talked so much about wanting to be a writer, it never occurred to before that I might already be one. For better or worse. Down to my bones.

So, this blog triggered the events that led to my downfall. To even things up, I'm hoping that it might also kick-start my climb back up.

I am writing, more than I ever have. I will keep writing. It is what I do. I will work hard at it no matter what, because if I don't then I am not doing what I am here to do.

That's all I can do. I hope it's enough.

Comments
Glad to know you, Ruby Tuesday. I'm proud of ya. j x
jackson_e_griffith

Hi, Jackson! Yeah, me too – well done, Chew.
Nishi_S

It looks to the naked eye as though we're back where we started, but it all feels so different. I'm sitting opposite Anna and Nishi in Macari's, and I am eating a bowl of chips.

Some of the differences are immediately obvious. Anna has cut her hair off in a brutal crop that would make any other girl look like an ugly boy, but that makes her look like a cross between Edie Sedgwick and a stray cat, or a cool version of Mia Farrow. She says it's just because she suddenly fancied a change, but I like to think it represents the newly independent spirit she has discovered since our Glastonbury adventure. The great irony is, if I ever tried to get a haircut like that, with my lack of cheekbones and collar bones or any other kind of defining bones, I know that the scariest meathead boys my age would shout out in the street that I looked like an 'ugly butch dyke'. Whereas if those same boys discovered that Anna was gay, they would probably jump off a cliff.

By coincidence, this is the longest in at least three years I've been without dyeing my hair. The red is fading down to a dull orange and the bleach beneath it is growing out to dark-brown roots. It looks horrendous, but it feels right somehow.

Every time I dyed my hair, I used to think that this would be the time I would find my perfect colour – the one that would make me pretty *and* interesting, the one that would sum up my perfect style so that people would recognize me at first glance. I longed for a signature look that I could stick with for longer than a week, and

I believed that every new possibility might be exactly that. I even had my next new colour all picked out – a dark purple, a bit goth to take us into the autumn and represent my new maturity. I was all set to do it, but then I realized that it would really make no difference to my life, or to my pale moon face. If that sounds depressing, it actually isn't. The little plastic bottle is still in the bathroom cabinet, its snap-off nozzle intact.

Of the three of us, Nishi is the only one who remains gloriously the same. She was always completely herself to begin with.

'Come on, Nish. You've got to eat something,' Anna urges, brow all furrowed.

Luckily – or not – unlike Nish, anxiety does not stop me from eating. All that's left of my 'brunch' – although we all agreed that we hate that word and will instead call it 'lunkfast' – is a single crust and a few manky brown chips left at the bottom of the grease-smeared bowl. Nishi has barely touched her toast, and is unlikely to now it's gone all cold and hard. She has consumed nothing but black coffee all morning, and is thus constantly jiggling one foot against the table leg, but we can't bring ourselves to tell her that it's deeply annoying. She has already excused herself three times to go and be noisily sick in the cafe's loo.

My usual gargantuan appetite aside, I genuinely feel quite calm. Maybe it's because there's no hope and I am past caring. Today is results day. We're on our way into college to find out our final scores. Nishi is practically chewing her fists off with fear. I know this seems excessive, given that she's expected to do better than anyone – but it also means more to her than it does to anyone else.

In between waitressing and hanging out with Nishi and making the most of being with my mum, I've had a lot of time to think this summer. I haven't come up with any earth-shattering revelations. But I've had enough time to make myself OK with everything that has happened.

As we leave the cafe and walk towards college, it's a walk we've done a hundred times before and I am hit by the fact that this will be the last time. However bad my results turn out to be today, I know I won't be going back there. I'm ready for the rest of my life to start. I don't want to hang around or go back. I'll get resourceful if I have to.

We have to go to the main office, but I spot Ms Foxe, my English teacher, straight away. I haven't even seen her since the exam fiasco, but I stuck a brief note of apology in her pigeonhole. She smiles at me with a hint of sadness – we've got on well for the past two years.

'Tuesday, it's obvious I'm not going to be telling you anything you don't already know – more's the pity. You've just about passed, as your coursework bolstered you up, but you didn't get anywhere near your predicted grade. It's a real shame for you, but you've got talent, Tuesday. I hope this doesn't mean you forget that.'

Knowing all of this for sure isn't exactly a shock. I've passed everything, but I was never expecting to do extraordinarily well in anything but English, so it turns out that I haven't done extraordinarily well in anything at all. It's fine.

I turn around to see Nishi crying openly, hugging Anna, a huge smile on both of their faces. I knew she'd do brilliantly, but I'm still so happy to see that she actually has. She'll be going to Oxford in the autumn. It's not that far away from us, really easy to get there on the train, so she and Anna are coming up with very sensible-sounding ground rules and visiting schedules. It's something I love about Nishi – when she says she's going to do something, she always does it. She deserves every bit of this.

Nishi's parents are taking her and Anna out for a swank celebratory lunch. My mum comes to collect me, having gone to work this morning – she knew I wanted to go in with my friends, but she offered to pick me up. Now that we're friends again, she's really going out of her way to show that she's on my side. Even though it's not exactly the funnest place to be at the moment.

As she pulls up she takes one look at my face and I shake my head just to ensure that there can be no confusion.

'No,' is all I say.

Unexpectedly, given that we have been expecting precisely this all summer, my mum's eyes fill with tears.

'I'm sorry,' she says. 'I know I'm being silly. It's just I had this ridiculous idea that there might be a miracle at the last minute. If this was a film, that's what would happen. I know it never really does in real life.'

I have to laugh.

'Oh, Mum . . .'

She offers to stay at home with me for the afternoon, but I tell her that she should go back to work. As well as the fact that it just wouldn't help, I really want to be by myself.

I think of Richard telling me to 'be proactive' above all, but I just can't bring myself to think about it straight away. Once my mum has dropped me off, I put on my pyjamas and get a pack of Jaffa Cakes out of the kitchen cupboard.

I have Jackson to thank for one big thing: I think he's cured me of rebellion for evermore. Before I met him I could feel it bubbling under the surface a lot of the time and occasionally it would burst through like a rash. I'm totally over it all now. Amid the stress of today, I don't want to go out partying, or binge on vodka in the park until I pass out; I don't want to smoke fags out of the window or even nick that open bottle of wine my mum has on the go in the fridge.

Instead I put the film version of *The Fault in Our Stars* into the DVD player – it's my new go-to when I want to force myself to cry and can't be bothered to read the book. It's always a good shortcut. Being this calm about the fact that I don't know what I am going to do with the rest of my life cannot be normal. I don't know why I feel so calm and quiet, and if it lasts much longer, it might just go on forever and I will end up eating biscuits in my pyjamas in the middle of the afternoon for all eternity. Not even proper biscuits – people can never seem to decide what a Jaffa Cake is supposed to be.

Anyway, *The Fault in Our Stars* usually does the trick. If that doesn't work, I might watch *Up* or maybe *Titanic* next. I really think if I can just make myself start crying, or at least start feeling *something*, then it will trigger off some kind of epiphany. A sad film should be able to make you draw some deep conclusion about your own life, surely.

It doesn't seem to be working. Once I've finished the Jaffa Cakes, I need some other extra distraction. So I start looking at the clearing website on my laptop. That does the trick much more quickly than all the death and weeping on the TV screen. I scroll through lists of incomprehensible abbreviations and complicated calculations. My stomach drops out from under me, right where I'm sitting. I keep scrolling blankly until my eyes blur, and I can't figure out if it's from unshed tears or eye strain from all those weird words that I can't even recognize passing in front of my eyes. No wonder I'm too thick to go to university.

I know I should look at this properly, as I have no other plans, but my brain shuts down and there would be no point anyway. So I get distracted by looking at the *Daily Mail* website, which makes me feel even grosser than eating Jaffa Cakes when I'm not hungry does. So then I look at Rookie and xoJane to correct the balance and fill my brain with some decent stuff.

I have a look at my email, as I haven't done so for at least twenty minutes. Nothing from Jackson or anyone else of particular note. Quite a lot from Amazon, as usual, and a lot of newsletters that I should never have signed up for about pizza deliveries, low-cost holidays and horoscopes.

Then I spot one lone email, from a name I don't recognize. My heart soars into the back of my throat before I can stop it. A few weeks ago, with Richard's words ringing in my ears, I looked up the heads of English at the universities I most wanted to go to. I sent them all a grovelling email, including a link to my most recent blog post, the one about wanting to be a writer since the dawn of time. I never heard back and just told myself that at least I hadn't lost anything by having a go.

Now, from the title of the email in my inbox, it looks as though somebody has finally replied.

Re: A Writer, of sorts

Dear Ms Cooper,

I read your email with interest and I went on to follow the link and read your blog. I must admit that I was sufficiently intrigued to keep reading; afterwards, my twenty-four-year-old daughter kindly explained to me your recent media exploits. Last time I went to Glastonbury festival, I think it cost £1 to get in and Marc Bolan was headlining! I digress . . .

I was impressed that you had the wherewithal to find my details and get in touch – a proactive spirit is surprisingly rare in eighteen-year-olds, I find. I enjoyed your writing and I do think you have talent. Your musings – or I should perhaps say 'ramblings' – are often amusing and occasionally quite astute.

Most importantly, I believe that you have learned your lesson and would be prepared to work hard. This combined with your excellent coursework and predicted grades indicates to me that you might be worth taking a chance on.

Perhaps you just caught me in a good mood (which if you take my course you will learn is an infrequent occurrence), but if you hadn't tried you would never have known. I commend you for 'having a go'.

Give me a ring, and let's discuss. My details are in the signature below.

Packing up my room has been like an archaeological dig. It's taken me three times as long as it should have, as a result. Mum's been wigging out, as I've spent most of the past week sitting cross-legged on my bedroom floor, reading old Harry Potter books, trying on clothes I'd forgotten about and sorting through shoeboxes full of things like old cinema tickets and passport photos with all four of us crammed into the booth.

Well, Mum says I can't take it all with me, and she's threatening to convert my room to either a yoga studio or home cinema as soon as I'm out the door. I don't blame her; space is at a premium, and I'm probably not going to be back much. So I might as well wallow in the relics of my childhood while I have my last chance. After all, I've lived in this house all my life. This house and my mum have basically been the only constants, and now, for the first time, I'm leaving both of them behind.

Actually, I can probably add Nishi to that list – I've known her since I started school and we've been best friends since day one, so I don't have many memories of life without her. It's obvious that Nishi herself is in a panic about starting at Oxford – we know all her telltale signs by now – and her refusal to talk about it is only making it worse. Fortunately, though, Anna has got pretty good at dealing with her these days. Failing all else, she has also got far better at rolling her eyes and laughing things off in a way that Nishi is still getting used to.

Anyway, I can't quite believe that this is going to be my last whole day of technically 'living at home'. I am eighteen years old and my A levels are done, even if they didn't quite go to plan, and this is it. Tonight will be my last night of sleeping in my own bed.

'Chew, you're not actually planning to wear that, are you?' My mum looks genuinely perturbed.

'Why not? It's so awesome I'm not sure why it's been shoved to the back of my cupboard for the past five years.'

The garment we are referring to is a Technicolor 1960s monstrosity that I remember buying in a charity shop (where else?) when I was about thirteen. I don't know why I would have bought it then – it's still enormous on me now. Then again, there has never been much in the way of rhyme and reason to my chazzing habits – sometimes I just want something so that nobody else can have it. I am always filled with good intentions to alter the fit or 'use the fabric', which invariably come to nothing. One day I hope I can become the kind of person who actually does that sort of thing. In the meantime, I have discovered that I own an entire wardrobe stuffed full of ill-fitting, mismatched and moth-eaten clothes that are of no use to anyone – and I love them all.

It feels just right for today. I don't know yet how I will feel at university. Maybe I'll want to start wearing black polo necks and dressing like a Serious Writer. Maybe my personality will change entirely and I will start wearing small hoop earrings and picking delicately at my food. I doubt it. Still, today will be the last day for a while when I am surrounded by people who know me this well.

'You're starting to look worryingly like Mama Cass,' my mum notes.

'Funny, I could murder a ham sandwich . . .'

I've never been sure if that story was an urban legend or not, but we really do have ham sandwiches. As well as Marmite, tuna and Nutella. All my favourites. I was up until two in the morning making an epically gigantic three-layered chocolate cake. It's probably too much food just for me, Mum, Nishi and Anna, but it feels fitting. Today is supposed to be a celebration of us all.

'Dude, what do you think you look like?' is all Nishi says when she turns up, before she has even got through the door.

Anna is more polite and at least gives me a hug as she hands over a box of flapjacks she has made.

'Hey, what's with the soundtrack? Not pining, are you?'

'No!' I feel myself blushing, even now. 'It's just the End of Summer Mix Tape I've made. I've done you all a copy. You've got to admit that it's fitting.'

As Anna noted straight away, Jackson's voice is coming from the kitchen stereo. I couldn't exactly leave him off my official End of Summer Mix Tape. If his voice has any effect on me, then it's definitely just an involuntary physiological reaction by now – honest.

'Hi, girls!' my mum announces herself with exaggerated fanfare.

Nishi and Anna both burst out laughing as Mum enters the kitchen. That's when I see that she has followed my lead and also put on a variety of my charity shop acquisitions – a floppy purple hat and some shorts with braces that I used to really like, plus my first Nirvana T-shirt.

'Mum, you look awesome!' I say, doing my best to keep a straight face and make it sound like a sincere compliment.

Of course Nishi and Anna then end up raiding the bin bag of clothes that my mum has earmarked to go back to the charity shop 'if they'll even have them'. Nishi looks the weirdest I have ever seen her, in an old-lady 1950s housecoat that I have been meaning for ages to adapt into some sort of cute dress. Anna, though, somehow manages to look just as stylish as ever in a slightly manky 80s prom dress, from my unfairly maligned Madonna-in-*Desperately-Seeking-Susan* phase.

'Oh, come on, girls,' my mum says, getting a bottle of champagne out of the fridge. 'You're all so sensible these days – let's have a glass.'

'Well, the last time Nishi got drunk,' I explain helpfully, 'she told me in the pub toilets that she hated me and never wanted to speak to me again. So don't let her have too much.'

'Unlike Chew,' Anna chips in, 'who's *so* sensible she marries pop stars in fake Las Vegas wedding ceremonies in a field.'

'Oh, by the way,' says Nishi, 'I saw Seymour yesterday. He's going out with that girl Sophie now, and he's working in that annoying men's clothes shop in town. You know, the one that sells all the pointy shoes.'

'Probably saving up his money for "going travelling",' I cackle – meanly, yes, but I feel I've kind of earned it. 'Then he'll come back wearing wooden beads around his neck on a bit of string, and he'll change his Facebook cover photo to a picture of, like, a Vietnamese temple.'

'Oh, turn this one up!' Nishi interrupts unexpectedly. 'It's actually a really lovely song.'

'I know I probably shouldn't admit this, but it really is, isn't it?' agrees my mum.

I could never have predicted their reactions, but it's the song that Jackson wrote about me: 'The Last Tuesday'. I felt a bit silly putting it on the mix in the first place, but I couldn't leave it off either. It wouldn't have felt right.

Maybe it's the champagne that's done it, but we're all singing along. I swear there's even a tear in Nishi's eye by the time we get to the final chorus. I'm sure it's nothing to do with Jackson Griffith, or me – that's the beauty of a great song. You can project yourself on to it.

It's a novelty for me not to have to, for once. It's about me. It's mine and it always will be. What a gift.

In fact, I've long suspected it, but now I know: if there are two things I'd hang my hat on in this life, it's true friendship and the power of a perfect two-minute pop song.

Acknowledgements

Huge gratitude to my brilliant agent Caroline Hardman and my brilliant editor Rachel Petty – thank you both so much. Thank you also to Joanna Swainson and to the amazingly lovely team at Macmillan. You have all made this such a joy I cannot ever thank you enough!

Predictable but heartfelt thanks to all my family and friends who have helped me so much – too many of you to name (sorry), but especially Mum, Dad, Katy, Nan, Ali, Tom, Ruth and Jimmy. Thank you to Ann Pitts for early encouragement and ongoing friendship.

Thank you to Alexis for taking my photograph (and sh*t).

Very modern thanks to all my Twitter and Facebook friends for support, comedy and distraction – and special thanks to Evan for giving me a tiny spark of an idea (and the soundtrack to the writing of this book).

Author Note

I have always wanted to write a book set at a music festival. Writing and music have always been my great loves in life, so this was probably the logical conclusion.

When I was eighteen, I celebrated the end of my A levels with a trip to Reading Festival. I had found the ideal outfit for the occasion: a ridiculous charity shop wedding dress (fetchingly paired with Adidas Gazelles). So my friend Russell (in a three-piece suit) and I told everyone that we had got married and were at the festival for our honeymoon. We even had fake bridesmaids! Hilarity ensued and we loved all the attention – we happily posed for photos and answered people's questions with increasingly ridiculous answers ('Yes, we are planning to come back every year for our wedding anniversary and bring our future children!').

I staggered home on Monday morning still in my mud-caked wedding dress. At first I thought my parents' horrified faces were due to my haggard appearance, but in fact they had read about my festival 'wedding' in the *Telegraph* and the *News of the World* – and had spent the whole weekend worrying that the reports were true!

The story stuck in my memory (and my dad's – who still likes to bring it up whenever possible as proof of my 'difficult' teen years!). Fast-forward a decade and it was the first thing that sprang to mind when I was writing this book.

The world has changed a lot since I used to run off to festivals for the weekend without so much as a mobile phone. In the interim, I was an early adopter of blogging and turned into a total Twitter addict. One day last year, wasting time on Twitter when I should have been writing, I somehow got into a Tweet-conversation with a popstar from my teenage days – one who I had seen at all those long-ago festivals and even had a poster of on my bedroom wall. When he started replying to my Tweets – and followed me back – I couldn't believe it!

Amazingly, we carried on chatting and sort of became friends. We talked about music and films and stuff, and planned to meet up when he came over to the UK to play at Glastonbury.

In the end, we didn't. But it was so exciting to me that I could talk to this person – who was not only thousands of miles away, but a genuine (gorgeous, talented, famous, etc.) *rockstar*. When I was a teenager, it just wouldn't have been possible.

I suddenly realized that this might complete the idea for the romantic festival adventure I had always dreamed of writing. The pieces instantly fell into place and I wrote the whole book really quickly – in about two months. It was one of those brilliant things where the real-life sparks of inspiration – as if by magic – turned into a fully formed fictional story with its own dramas and characters. I loved every single minute of writing it, and I fell in love with Tuesday and Jackson along the way.

After that, it was a whirlwind. A couple of months later, I found myself at the Macmillan offices eating cupcakes decorated with miniature vinyl records while I signed a contract for two books.

Since then, all the behind-the-scenes hard work has been going on, while I have been counting down the agonizing wait to finally have the finished book in my hands. The whole experience has been such a total joy, I can't even tell you. I am so grateful to everyone who has supported me, and thank you so much for buying this book! I hope you enjoy reading it as much as I adored writing it.

Combining my love of books and music has always been my dream and there's so much more to write about – my days of playing bass in a (terrible and very short-lived!) band is the next spark of inspiration . . .

I wish I could go back to Reading Festival 1999 and tell my teenage self all about it. If I had told her that I would one day be writing books inspired by the music I love, I don't think she would have believed me.

Ellie x